A Worthy Adversary

She met his gaze evenly. It was as strong as his arms which had lifted her onto his horse with as little effort as if she weighed no more than milkweed fluff. She could not halt herself from admiring his muscular shoulders and arms, which had swung his broadsword with ease. His blue-gray eyes slowly narrowed when she did not answer.

This assignment would have been so much simpler if his features were not even and strong. Especially his jaw, which hinted at a stubborn nature. She must not allow that to trouble her, for she could be obstinate too. . . .

Praise for *A Knight Like No Other*

"Fast, fresh, and fun!"
    —*New York Times* Bestselling Author Mary Jo Putney

"Historical romance at its best!"—May McGoldrick

"Lively and entertaining."—Margaret Evans Porter

A Knight Like No Other

Jocelyn Kelley

A SIGNET ECLIPSE BOOK

SIGNET ECLIPSE
Published by New American Library, a division of
Penguin Group (USA) Inc., 375 Hudson Street,
New York, New York 10014, USA
Penguin Group (Canada), 10 Alcorn Avenue, Toronto,
Ontario M4V 3B2, Canada (a division of Pearson Penguin Canada Inc.)
Penguin Books Ltd, 80 Strand, London WC2R, 0RL, England
Penguin Ireland, 25 St. Stephen's Green, Dublin 2,
Ireland (a division of Penguin Books Ltd.)
Penguin Group (Australia), 250 Camberwell Road, Camberwell, Victoria 3124,
Australia (a division of Pearson Australia Group Pty. Ltd.)
Penguin Books India Pvt. Ltd, 11 Community Centre, Panchsheel Park,
New Delhi - 110 017, India
Penguin Group (NZ), cnr Airborne and Rosedale Roads, Albany,
Auckland 1310, New Zealand (a division of Pearson New Zealand Ltd.)
Penguin Books (South Africa) (Pty.) Ltd., 24 Sturdee Avenue,
Rosebank, Johannesburg 2196, South Africa

Penguin Books Ltd, Registered Offices:
80 Strand, London WC2R 0RL, England

First published by Signet Eclipse, an imprint of New American Library,
a division of Penguin Group (USA) Inc.

First Printing, March 2005
10 9 8 7 6 5 4 3 2 1

For Jennifer Jackson
Thanks for your enthusiasm for this project—
and never suggesting I'm crazy for trying something different

Chapter 1

The attack came out of nowhere.

One minute, Avisa de Vere was talking with one of her students in the Abbey's kitchen garden. The next, they were under attack.

The student, a slight girl who was barely more than a child, screamed and ducked behind the well house. Her sword clattered on the stones as she dropped it.

Avisa pulled her own sword and whirled to deflect the man's blow. The concussion streamed up her arm, but she tightened her grip on the hilt.

What was a man doing, unannounced, within the walls of St. Jude's Abbey? Was he a thief? A madman? Or—and she did not want to allow the thought to form—could England itself be under attack?

She clenched her teeth as she parried his next motion, sending the tip of his sword clanging against the stones. She slashed her sword up, but he was quick and blocked her blade.

She matched his swings as he backed her through the garden. The swords rang out wildly as plants that had withered beneath the snow were crushed beneath her feet. Every lesson she had learned, every lesson she had taught, filled her mind.

Force your opponent to raise and lower his sword. That will tire him quickly and make it a more even match. You must lessen the disadvantage you will certainly face, for you are not as big or as strong as most men.

She was the best swordswoman in St. Jude's Abbey, but he was challenging every move she had mastered. She might be doing better if her arms and shoulders were not exhausted from hours of teaching, slowing her sword.

With a fierce blow, he knocked her backward several steps. Her right shoulder burned with the impact, but she did not fall. She ignored the ache as she met his next blow. He swung at her legs. She jumped over the blade's wild swing, and his sword cut through the hem of her gown. Fabric flew toward the well house as more pain coursed up her leg.

She was losing. She must not lose. Tightening her hold on her sword, she leaped in the air again and struck out at him with her right foot.

Her low boot hit his wrist, and his sword flew from his hand. He stared after it in shock. When he took a step toward it, her sword halted him. His eyes widened as she placed the tip to his throat.

"Who are you?" Avisa demanded, watching him closely, because he might be stupid enough to try to get his sword. "Why are you ambushing two sisters within St. Jude's Abbey?"

His eyes shifted to look past her, but she would not be fooled by that tired tactic.

"Who are you?" she asked again. "Speak, man, of your intentions within these walls. We of St. Jude's Abbey do not offer a welcome to intruders who try to kill us." She did not want to thrust the sword into him, but she would do so to protect the Abbey where she had lived for all the years she could remember.

The answer came, not from the man but from behind her. A melodic feminine voice said, "Well done, Avisa de Vere. You are proof that this abbey has accomplished the very aim I gave it at its founding."

When the man in front of her knelt, Avisa turned. The kitchen garden was enclosed on three sides by walls that matched the gray stone of the Abbey's main building. Now the plants were hidden under the snow. It crunched beneath the feet of a tall woman, flanked by two men-at-arms whose swords remained in their sheaths. A redheaded lad stood next to the well house.

Visible beneath the woman's ebony cloak, the hem of her blue silk gown was decorated with exquisite embroidery. Threads of gold and silver had been sewn into an intricate pattern. Rings of the same precious metals brightened her fingers. Around her neck, a heavy gold cross was encrusted with gems. Her hair was hidden beneath her wimple, but a ruddy wisp had escaped to curl along her angular cheekbones.

Although she had never seen the queen of England, Avisa recognized Queen Eleanor from the portrait hanging in the abbess's house. She dropped to her knees, laying her sword at the queen's feet. She tried to slow her breathing and her heart, hammering against her chest. She had not been as apprehensive while fighting the intruder as she was at being in the queen's presence.

"Rise, Avisa de Vere," ordered Queen Eleanor, her voice proclaiming her birth in Aquitaine.

Avisa obeyed.

"You appear surprised, Roger," the queen said to the man picking up his sword. "I warned you to be well prepared before you presumed to fight a woman within these walls."

The man shook his right wrist as he awkwardly shoved his sword back into its scabbard with his left hand. "That you did, your majesty." He regarded Avisa with amazement. "I would be grateful if you were to teach me that trick."

"Maybe later," the queen said before Avisa could answer. She motioned toward the well house. "You need not hide any longer. Come out."

Avisa's student, a girl who looked younger than her dozen years, inched around the well's wooden door set among the stones, then knelt. She bounced back to her feet at the queen's command. Giving Avisa a fearful glance, she gulped so loudly Avisa could hear it. Beyond the few words spoken here, the kitchen garden had become as silent as if some great wind had blown through the Abbey and swept everyone else away.

Queen Eleanor bent and lifted Avisa's sword. Holding it flat in her hands, she said, "Your skill with this is an excellent reflection on the Abbey and what you have been taught. Are you as proficient with a bow?"

"Almost, my queen," Avisa replied.

"Almost? Your humility serves you well inside the walls of the Abbey, but I wish to know the extent of your skill." She gestured to the man standing on her right.

He held out a bow and a quiver.

Avisa sheathed her sword before taking the bow and quiver. She slid the quiver's strap around her left shoulder. She set one end of the bow on the ground, balancing it with her foot as she reached for the other end to set the string. The string jerked out of her hand before she could place the loop over the notch in the wood. Her palm burned. This bow was not as pliable as the one she was accustomed to using.

Was this another test? If so, she would not fail her queen and the Abbey. Gritting her teeth, she grabbed the string again and bent the bow until she could slip the string into place. She paid no attention to the line gouged into her seared palm as she reached over her shoulder to draw an arrow from the quiver on her back. Setting it to the string, she glanced at Queen Eleanor.

The queen pointed to a wizened apple hanging from a tree just beyond the kitchen garden's stone wall. "That is your target, Avisa de Vere."

Whispers flowed outward like ripples created by a pebble dropped into a pool. Most of the Abbey's residents had gathered near the kitchen doors to watch. She was not surprised that word had spread through the Abbey of Queen Eleanor's arrival. There were no secrets here.

Avisa paid her sisters no mind as she raised the bow and sighted on the apple. The distance was about the same as the targets she had used for practice, but the apple was far smaller. Taking a deep breath and releasing it as she had been taught by Sister Mallory, who was the best archer in the Abbey, she drew back the string. It twanged as she released it, and she reached for another arrow. The second arrow followed, striking the apple only seconds after the first hit the branch next to it.

Around her, gasps of astonishment were quickly quelled. There would have been cheers of congratulations if the queen had not stood among them. No one knew how to act, for the queen had not come to the Abbey before this—as far as Avisa knew.

"Two arrows?" asked Queen Eleanor.

"As soon as the first arrow left the string, I knew it would miss." Avisa leaned the bottom of the bow against her shoe. When it brushed her leg, she winced. Looking down, she saw blood staining her stocking where her dress's hem had been cut away by the man's blade. She paid no attention to the pain. She had been hurt worse while practicing.

"It still struck close enough to render a man useless," said the red-haired lad beside the queen. "You have an excellent eye, Lady Avisa."

In spite of her determination to do nothing that would disgrace the Abbey, Avisa recoiled. The title of *lady* was rightly hers, but she had not been addressed as anything other than *sister* since her arrival at St. Jude's Abbey.

Queen Eleanor put her hand on the lad's shoulder. "That is enough, Richard." Looking again at Avisa, she continued, "However, I do concur with my son—and with you. You are *almost* as skilled with a bow as with a broadsword."

"Thank you, your majesty." She bowed her head so no one could view her pride. The ones within the Abbey's walls were instructed that pride gained nothing but trouble. Yet, she could not rid herself of it.

"Come with us, for I wish to speak further with you, Avisa de Vere."

Questions inside her demanded to be asked, but she silenced them. When the queen spoke a command, it must be obeyed.

Gazing at the water-stained walls of the Abbey and its narrow windows, Avisa repeated the prayer of thanksgiving she had spoken so many times. When her family sent her to the Abbey before her second birthday, they could not have guessed what she would learn within the cloister. Their thoughts, she surmised, had been focused on gaining the queen's favor by offering their youngest daughter to lead a life of religious contemplation. It was her good fortune that St. Jude's Abbey offered its sisters a very different type of training.

Her family had a tradition of bravery, and her father was no exception. It was said that the baron had protected the king's interests on many occasions. He had dared to confront the king's foes and had emerged victorious and covered with honor. He would be proud of her—if he knew she had gained a knight's skills and more.

She ran her finger along the rounded hilt of her sword. The blade was shorter than a man would use, so she had learned to find ways to compensate. Now she was teaching what she had discovered to others who showed an aptitude. No novice was compelled to study weapons, and there were some women in the Abbey who preferred the ways practiced in other religious houses. But that life would never have satisfied her.

As Avisa followed the queen into the abbess's house, the men fell in behind her. She was tempted to glance over her shoulder, unsure if Queen Eleanor had other surprises in store for her. She would not be ambushed a second time. The man had fought well, and if he lunged at her with his sword, she could not disarm him the same way again. She let a smile edge along her lips. That was not the only way she had learned to defeat a swordsman.

The halls of the abbess's house were well lit against the early winter darkness. Beneath her feet, rushes had been twisted into mats. They rustled on each step, releasing the heady aromas of the herbs spread among them.

Seeing the queen's son glancing about with curiosity, although the queen looked neither to the left nor to the right, Avisa fought back another flush of pride. The Abbey was built well, and its walls were covered with tapestries that would be the envy of any of the king's lieges.

The abbess's private rooms were upstairs, so they went up the curving staircase that grew narrower as they climbed. At the top, it was not wide enough for two people to pass. The windows were set back so far into the thick wall that Avisa could have barely touched them with the tip of her sword.

They emerged on the upper floor, which was identical to the lower one. Avisa said nothing as the queen strode without hesitation in the direction of the abbess's private chambers. Had the queen come to St. Jude's before? Impossible! The Abbey would have buzzed like a hive of maddened bees with such tidings.

Queen Eleanor smiled as she glanced back. "Do not be astonished, Lady Avisa. While this Abbey was being built, I became quite familiar with its design, so that I might be able to find my way about by myself, if the need arose."

The abbess must have been alerted of the queen's arrival, for she waited in the arch of the doorway at the end of the hall. The abbess's head barely reached the queen's shoulder. Her smile was wide as she curtsied and then was kissed on both cheeks by the queen. Motioning for the queen to sit on the padded bench in front of the room's only window, she greeted the young prince.

This chamber with its arched and timbered ceiling had more furniture than most rooms in the Abbey. A long table's legs resembled beasts of the woods. While the artisan had carved the animals during her third year at the Abbey, Avisa had skulked into the abbess's private room to watch. The abbess often sat there when she was reading or writing. Four chairs and another bench faced the hearth, where a fire crackled. A prie-dieu huddled in one corner beneath a niche where a cross glowed in the light of a candle set beneath it. In the opposite corner, a trio of cats slept. They kept mice out of this room.

So many times Avisa had come here to discuss a new novice or to report on a student's progress. Each time, she had imagined what it might be like if one day these rooms and the burden of running the Abbey were hers. Although the abbess had said nothing about future plans, many who lived within the Abbey believed Avisa was the obvious choice to assume the duties. It was not an honor she sought. Teaching and honing her own skills brought her great satisfaction. The idea of putting aside those tasks to deal with the administration of the Abbey did not appeal to her.

Now Queen Eleanor was here. Her arrival must signal something, but Avisa could not guess what. If the queen had come to ask the abbess to oversee the establishment of a daughter abbey—another idea that had circulated through St. Jude's Abbey in recent weeks—everything Avisa loved might change.

A door at the far end of the room opened, and a woman stepped forward at the queen's command. She bent from the waist in the bow of her land, far east of the borders of distant Persia. As she straightened, long, straight black hair slid along her shoulders like silk. Her exotic face, so different from the others in the Abbey, was placid, but Avisa knew her teacher and friend well enough to sense Nariko's tension at speaking to England's queen.

"You are Nariko?" asked Queen Eleanor.

"I am." Her voice held only the barest hint of her homeland at the world's far edge.

"Did you teach Avisa de Vere the trick that unarmed my knight-at-arms with a single blow of her foot to his wrist?"

"Yes."

"It was a great surprise for him."

Nariko smiled, her eyes slitting above her flawless cheeks. "The warriors of this country think to fight only with weapons of wood and iron and steel. I teach how to use one's body to overcome a foe."

"And you have taught your students well, Nariko. Thank you."

Bowing again, Nariko backed away and left. Avisa knew her friend was eager to return to her students, as Avisa was.

The abbess ordered food and wine brought for their guests. While the abbess and the queen spoke of the weather and the discomforts of a long journey, Avisa remained by the door. She could not leave until dismissed. Had they forgotten she was there?

"I did not expect so many years to pass before I returned," the queen said. Seated on the bench, she looked every inch a queen. Her head was high, and her hands folded prettily in her lap.

The abbess drew a chair around the table and sat on it. "I have prayed that you would have no need to return."

"As I have. Unfortunately in these dire times, not all prayers can be answered as we wish." She glanced toward Avisa.

"Come closer, Sister Avisa," the abbess ordered quickly.

"*Lady* Avisa," the queen corrected.

The abbess shuddered so hard that Avisa feared she had taken an abrupt chill. Rushing to her side, Avisa plucked a cloak from a peg. She draped it over the abbess's shoulders.

"What is this for?" asked the abbess.

"You looked as if the cold had bitten into your bones."

Patting Avisa's hand, she tried to smile but failed. Her eyes were dim, their customary sparkle banished, as she looked back at the queen and said, "This is most unexpected, your majesty."

"Why?" asked Queen Eleanor, clearly perplexed. "You knew the time was certain to come when I would need to call upon the services of the ladies of St. Jude's Abbey."

Avisa wanted to ask what the queen spoke of, but bit back her query when a novice, wide-eyed as she stared at the queen and her son, entered with a tray. On it, a goblet encrusted with gems as glorious as the ones on the queen's fingers was set next to simple cups and a bottle of wine. Another girl followed with bread and meat. Both trays were set on the table.

Not needing an order from the abbess, Avisa went to the table and poured wine into the glasses. She bowed as she handed the jeweled goblet to the queen and a simpler cup to her son. Then she served the abbess. Drawing the second bench between the queen and the abbess, she placed on it the tray with the food. She stepped back and waited for them to enjoy what had been brought. When her stomach threatened to growl, reminding her that she had not stopped for a midday meal, she shifted her left arm in front of her. She slipped her hand into her drooping sleeve and pressed surreptitiously against her belly.

It was useless. The sound emerged, eliciting a giggle from the prince.

"Come and have something to eat, Lady Avisa," the queen ordered. "I was told, upon my arrival, that you have labored long today in an effort to share with others the knowledge of weapons you have gained here."

"Thank you." She picked up a piece of the warm bread and took a grateful bite.

"Ask the question I see in your eyes, Lady Avisa."

Wondering if she should demur or speak honestly, she squared her shoulders. "I am astonished at how you address me."

"It is the title you possessed before you entered St. Jude's Abbey, is it not?"

"Yes, your majesty, but once I was within these walls, I happily accepted the title of sister."

Queen Eleanor lifted her goblet and took a sip. "Even within these walls, you must have heard of the ongoing trouble between my lord husband and Becket, the Archbishop of Canterbury."

Avisa was about to reply, then realized the queen was looking once more at the abbess. Did Queen Eleanor believe that she had answered Avisa's question? Avisa was even more baffled.

"I have heard of the trouble," answered the abbess.

"My lord husband is now in Bayeux on the far side of the Channel, but Becket has returned to England. There will be trouble."

Avisa knew she should hold her tongue, but she began, "In the past—"

"This is not like the past. When last they parted, the archbishop told my lord husband that they would not meet again on this earth. One of them is doomed to die soon. I do not wish it to be the king." The queen sighed. "If the archbishop would retract his condemnations of those who serve the church *and* the king, this matter might be settled peacefully." Her smile returned, as cold as the air outside the stone walls. "But no one will heed the counsel of a woman, be she queen or abbess or peasant."

The abbess set her cup down and handed young Richard another slice of the bread as well as some beef. "It is because of this that you wish the help of St. Jude's Abbey, I surmise."

"Yes."

Avisa bit her lip to keep her questions from bursting out. What help could an abbey offer to bring about a reconciliation between the king and his archbishop? What help could *this* abbey offer?

As if Avisa had spoken, the queen looked at her and said, "Lady Avisa, I have a task you are well suited for."

"You need only ask," she answered dutifully.

Queen Eleanor smiled at Richard, then said, "My dear son, join our retainers who wait in the hall."

Rebellion burned in his eyes for the moment before he nodded. He grabbed another piece of bread before leaving.

"I would prefer Richard not be privy to what I have to say," the queen said as soon as the door closed behind him. "He is but a boy, and he sometimes forgets to guard what he says. I hope he learns discretion by the time he is a man like my godson Christian Lovell." Affixing Avisa with her cool gaze, she went on, "I came here to seek your help in protecting my godson."

"Protecting him?"

The abbess fired a frown at her, and Avisa silenced her next question. None of this made sense. Yes, she had gained a knight's skills within the Abbey, but how was she supposed to *protect* this man? And why couldn't he take care of himself?

"Christian is as precious to me as my own sons." The queen ran her finger along the top of her goblet. "I do not want him involved with what surely is to happen in Canterbury." Holding up her hand, she added, "Do not speak the doubts I see in your eyes, Lady Avisa. I know I have told you little, but I shall give you no answers this day. I have not come to St. Jude's Abbey to explain or justify the actions of my lord husband. I have come to find someone to keep my godson far from Canterbury." The queen appraised her, then nodded. "My godson has, it is said, a penchant for pretty blond ladies. You are both comely and fair-haired as well as adept with a sword. You should do well."

"I will endeavor to do as you wish."

Setting her goblet on the table, the queen rose. "Do not mistake my concern for my godson as a suggestion of weakness on his part. He is capable of doing my lord husband's bidding, but I do not wish to see the blood of the Lord's servant on Christian's hands."

The abbess drew in her breath sharply, but clamped her lips closed when the queen glanced at her.

"I understand," Avisa said, surprised that she did. Although she was cloistered, she was not unaware of worldly concerns, for the abbess spoke with her often of matters that consumed the world outside the Abbey. The hostility between the king and the Archbishop of Canterbury was long-lived.

"Then take up the task, Lady Avisa, of keeping Christian

Lovell away from Canterbury until the king returns to England."

"I can escort him here—"

"Here?" Queen Eleanor laughed. "You mistake my command, Lady Avisa. You are to keep him far from Canterbury at the same time you allow nothing to connect you to St. Jude's Abbey. The value of the Abbey to me would be lessened if anyone else was to learn of my true intention in founding it and having young women trained to serve me in times of trouble."

Avisa glanced at the abbess, who nodded with a gentle smile. The queen's words made sense. Avisa had never given thought to *why* she had been taught a warrior's skills. She had grown up here, and the life had seemed ordinary— until now.

"Do others know the Abbey's true purpose?" she asked in barely more than a whisper.

"Only the abbess and now you." The queen arched a brow as she faced the abbess. "You will need to concoct an excuse for Lady Avisa to leave the Abbey, an excuse that will create no suspicion in the hearts of those who remain behind and no questions when she returns."

The abbess nodded.

"As well, you must be prepared to send her any assistance she needs."

The abbess nodded again.

"Christian is traveling from his father's lands to the west. He is accompanied by his brother, Guy Lovell, who does not share Christian's serious nature. His page will be with him as well, a lad with hair as red as my Richard's. I would advise you to meet Christian and persuade him to avoid Canterbury." She withdrew a rolled page from beneath her cape. "This will give you the information you need to intercept him."

Avisa took it, forcing her fingers not to tremble. She was about to leave the Abbey. The last time she had traveled beyond its walls was when she came to the Abbey as an infant.

"You must do whatever is necessary," Queen Eleanor added.

"I understand. I will not disappoint you, my queen."

"See that you do not. I would not wish to think my patronage to this Abbey has been in vain."

As the abbess escorted the queen to the door, Avisa stared down at the page. She understood what she must do, and she understood that if she failed, she could doom St. Jude's Abbey.

You must do whatever is necessary.

She touched the hilt of her sword. She would follow that order, and she would safeguard Christian Lovell . . . and the Abbey.

Chapter 2

Christian Lovell cursed the wintry afternoon, although it would do him no good. God's breath, it was freezing. This was a day best suited for sitting next to a fire with something warm in his tankard and someone even warmer on his lap.

He pulled his cloak more tightly around him and shifted on the hard wooden saddle. For this long journey, he missed Respin, his destrier. The horse, trained for battle, had served him well while on the Continent. But Respin had pulled up lame the day before Christian departed Lovell Mote for the wedding of Philip de Boisvert, his father's friend, in Canterbury. So he rode Blackthorn, a fine horse, but one without the stamina of his warhorse.

"How much farther?" asked his cousin Baldwin. The red-haired lad, who was barely beyond his first decade, served as Christian's page. This was Baldwin's first trip away from the estate where he had been born, and he was reveling in every aspect of the journey, even through this cold and windy wood.

"We will travel until it is nearly dark, then look for a place to spend the night."

His brother, Guy, groaned. "By your answer, I suspect we will not reach Bart-by-Water before sundown."

"'Tis unlikely." He looked at where the sun was close to the tops of the trees. The hours of sunlight grew fewer each day. Once the winter solstice and Christmas were upon them, the darkness would lay claim to less of each day.

"If we were to hurry, we might reach it," his brother replied. "I do not wish to remain on this road where there are too many who would be willing to slit our throats and steal the clothes we wear."

Christian frowned at his brother. Guy was a well-favored man, tall and dark-haired as most Lovell men were. His skills with a sword and a bow needed refining, but he was the first to admit he was fortunate to be the second-born son. He preferred lying with his head in some woman's lap as he sang to her of a love that would last until she welcomed him into her bed and he grew bored with the conquest. Then the chase would begin anew. He gleefully reminded Christian on every possible occasion that he would not have, after their father's passing, the boring responsibilities of the family's lands and title.

"Tarnished title," Christian muttered. He chided himself for the taint of bitterness in his voice. How could he forget the shame heaped upon their family when every day brought another reminder? Not even more than a score of years could erase the disgrace that his father refused to speak of. Others were not so circumspect. Too many of Christian's memories were besmirched with whispered conversations where the words *coward* and *failed the king* were repeated.

He did not want to believe that his father had lost King Henry's favor by failing to halt King Stephen when Henry and his mother, Matilda, had fought for the English throne. On that sojourn to England in 1147, Henry had been defeated so utterly that Stephen had paid his passage back to Anjou. Henry would not have had to endure such humiliation if Lord Lovell had not fled the battle. Christian's father had never shown other signs of a lack of courage, but after that he was shunned by his fellow barons. The shame would become Christian's when he assumed the title unless he proved himself worthy of being called a hero.

"We could stop at Messingham Hall," his brother said,

interrupting his grim thoughts. "I doubt even *he* would turn us away on such a frigid night."

Christian did not answer. He had not set off on this journey to learn the niceties of speaking velvet-covered lies to gain power and prestige—the only accomplishment Lord Messingham seemed to possess. He did not want to be obligated to any of those who enjoyed reminding the king of the Lovells' ignominy. Lord Messingham had been the first to turn his back on the Lovell family, and he convinced others that they should do the same. That they had found shelter last night behind the stone walls of a fortified house had been close to a miracle. Even so, the welcome had been reluctant and the farewells eager. On both sides, because Christian had been glad to put an end to an argument between his brother and an old man who accused him of robbery. Christian had chided his brother for teasing the decrepit man, who was, they had been warned upon their arrival, quite insane.

Christian hoped their journey would bring adventure and glory and the chance to prove he was a man of courage—and to wipe away the stain of cowardice. So far, he had made no decision more difficult than where they would spend the night. He had done nothing that would win him honor and perhaps a place among the king's advisors. Such a post would be proof that he had not inherited that stain of cowardice.

His horse whinnied softly. Blackthorn made that warning sound when he sensed trouble.

Christian peered into the shadows gathered beneath the thick trees edging the road ahead. Raising his hand, he signaled for his companions to halt.

"What is it?" asked Guy through a yawn. "I wish no further delay in finding a place to sleep where the cold does not numb my hands and toes."

"Hush!" He put his hand on his sword. It slid easily from its wooden scabbard, for Baldwin kept the leather interior smooth and supple.

"Do you see something?" Baldwin inched closer as if he could see better from Christian's perspective.

A scream ripped out of the shadows. A woman's scream for help!

Christian's horse sped toward the trees as he raised his sword. A brook cut through the road, but they cleared it with ease.

Another cry drew his eyes toward the center of the darkness. He saw a woman surrounded by a quartet of men. One man was reaching toward her, and she lashed out with a short knife. She swung it at him, then looked past her attacker toward Christian. She aimed the blade at the man trying to take it from her. With a laugh, the man struck her arm and sent the dagger arcing away. She shrieked again.

Christian slapped the flat of his sword at one man, knocking him to the earth, and tugged back on the reins. He did not want to draw blood until he knew what was happening. Blackthorn rose, pawing the air. The other men ran away. The man on the ground leaped to his feet and fled with his comrades, who were fading into the trees.

Jumping down, Christian rushed to where the woman crouched on the ground, her arms over her head. He knelt beside her, and she moaned.

"I shall not hurt you, woman," he said. "They are gone."

She shook her head, threatening to dislodge the narrow strip of her barbette. Wrapped atop her hair and over her ears and under her chin like a bandage, its blue fabric matching the embroidery on her gown could not diminish the golden wealth of her hair, tightly plaited and half hidden beneath the barbette. Its color, until now, had existed only in his fantasies.

"Fear not," he said. "They are gone."

"Truly?" she whispered.

"You need fear them no more."

She lifted her head, and he wondered if the sun had abruptly changed its direction to rise beyond the trees, because her face glowed. Not with the sun's light, but with her smile.

"How do you fare?" He held out his hand.

"I am safe, thanks to you." She put her hand on his glove.

As he drew her to her feet and out of the shadows, her hair shone gold in the thinning sunshine. He sucked in his breath as he stared at her finely drawn features. Her eyes were the color of a still pond on a summer's morn, and her cheeks had been burnished with the day's chill. Yet her lips held his gaze, for they were as red as the trim on her cloak. When they parted in a soft invitation, his arm swept around her waist, drawing her against him, before he had time to form another thought.

Her eyes widened with an astonishment that suggested she was a maid who had never known a man's embrace. The idea sizzled in his head and along him. He did not resist the invitation she offered, bending to capture her mouth.

With a gasp, she pulled back. "Brave sir, I thank you for your kindness in saving me. Yet I must repay your benevolence by begging another boon."

"Ask what you will, woman." He did not halt his hand from sliding up her back beneath her cloak. Her pliant breasts brushed him on every quick breath she took. Her rapid breathing or his? It must be hers, for the very sight of her stole his breath from within him.

"'Tis my sister." Her voice trembled, but she met his eyes evenly. "She is in need of succor from the wicked man who stole her from her bed to take her to his."

Christian tried to concentrate on her words, but the breeze, which seemed to have lost its chill, brushed her tawny strands against his cheek in a sweet caress. If this woman's sister was half as fair as she, he could understand why a man would abduct her to have her for his own.

"Will you help me save her?" she pleaded.

A laugh silenced his answer, and he looked past her to see his brother and young Baldwin dismounting. Guy chuckled again before saying, "'Tis a fair armful you have there, brother. Did you reap your reward of a kiss for saving her from the outlaws? Or are you negotiating for more than a single kiss?"

Christian released the woman, and she went to get her dagger, which had fallen in the road. He wanted to curse at his brother, but Guy's arrival reminded him of the need to control himself. He had not rescued this maiden from those men only to ravish her himself, no matter how tempting the idea might be. When she bent to pick up a pack, he was astonished to see her grasp another blade far longer than her knife, yet shorter than his broadsword.

"Why didn't you use that against your attackers?" he asked.

"They surprised me," she replied. "I did not have time to draw it."

"You should not carry a weapon you are not prepared to wield. It could have been turned against you."

Her eyes twinkled. "Truly good advice, kind sir. I shall recall it if I chance to meet more outlaws on my journey."

"What is your name?" Christian ignored his brother, who was listening with a broad smile.

"Avisa de Vere." She leaned the sword so its tip rested on the ground, and he realized it was the perfect length for her. He could not help but wonder what smith had crafted a sword for a woman's use. "And may I know the name of my rescuer?"

"Christian Lovell, knight in service to our liege King Henry." He bowed his head. "I travel with my brother, Guy, and my page, Baldwin."

"I am in your debt."

"You said something about your sister . . ."

Guy crowed, "She has a sister? As winsome as you, pretty Avisa? It would ease the cold of this night if you were to take us to where you and your sister live."

Even in the twilight creeping from beneath the trees, Christian could see a flush climbing Avisa's cheeks. Was it anger or embarrassment at his brother's barely veiled suggestion that she and her sister should welcome two strangers into their beds tonight?

"I would gladly take you there," she said, startling him until she added, "I welcome any help in saving my sister from Lord Wain of Moorburgh's lascivious hands."

"What is this?" Guy frowned at Christian as if he had conspired with Avisa to entrap Guy into agreeing to what might become dangerous.

Baldwin grinned. "Are we going to rescue this woman's sister?"

"Baldwin, take the horses to the stream and let them drink," Christian said.

"I shall go with him." Guy grabbed the ring tying his horse's reins together. "If you wish to immerse yourself in nonsense, brother, I trust you will remember that I do not aspire to heroic deeds."

Avisa's face revealed her despair as she watched the two lead their horses away. Closing her eyes, she said, "I can understand your brother's reluctance. Lord Wain is a fearsome foe, and others have tried in vain to defeat him. Only the bravest within England's shores would dare to confront him."

How did she know the very words to tempt him into offering to help her? To rescue a maiden from a man, lord though he might be, was the duty of every knight. To free her from a man loath to release her would be every knight's honor. To defeat a man who had been the victor in other such battles would bring great glory to any knight. Maybe even enough glory to redeem his family's name.

"Where did this rogue lord take your sister?" he asked.

Those remarkable eyes came alight once more. "Are you willing to help me?"

"I have yet to decide, for my journey takes me to Canterbury for a wedding."

"Yours?" She hastily looked away, and he suspected she was disconcerted that a man on his way to exchange vows with his betrothed would have held her with desire.

"Not mine, but a friend of my father. Philip de Boisvert."
He could not keep from staring at that silly short sword. A
woman brave enough to have such a weapon needed someone to save her from her delusions that she could defend herself on her own. She might be unwise, but he had to admire
her courage—and her beauty that tantalized him.

Suddenly she raised her sword. His hand went instinc-
tively to his own.

"Look behind you!" she shouted.

Christian drew his sword as three of the outlaws burst
from behind the trees. Hearing the clang of iron, he saw,
from the corner of his eye, Avisa battling another man. She
handled her sword with competence. He slashed his own at
her attacker. The man fell back, then bellowed a laugh as
more men leaped out onto the road.

"Christian!"

He looked over his shoulder as Baldwin yelled again. He
did not bother to curse as a score of men raced after his
page, who was trying to flee and scramble onto his horse at
the same time. The runners' swords were drawn and their
wicked intent clear.

Hating the very idea of retreat, Christian knew he must
think of Avisa's safety before his honor. His family's name
would be defiled anew if he allowed her to die.

He swung up onto his horse, slicing into an outlaw. Again
he drew Blackthorn up on his rear legs. The men jumped
back as the front hooves struck at them, but they did not run
away as they had before.

The horse dropped back to the road, and Christian held
out his hand. Avisa seized it and swung up onto the horse
with an ease that amazed him. He settled her on his lap, and
the soft fragrance of some flower filled his breath. He would
have liked to enjoy it, but he had no time to think of anything but saving her life.

"Hold tight!" He motioned to Baldwin to follow as
Guy sped past them. "Let's go! Now!" He steered his

horse straight at the outlaws, laughing as he forced them to scatter.

He looked back as he drew even with his brother. The men were in pursuit. After them or—he glanced at Avisa, who was gripping her sword, ready to fight—or after her? Her sister had caught the eye of a baron. Could these be his men come to steal Avisa as well?

"Who are they, Avisa?" he demanded. "Who is their lord?"

"They are landless, horrible thieves. Turn into the woods!"

"What?"

He cursed when arrows flew past, striking trees and the road. He heard a screech behind him, but when he looked back again, his brother shouted for him to keep going.

"Turn into the woods," she ordered again.

"We can outdistance them more quickly on the road."

"But not their arrows!" she cried as more arrows whistled past.

Steadying Avisa, he sent the horse into the forest. She was correct. Their only escape might be where the trees would shield them.

Once they were deep within the wood, he turned his horse in the direction they had come, glancing behind to make sure Guy and Baldwin followed. He thought Avisa might ask why he was riding toward their pursuers, but she remained silent, her fingers tight around her sword.

Steering his horse into the stream, he motioned for his brother and page to follow. Water splashed up onto his boots. He heard Avisa sputter. There was no time to apologize for getting cold water in her face.

"Follow the stream another half mile," she said, her voice taut but hushed.

He tried not to let his mind linger on how pleasurable it would be to have that dulcet voice brushing his ear as he held her and explored the soft body now pressed against him on the narrow saddle. "Why? What is a half mile from here?"

"With luck, a way to evade our pursuers."

He nodded, hoping she knew this countryside better than he did. Watching that the stream did not deepen into a pool that could cause the horse to lose his footing and send them flying over his head, Christian glanced to his right when she did.

"There," she said. "Go that way."

Christian had to admit she was woods-wise, for she was pointing to a rocky section of the bank already splashed with water. Their passage could be missed. He guided the horse up onto the icy rocks and behind bushes edging the stream. There he drew to a stop.

"This should be good," he said.

"It will be better if we hide in that thicket there." She started to slide off his lap.

His breath caught as the motion was a reminder—even though he needed none—that a lovely lass perched on his lap. His arm closed around her, and she looked up at him. Whatever she had been going to say went unspoken when he caught her gaze and held it.

Something about those fiery blue eyes was familiar. Had he seen her before?

He did not realize he had asked the question aloud until she said, "No, that is impossible."

"We must—"

She put her finger to his lips, and his heart threatened to explode from his chest. The chaste touch, innocent and yet wise, sent his head reeling as if she had struck him. It was futile to try to hear what had alerted her, for his pulse raged in him. Even when she drew her finger away, he could feel its warmth against his lips.

Christian shook his head to clear it. He kept his arm around Avisa as he slid awkwardly from the saddle. A groan escaped his clenched teeth when he landed too heavily on his right leg. Pain seared up it. That had been foolish, and this was the worst time to be a fool.

"Are you hurt?" she asked, warning that she was aware of every nuance. As she must be. The slightest mistake and they could be defeated by a more numerous foe.

"I shall be fine."

"Good. You must be able to walk, even though we are not going far."

"Are you suggesting we fight them *here*?"

"No."

"Then what?"

"Come with me." She held out her hand. When he took it, she smiled. "We are not the first to hide here."

He was unsure what she meant until he saw broken branches on the edge of the thicket. He guessed a creature about the size of a stag had sought sanctuary within it.

Limping, he went with her around the rocks and parted the bushes so she could slip through. He heard other branches clattering. Guy and Baldwin must be hiding as well. For once, he was glad his brother had no yearning to be lauded for bravery.

"Wait here," he said.

Her eyes narrowed, and she frowned. "Where are you going? The robbers may be afoot, but they will be swift, for they want the prize of my purse."

"I am going to secure the horses. If they make noise, they may betray us."

"I can secure them. You are too slow with that twisted ankle."

He was about to argue, then realized she was right. Sitting while she slipped back through the briars was aggravating. What sort of man allowed a woman to face danger alone while he hid in safety? He started to follow her, then paused when the branches rattled. Pulling his sword, he lowered it when Avisa slipped in to kneel beside him.

"I lashed the reins to a tree behind us," she whispered, leaning toward him. That luscious, flowery scent sought to distract him again, and again he struggled to ignore it. The scent of roses, if he was not mistaken. How perfect for this woman who was as supple as a rose petal and as prickly as the sharpest thorns. "Your companions are well hidden."

"Good." He flinched as he shifted to see past the briars.

She leaned forward to touch his right ankle. Even through his leather boot, he could sense her fingers' warmth. Putting his own beneath her chin, he tilted her head back.

"I should check your ankle," she whispered. "If you have hurt it badly—"

"I would rather that you kissed me to make me feel better."

"This is no time to think of that." Her tone became a scold, but fire burned more fiercely in her eloquent eyes.

"No, but it is all I can think of." He ran his fingers up her arms and let them curve around her face.

At the sound of shouts, she stiffened and drew away.

He started to move to peer past the tangled branches, but she put her sword across his knees, halting him.

"Stay where you are if you want to keep from being skewered," she ordered.

"We must be prepared. If they find us here—"

"They shall not, if you do as I say," she said with an air of quiet authority. "Be still, Christian Lovell, or be dead."

Chapter 3

Christian's eyes widened at Avisa's hushed threat, but he said nothing more. Good. She did not want to argue about every order she gave.

The situation had become as tangled as the briars around them. After exploring the roads and woods in this parish, she had thought it seemed a good idea to allow the queen's godson to chance upon her when it appeared she was in need of assistance. Talking at a local inn about having gold in her purse had been enough to lure the thieves from their lair, but she had not guessed there were so many outlaws in the forest.

Branches rattled, and she hissed for silence as splashes and shouts from their pursuers grew louder. She looked to her left and saw the man who had been riding with Christian and the boy. From the description the queen had given to her on the rolled page, she would have recognized him as Guy even if Christian had not spoken his name. His face was as gray as the sky at dawn. Was he frightened? The queen had said nothing of him other than that he rode at his brother's side. He started to speak, but Christian held up his hand for silence.

When Christian draped his dark cloak over himself and Avisa, she tried to edge away. He flashed her a scowl.

"I need my sword arm free," she whispered.

"Better that they do not detect us here."

Avisa had to admit he was right. They were well hidden by the cloak, which was almost the same color as the bare branches. She recalled the queen's words not to underestimate her godson. She would not make that mistake again.

When the outlaws waded through the water not far from them, she tensed. Christian slipped his arm around her shoulders, shocking her and sending a quiver racing along her. In the Abbey there had been hushed conversations about what men and women shared in the secular world. She understood the desires that brought them together—or she had thought she did. His touch told her how little she truly knew.

But she was not here to learn. She was here to keep him from going to Canterbury. The queen's command must take precedence over everything else. Obeying it would mean the Abbey's continuing to receive her majesty's benevolence.

His hand inched around her waist, and that unknown throb surged through her again. Her gaze slipped from the stream to his eyes' fascinating glow. A hint of a smile tilted his mouth, and she found herself imagining those lips on hers.

Hearing a curse, Avisa looked back at the stream. She watched with satisfaction as the outlaws ran past.

"Sometimes the old tricks are the best," she whispered.

A slow sigh drifted from Christian's lips.

"What is amiss?" she asked.

"There is no honor in besting fools."

"I was not seeking honor. I was seeking to keep them from robbing me."

"Or worse."

She nodded grimly. "Or worse."

After the last of the thieves had vanished along the stream, Christian stood and pushed aside the briars. "We must leave before our pursuers realize they have been deceived and return. Do you know the shortest way to the road, Avisa?"

"Yes, but first . . ." She looked at his companions. "How do you do?"

"I am fine," the lad Baldwin began as he emerged from the thicket, "but Guy . . ."

Christian swore, and she saw his brother's tunic was red with blood. When he knelt beside Guy, he asked, "What happened?"

"An arrow," groaned Guy. "In my hip."

Avisa muttered a prayer under her breath. She should have thought of a different way to make sure Christian's path crossed hers.

"Where can we get help for Guy?" Christian asked.

"I know a place," she replied, "but it is a distance from here." She hoped she could find the clearing she had discovered several days before. Nothing looked familiar now that daylight had been banished from beneath the trees.

"Lead us there."

She met his gaze. It was as strong as his arms that had lifted her onto his horse as if she weighed as little as milkweed fluff. She could not halt herself from admiring his muscular shoulders and arms, which swung a broadsword with ease. His blue-gray eyes slitted when she did not answer. This assignment would have been simpler if his features were not even and strong. Especially his jaw, which hinted at a stubborn nature. She was tempted to warn him that she could be obstinate, too.

"Is your ankle all right? Can you walk, Christian?" She glanced toward the stream. "Those outlaws will be back, and they will be in a fouler mood than before."

Christian's dark brows lowered. "I will walk as far as I must, but do not forget we have horses."

"Where we travel, it will be easier to lead them."

"Then let's go, unless you are planning to stay here to greet the thieves on their return."

She ignored his sarcasm when she saw his page's grin. "Of course not. Your brother needs help."

"He shall get it."

"And so do you."

"My brother first."

She squatted next to Guy Lovell. He started to cringe away, but she put her fingers gently on his arm as, with care, she drew aside the folds of his tunic. The broken shaft of an arrow protruded from his hip.

Christian grasped the end.

She put her hand over his before he could yank the arrow out. "Take care. You may tear the flesh more."

"Are you a healer?"

"No, but I do have some knowledge of wounds." She did not look at him. She had to avoid any questions that might reveal the truth about her training at St. Jude's Abbey. "Come with me, and I shall show you."

"Come with you? Where?"

"Where I may repay you for saving me from those thieves." She dipped her head, but noted the quicksilver sparks in his eyes. "But we must go now. Help Guy, young Baldwin, while I assist Christian."

The lad bent to bring the hurt man to his feet, then straightened. "'Tis not your place to give orders."

"Hush, Baldwin," Christian replied, his voice strained. "Avisa is offering us assistance, and we would be wise to take it."

"Will you stop arguing and get this damned arrow out of me?" grumbled Guy.

She bent to help Christian to his feet. His palm curved along her cheek, and she found herself drowning in his eyes' depths. His thumb caressed her jaw. Her hand rose to stroke his cheek, but she paused when his lips parted. Whatever he might have said vanished beneath splashing in the stream.

Avisa did not wait. She drew her sword and, unlashing the horses, held out the reins to Christian. He did not take them. Instead, he put his arm under his brother's shoulders to help his page.

"Go!" she whispered. "They will give you no chance for excuses if they find you."

"Won't they follow?" Christian asked as quietly. She had

to admire his good sense in listening to her . . . when he had no other choice.

"They believe the tales of restless spirits which inhabit the forest on this side of the stream. Even if there is one among them who has the slightest amount of valor, they have little skill as trackers. They would rather prey on those who travel the roads."

"You know much of them."

She nodded, but gave him no chance to ask another question. Slipping through the trees, making sure the horses' bridles made no sound, she wondered how many more lies she could speak before he saw through her tales. It was the truth that the robbers would not spend much time seeking them when other victims would soon spring their trap. The rest of it was as false as her claim that she needed help to save her sister. Each lie was bitter on her tongue, but she had told the queen that she would do whatever she must to protect her godson.

Crouching, she pointed in the direction she wished the men to go. Christian began to help his brother walk, each step obviously painful for both men. She shoved the reins into Baldwin's thin hand. When he started to speak, she put her finger to her lips. He nodded and followed the men.

Avisa edged back toward the stream. She had to make sure the robbers did not chase after them. Again she risked a glance at Christian, who was struggling with his brother. Guy moaned at each step, the sound threatening to alert the thieves. She could understood why the queen was worried about Christian. He seemed reluctant to disengage from any battle. Nor was he willing to follow others' orders, although he easily gave them.

When she heard angry voices in front of her, she dropped to the ground and crawled toward them. Fingering her sword's hilt, she gnawed on her lower lip.

"They must be here," grumbled a man whose back was to her. "They cannot disappear."

Another man began, "If the woman is a witch—"

"Bah! No witch is that lovely," the first man argued.

"A lovely witch can steal a man's mind from him."

Rumbles of agreement ended abruptly. She did not see the signal that their leader, a man with few teeth remaining, made, but the thieves went toward the road.

She inched away toward where Christian and his companions should be. They had not gotten far. Christian was now walking with barely a limp, but his brother did not seem able to continue.

"Where did you go?" Christian asked as he paused to let his brother lean against a tree.

Baldwin wore a grateful smile as he stepped back and rubbed the shoulder that had been holding Guy up.

"I wanted to be sure we wouldn't be followed." She saw no reason to lie.

"What?" Disbelief sanded away the harder edges of his face.

"I watched the thieves give up the chase."

He grasped her shoulders, jerking her closer. "How could you be so stupid? If they had seen you—"

"They didn't see her," his brother snarled, then groaned. "Have your lovers' quarrel later. First, take me somewhere where you can get this accursed arrow out of me."

Avisa moved away from Christian, who scowled at his brother. For interrupting or because he was furious with Guy *and* her?

"Bring Guy's horse, Baldwin," Christian ordered. "He cannot walk any farther."

It took the three of them to get Guy up to lie across the wooden saddle. Avisa was unsure if Guy did anything beyond complaining that they were hurting him worse. She wanted to ask if he always whined like this, but she could not risk angering Christian to the point he decided to leave her to rescue "her sister" on her own.

As she took the reins of the other horses, Christian said quietly, "Don't be stupid and run off like that again, Avisa, or you shall make me regret coming to your rescue."

"They did not see me, and we needed to know they were not trailing us."

His jaw set in a rigid line, and she knew he agreed with her. Again she could not guess if he was furious because she was right or because she had endangered herself.

She realized she was wrong about both when he said, "I expect all of us to stay together to protect each other."

"With you as our leader?"

"Yes."

She fought not to bristle. Within the walls of the Abbey, she was acknowledged for her skills and how well she commanded others. The abbess had warned her, before her departure, that she must expect circumstances to be very different outside the Abbey and that she must act accordingly. It galled her to acquiesce, but arguing further might raise his suspicions and lead to questions she must not answer.

"Will you agree, Avisa?" he asked when she remained silent.

Before she could answer, his brother demanded, "Can't you debate this *after* you get the arrow out of me?"

Christian apologized to Guy, but kept staring at her. Did he think to intimidate her with that stare? She almost laughed. He might be able to daunt other women with such tactics, but she knew how to use the same tactics herself.

A bird squawked as it flew up behind Avisa. She looked at the lad. Baldwin wore a guilty frown. If they were betrayed by his thoughtless blundering through the underbrush and the outlaws decided to hunt them anew . . .

She gasped when Christian put his hand on her arm. The heat from his fingers sifted through her wool sleeve, reminding her how his arms had held her gently against the warmth of his chest. Why was she thinking of *that* now?

"It will be fine," he murmured and motioned for her to lead the way.

She swallowed roughly. Pushing through more briars tangled among the trees, she was glad to keep her back to him.

Christian had not reacted to touching her. Maybe he had not sensed the connection that filled her with sudden pleasure. She must emulate him, because she could not be silly while the queen depended on her.

No one spoke as they went through the wood. Darkness obliterated any path through the bare-branched trees, and Avisa was relieved when the moon rose to shed cold light upon them. If she were injured, Christian would most likely find her a place to heal while he continued on his way to Canterbury.

She smiled when she recognized a large boulder placed atop another. She had not been certain she would need this sanctuary when she set her plan into motion, but she was glad she had earlier scouted the clearing ahead of them.

"Wait here," she said, holding up her hand as she looped the horses' leading reins over a thick shrub.

"For what?" asked Christian.

His question did not surprise her. He had challenged everything else she had said.

"Just wait." She pointed to the thinning trees. "I want to be certain no trap awaits us in the clearing ahead."

He stepped forward, drawing his sword. "Let me check."

She gestured for him to lower the sword. "I know these woods. You do not. I will be able to tell if something is amiss. You could lead us right into a trap."

"How do I know you aren't leading us into a trap?"

"Do you think I am allied with the outlaws?"

She gasped when he gripped her plaited hair at her nape. Tilting her head back, he stepped closer to her. The flat of his broadsword brushed her skirt. Instead of being frustrated with his overbearing determination to keep her in a woman's place, she should have gauged *his* frustration.

"I do not know with *whom* you are allied, Avisa de Vere, but you know these woods too well for someone traveling through them." His mouth was a straight line as he ground out each word. "You are not being completely honest with me."

"Of course not!" She hoped it was not just bravado and her lies that strengthened her voice. "For all I know, you arranged for me to be set upon by the robbers so you could rescue me and persuade me to let my guard down. For all I know, you may be Lord Wain's lapdog, sent to hurt me as he wishes to hurt my sister."

With an oath, he released her. "You have a honed tongue, woman. Be wary, or someone with less patience than I will cut it out."

"I will try to remember that." Before he could retort, she added, "Be that as it may, for now, you have to trust me."

His laugh, although hushed, resonated through her like thunder coursing across the hills. "Trust you? Why should I trust you when everything you have told us may be untrue?"

Guy chuckled tautly as Baldwin drew the horses closer. "Maybe you are the one who should be wary, brother. You have met your match in this woman."

"As long as we do not meet our ends at her hands."

Avisa smiled. "Have faith in my determination to keep my head on my shoulders."

As she started to walk toward the clearing, Christian seized her arms and twisted her to face him. She fell to her knees in front of him. When she tried to get to her feet, his fingers tightened on her arms. He held her in place easily when she struggled to escape.

"Heed my words well, Avisa de Vere, if that is your true name—"

"It is."

He spat on the ground, and she stared at him, wide-eyed. This cold man was unlike the kind one who had believed she needed to be rescued from the outlaws.

"Heed me," he repeated. "If you betray us, you shall not live to betray another."

Baldwin whispered, his voice filled with anxiety, "Guy needs help soon."

Avisa eased out of Christian's grip and stood. Pushing her crumpled sleeves back over her wrists, she said, "Stay here until I signal it is safe." She smiled as icily as Christian had. "Even then, be cautious. The ones we met are not the sole outlaws in the forest."

Ducking, she slipped through the thick bushes at the edge of the clearing. She scanned the woods around the open space cut through on one side by a stream. Whether it was part of the one they had crossed before, she did not know.

She turned and waved to the men to follow her. As they emerged from the sentinel trees, she was not surprised to see Christian carrying his sword. The boy beside him held a knife.

"There is no one here but us," she said when they drew even with her. As Baldwin helped Guy from the horse, she added, "With the bright moonlight, I believe we are safe to have a small fire. If we use green wood, the smoke will be thick and not float far, so nobody will follow its trail here. Such a low flame will not alert others we are here, and we need to sear the edges of Guy's wound so it will heal."

Christian sent his page to gather wood and kindling before turning to his brother. The moonlight washed out Guy's gray, pain-lined face more as he held tightly to the horse to remain on his feet.

"How do you fare?" Christian asked.

"It would seem our journey has taken an unexpected turn," Guy replied with another moan.

"We can leave as soon as you are tended to, if that is your wish."

Guy smiled. "How could I give up the chance to discover more about our fair Avisa?"

Avisa stared down at the ground. Guy Lovell had an arrow in his hip, and yet he seemed to be regarding her with lust. She must be misreading his expression. She suspected this was another thing she did not understand about men. Returning to St. Jude's Abbey, her task completed, had never sounded as splendid as it did now.

"If you will bring him to where your page is lighting the fire," she said, "I shall tend to his wound."

"Baldwin will do that." Christian's tone warned she would be foolish to argue.

She did anyhow. "But I told you that I have some experience with this."

"As Baldwin does." He wore a cool smile. "A wise page learns to tend all sorts of wounds. Why don't you prepare us something to eat?" He pulled some packages from behind the saddle of his brother's horse. Tossing them to her, he said, "Prepare these."

"I am a better healer than a cook."

"You do not need to cook anything. Just open the packages. The meat and bread are ready to be eaten. Let us men attend to the wound."

Avisa bit back the curse that no sister in St. Jude's Abbey should even know. She had learned it at a decrepit inn on the way to where she met Christian Lovell. Was this how all men treated women, or was he trying to humiliate her because she had questioned his orders?

Whirling so her skirt belled out behind her, she walked to where the low fire was burning. She threw the packets on the ground beside it and kept walking. How tempted she was to tell him that she had been sent here to protect *him*! That fact would erase the arrogant smile from his lips.

Her steps faltered at a roar of pain. She looked back at where Baldwin was bent over Guy. "Oh, dear God," she whispered, then almost screamed when a hand touched her cheek. She took a calming breath as it steered her face toward Christian. She had not realized he was following her.

"Do not look horrified," he said with a tight smile as he stepped between her and her view of the fire. "Guy shrieks when drawing a splinter from his finger. He will be fine."

Another screech sent a shiver swirling up her spine. "Are you certain?"

She saw the truth in his eyes. Christian was trying to prevent her from seeing what was happening. She pulled away and ran to where Baldwin was tossing aside the blood-coated arrow. A gash was torn across Guy's leg.

Baldwin's smile was strained as he reached for a pouch on his belt. "He will be fine once I clean it. I will stitch the wound closed."

"If you are suffering from a weak head," Christian added, as he came to stand beside her again, "you should sit before you faint."

"De Vere women do not faint," Avisa asserted, but her head did seem oddly light.

"On that I agree, for courage you have in great quantities." He motioned toward the brook. "Will you join me while I wash the dust of the road from my mouth? It will give us both the opportunity to learn more of each other in a civilized manner."

"Very well." Better to relent a little. Deciding what to tell him would free her mind from focusing on his skin's teasing caress when he had cupped her cheek.

They crossed the clearing. The water had become silver in the moonlight. The stones trailed patterns in the slow current dancing around the dead plants.

She looked at the opposite shore. A motion sent her hand to her sword, but she relaxed when she saw several deer.

Christian knelt to scoop up some water. "If you fear the outlaws will follow us, Baldwin and I will take a turn on watch."

"An excellent idea."

He stood. Water glistened on his lips, luring her gaze to them. She looked again at the tips of her shoes as he said, "My offer is for one night only. I do not want Guy's rest disturbed tonight. Nor do I want to wake with a knife stuck here." He touched the center of her chest. When she stepped back, shocked, he chuckled.

"You are bold, sir."

"So are you!"

Avisa bit back her retort. Was Christian's concern truly for her and his comrades, or was he just trying to unnerve her? If it was the latter, he was succeeding far better than even he might suspect. The stroke of his finger against her breast, brief as a heartbeat, had sent heat flashing through her with the speed of a summer storm. Fast and breathtaking and frightening as it swept all thought from her head.

Struggling to keep her voice even, she said, "Having a guard is a good suggestion." She must handle this situation delicately, for she did not want to create a chasm between them. If she did, he might leave without her, and she would have failed the queen and the Abbey. Maybe assuming the woman's role and opening the food packets would ease the tension between them. "Excuse me. I must—"

He caught her hand and kept her from walking away. "I deserve an explanation, Lady Avisa."

"Lady?" she choked. "Please do not call me that."

"Why? It is your name, isn't it?"

"Why do you think that?"

He tapped her scabbard. "Your sword was made by a master craftsman." He rubbed his fingers on her drooping sleeve. "This fabric has not been embedded with smoke and ash from long hours of being near a smithy's forge, so I doubt you are an ironsmith's daughter. Although I have to consider you might have stolen your sword, you know how to use it. That suggests the sword was made for you, and such an excellent weapon would belong only to a lord's daughter."

She wondered how else she had betrayed herself. Again she recalled the queen's warning not to misjudge her godson. "I have to—"

"Tell me the truth, or . . ."

Shock widened her eyes. "Or what?"

He drew her to him as his cloak flowed around her again, holding her within its dark wings. His voice became a low rumble. "Tell me, milady, why a lord's daughter hides in the woods."

"My sister—"

"'Tis more than that, for your father must have men to free your sister."

"No longer." She dampened her lips. The story she had

thought was simple and straightforward was becoming more convoluted as she invented answers to his questions. Sitting on a mossy hummock gave her a way to keep him from seeing her face, which might reveal she was lying as she spun the tale she had devised with the abbess. "Lord Wain attacked my home, and few survive. Those who do have sought sanctuary with Milo de Sommeville." The abbess had suggested the baron because he was well respected by the queen and his family was long allied with the de Vere family. "I must reach Lord de Sommeville and beg his assistance, but I cannot be certain he will grant my family such a boon when he could be Lord Wain's next target."

"How can that be so? When Stephen was king, such things happened, but now Henry is king, and he is bringing law back to the land."

"Lord Wain believes the only true law is his own. Will you help me reach Lord de Sommeville's stronghold and gain his assistance to save my sister? I know you are on your way to your father's friend's wedding, but I fear I cannot save her on my own."

"I suspect you could." He smiled. The expression transformed his face. The strong lines remained, but a gentleness slipped into his voice. "You have guile and wit as your two best weapons, so you might not have to draw your sword."

Avisa blinked as his laugh broke the spell his voice had woven about her without her being aware of it. Vexed, she fired back. "Do not belittle the huge task ahead of me! I admit I was foolish to believe I could save her on my own. Will you help me?"

Sitting beside her, he tossed a stone to plop in the water. His easy pose did not deceive her. His hand was not far from his knife, and his feet pressed against the mossy bank so he could jump up at the first sign of trouble.

"Before I agree to assist you, tell me the truth about one thing," he said, low enough so his words would reach no one's ears but hers.

"If I can."

"Why are you traveling—?"

A warning shout rang through the clearing. Avisa reacted without thought. Christian gasped when she struck him hard in the chest. With a curse, he fell back on the ground. She yelped as his arm swept around her to pull her down, too.

"What are you doing now?" he gasped.

"Saving you from that arrow."

His eyes widened when he looked past her shoulder to the quivering arrow stuck in the tree inches from where his head had been. "So I see."

"If the outlaws have returned—"

"It did not come from one of their bows."

"How do you know that?" She stared at him. "You recognize the fletcher by his work?" She reached up to pull the arrow out of the trunk, but his arm around her halted her. "Please release me!"

He smiled and twisted sharply from beneath her, flipping her onto her back. She cried out in amazement as he slid his sword from its scabbard. Was he going to slay her? Why? She had just saved his life.

She gasped again when he tossed it aside. She put up her hands to push away his heavy cloak. When her fingers brushed his hard chest, his thumb edged along her chin. She tried to turn away, but his fingers twisted through her hair.

"What is wrong?" she demanded.

"Very little at the moment, I would say."

"I thought you said we would behave in a civilized manner."

"We are."

"But you just drew your sword. Have the outlaws returned?"

"No."

"Then why—?"

"It would have been in the way." His other arm slipped beneath her.

"In the way? What do you mean?"

His laugh vanished as his mouth slanted across hers.

Shock riveted her at his brazen kiss . . . and at the luscious pleasure on his lips. Her breath sounded swift and eager in her ears as his mouth slipped along her neck. Each fevered touch was a separate pleasure, growing excruciatingly exciting.

She lifted her hands to shove him away, but as she touched his firm shoulders, he pressed her more deeply into the moss. Boldly, he explored her lips, and the tip of his tongue grazed the corners of her mouth, sending undeniable desire racing within her. A desire for more of these dangerous, delicious kisses. When he raised his mouth from hers, she stared up at him, her breath ragged.

He chuckled again. "How simple and delectable it is to hush you this way! I would be glad to think of endless ways to seduce you into silence."

"Are you quite finished?" She shoved him away and sat. How dare he be so presumptuous—and how dare he ruin her pleasure with a jest?

He laughed. "Now that is a charming thank-you when I wanted to show you how grateful I am."

"Do not foolishly assume I wanted such gratitude."

"It was not a foolish assumption when you were willing."

"Christian!" came a shout.

Baldwin ran up to them and pulled the arrow out of the tree trunk. His arrival kept her from having to devise a lie to conceal how close Christian was to the truth. His kisses had overwhelmed her, making her forget—for those wondrous moments—even her obligations to the queen and the Abbey.

"Christian!" Baldwin cried. "Are you all right? Guy should have known better than to try to fire at a stag when he cannot stand."

"Guy?" Avisa gasped. "Guy let fly that arrow at us?"

"How else would I have recognized it?" Christian asked with a cool serenity that threatened to unleash her temper. He took the arrow from his page. "See this notch at the end of each feather? That is the hallmark of my father's fletcher."

"Your own brother fired an arrow at you?"

"Do not worry yourself. We were not hurt."

"It nearly struck you."

"You saved me, and he did not let loose another."

Standing and brushing twigs from her gown, she said, "I saved you *again*. You are in my debt."

"And you wish me to even that debt by rescuing your sister?" His smile straightened into a frown.

"Yes."

He regarded her for a long moment, then nodded. "Very well. We shall help you as you have asked." Brushing his fingers against her cheek, he added, "But you must agree to one important thing, Avisa."

"What?" She wished her mind would function, but the sensations his fingertips had sent through her held every thought captive as surely as her imaginary sister in that imaginary dastardly baron's imaginary castle.

"That you will follow my orders. Do you agree?"

"Yes," she replied, knowing she risked his not helping her if she said anything else.

He tweaked her cheek as if she were a child. "I trust a de Vere does not break such vows."

"I do not break any vows I take."

When he smiled again and went with his page to where his brother began to apologize for firing the arrow, she did not follow. She would not break any vow, not to him and not to the queen. She would protect Christian Lovell as she had pledged, but, for the first time, she realized she would also have to protect herself from surrendering to her longing to be in his arms again. She was not sure which would be more difficult.

Chapter 4

Christian had never been more pleased to see the open gate of a castle than he was when he led the way through the gatehouse at Castle Orxted. When he had ridden past the holding yesterday, he could not have guessed the next day's sunset would find him entering its gate.

The massive gatehouse rose more than forty feet above the road. Narrow windows on the upper floors offered the baron's archers an excellent view of the road. If any enemy soldiers evaded their arrows and battered aside the outer gate, they would find no shelter under the breadth of the gatehouse. He looked up at the trapdoors that could be opened to pour hot sand and oil on invaders. There would be no escape into the ward, because the inner doors were thicker than Avisa's waist.

He growled a curse under his breath at the comparison he had not intended to make.

Her hearing must be keen because she looked over her shoulder. She took care, he noted, not to shift. Her kisses had tasted of innocence, but she must realize even a monk would be tempted if such an alluring woman was unable to sit still on his lap. He had considered having her ride with Baldwin, but the page would not be able to handle his horse, offer assistance to Guy, who was unsteady on his, and make sure she did not fall off.

Noise exploded around them as he led the way into the outer ward. The large area was filled with soldiers and women flirting with them. A pair of dogs raced past Blackthorn, causing the horse to falter. Christian's arm contracted around Avisa as he urged the horse toward the inner gate.

Her fingers bit into his hand, and he muttered, "No need to claw me. I will not let you tumble off."

"Let—let me—g-g-go!" she choked. "Too—tight."

Realizing he was keeping her from breathing, he loosened the arm clamped around her middle. She drew in a deep breath, and he watched her enticing breasts move. All he needed to do was stretch up his thumb to caress the right one's underside before exploring farther.

She grasped his arm with both hands and pushed it a bit lower, as if she had guessed the course of his fantasies. That unsettling thought was put aside when she said, "I appreciate your concerns on my behalf, but please do not try to protect me by keeping me from pulling in a breath."

"That was not my intention."

"I did not say it was."

He was glad she was looking from side to side, trying to take in every aspect of the outer ward, from the animals being herded through a small gate on one side to the blacksmith on the other. He did not want her to see his grimace at her retort. Avisa was giving him the chance he had hoped for to prove his courage when they rescued her sister, but she seemed determined to test his patience each step of the way. And his self-control, for as she turned to look to the right, her hair brushed his cheek. It urged him to bury his face in it as he showed her that the kisses by the stream were only a sample of what he could share with her.

"Take care," he said when her hair drifted across his chin again as her head swiveled to the other side. He spat out a strand that had slipped past his lips when he spoke.

"I am sorry." She reached to tuck her hair back into place. As she tilted her head, her smooth neck taunted him to let his mouth slide along it.

"It is nothing."

Something in his voice must have betrayed him, because

she looked over her shoulder, distress in her eyes. Eyes, he noticed again, that were the exact shade of the embroidery on her gown. Her lips could have been fresh strawberries, a luscious treat once summer returned. Would her mouth taste as sweet in the sunshine as it did in the shadows?

She blinked twice, fast, and he wondered if she was caught up in the spell, too, created when their gazes met. As she looked forward once more, he knew he would be a fool to ask. He had an opportunity he had not expected to show the rest of England what he knew in his heart, and he could not allow himself to be distracted by a pretty blonde. He gripped the reins as he silently repeated those words a second time.

Animal smells welcomed them as they rode through another gate to the inner ward. More odors, not much more appealing, came from a wooden building set to one side of the tall, narrow keep. The kitchen, he guessed, although he wondered why it had not been rebuilt in the same stone as the rest of the castle. Maybe it had not burned recently.

When a servant came forward to greet him and offer to take the horses to the stables, Christian motioned for someone to assist Avisa down. Having her slide across him would destroy any attempt to resist her soft curves.

A lanky man held up his hands. When Avisa put hers on his shoulders, he lifted her off Christian's lap.

"God's teeth!" the man hissed when her sword struck him before he set her on the stones.

Swinging down, Christian grimaced as his right foot touched the ground. Accursed ankle! No knight of legend had been hampered by a twisted ankle. So he would not be either. He took Avisa's arm and, hobbling, guided her toward where his brother was dismounting with Baldwin's help. Too many eyes followed their motions.

"They must not get many people coming through their gates," Avisa said quietly. "I realize that any visitor is a source of interest, but they are staring."

"They have probably never seen a woman wearing a broadsword before," he replied.

Her eyes were wide with astonishment. "You are jesting!"

"No."

"I find that hard to believe." She touched her sword's hilt, her fingers lingering on it.

He gulped as he could not keep from recalling that soft touch against him. "Believe what you choose to believe, Avisa, but ladies do not carry broadswords. They depend on their men to protect them." He smiled coldly. "They concern themselves with more feminine pursuits."

"The queen must have been armed when she went to the Holy Land."

"Maybe she was, but no one here saw that."

Avisa frowned. Again Christian was correct. Eleanor had been France's queen then, not Henry's.

He reached around and closed her cloak in front of her. "You have attracted enough eyes already."

Avisa bit back a retort while Christian put his shoulder under his brother's arm to assist him across the shadowed courtyard the wintry sun had already abandoned. Guy's bow fell to the ground, and he ordered Baldwin to retrieve it.

Christian called, "Hurry! I want to get something to wash the road's dust from my throat."

"There is no need to wait for me."

He fired a scowl at her as his brother chuckled. "I said, 'Hurry,' Avisa!"

By the four winds! He was a vexing man. Yet his words were a reminder she should not need that she must remain close to keep him safe.

She followed the men, looking around so she did not have to watch Christian's obviously painful steps. The castle had been constructed of the same stone as the Abbey and was surrounded by a curtain wall, but that was the only similarity. In addition to the gathering of small buildings she was accustomed to, the castle had an inner wall and a narrow keep even taller than the chapel at the Abbey. Windows, like the silhouette of a single finger, were scattered across its stone face. A trio of steps led up to double doors that were, she discovered as they passed them, so thick her palm could not have covered their depth.

The dark keep was lit by sputtering lamps in niches along the wall. Avisa paused as two women carrying trays of food crossed in front of her. She looked to the left and saw a dim doorway that must lead down to the kitchen. Harried voices came from that direction. Closer, she heard the coo of doves that must have decided escaping the evening's cold was worth the risk of being caught and prepared for the lord's dinner.

Where had Christian and his brother and page gone? She peered through the darkness. A staircase rose directly in front of her, and a pair of doors near it led to the right and the left. The keep was so enormous she could search through it for hours without finding them.

Her hands clenched at her sides. The queen had given her a task, and she had let it slip her mind while she pondered the fate of a pair of doves. If she was not so accursedly exhausted, she might be able to concentrate on what she must do. Sleeping had been impossible last night when Christian had been lying only an arm's length away. Through her mind, over and over, came the memory of the thrilling sensation of his mouth on hers. Each time, she had reminded herself of her vows to St. Jude's Abbey. Would a few kisses condemn her in the Abbey's eyes? She *was* a cloistered sister, but a cloistered sister bid by her queen to do whatever was necessary to protect Christian. And she had done so, for the kisses had helped seal the agreement that he would help her save "her sister," distracting him from his journey to Canterbury.

But the kisses had distracted *her*, too. She must keep her wits about her if he attempted to kiss her again. She was unsure how, but she had never failed at a task given to her. She would not do so now.

The sound of Guy's complaining came from her right, and Avisa almost cheered out loud. She had not thought she would be grateful for his refusal to bear his pain in silence. Hurrying in that direction along a corridor so constricted she could have stuck out her elbows and touched both walls, she quickly caught up with the others. Christian, she noted, was favoring his right leg more.

"Can I help?" she asked.

Christian said, "I think we have—"

"Of course you can," interrupted his brother. He gave Baldwin an ungrateful shove aside, paying no attention to how his arrows fell from the quiver and scattered on the floor, and held out his arm. "Come here, Avisa."

"Baldwin," ordered Christian, "help Guy. I will help Avisa."

"Help her?" Guy's gaze swept along her. "When did she get hurt?" His chuckle swooped along the low passage. "You should not be so rough with fair Avisa, brother. If you forsake your chivalry, you will never replace de Tracy as one of the king's favored knights."

"I am fine," she said as Guy continued to laugh. To Christian, she added, "I can relieve Baldwin, who has been tending to your brother all day."

"It is good for him." Christian took her arm and kept her from stepping forward as Baldwin, slinging the quiver over his shoulder again, went with Guy along the hallway. "A page must be prepared to work harder than he imagined when he first offered his services."

"But Baldwin is exhausted."

"Let me be the judge of that." He gave a tug on her arm. "Come along now."

"Do you enjoy commanding everyone around you?"

"Yes, when I know *I* know what is best."

She wished the queen had asked anyone else to complete the task of keeping Christian Lovell alive. No, she would not want this impossible man inflicted on any of her sisters.

She would do what she had vowed to do and then return to the Abbey, knowing that it retained the queen's patronage.

The shadows in the passage began to give way to light, and Avisa heard more voices. As she went with Christian into the castle's hall, she stared, openmouthed. Hearths were built into the outer walls, and another one was set in the middle. Smoke hung heavily from the fires because shutters had been closed over the windows near the rafters that marked the ceiling in precise rows. Other odors, far less agreeable than smoke, filled every breath and rose from the rushes on the floor.

"Oh, by St. Jude," she gasped when she saw a man relieving himself against a wall. No wonder the hall reeked worse than a latrine trough.

"Did you say something?" asked Christian.

"No, nothing." She did not want to discuss such bestial habits with him. From his tone, she guessed he saw nothing out of the ordinary about the man. He glanced toward her, and she looked hastily away, hoping her face was not crimson.

They walked toward tables drawn close to the hearths. The benches edging them were filled, save for one bench where an old man huddled over some broken bread. He was mumbling to himself, but he watched closely as they passed. She was uncertain if he was mad or if time had worn his thoughts to crumbs, as scattered as the ones in front of him.

Hearing a curse, she saw Guy's face blanch even further before turning a hideous shade of red. His gaze focused on the old man.

She was about to ask what was wrong when someone shouted, "Take care!"

Avisa jumped out of the way as servants wove from table to table, offering more food. She noticed the finest foods were being taken to a table set on a raised platform.

That table would be used by the lord, his family, and his favored retainers or guests. A pair of benches flanked the single chair set at its center. That chair belonged to the castle's lord. Not even his wife or heir would dare to sit in it. The abbess had reminded her of that custom along with others they did not follow in the Abbey.

But why didn't you tell me that no woman carried a broadsword? Maybe the abbess had assumed Avisa would recall that, but the few memories she had of the short time she had lived in her father's holding were of her mother's smile and her father's voice.

"Our host is Jasper de l'Isle," Christian whispered from the side of his mouth. "He is a man of little imagination, so try not to vex him."

"I will endeavor to be on my best behavior," she said.

"I was speaking to my brother." He glanced at her. "But I am glad you also are taking the warning to heart."

Avisa hated having to swallow another retort, but speaking now, even in a whisper, risked her words being heard through the hall because all the voices grew silent when Lord de l'Isle came to his feet. Benches screeched, shoved back on the stone floors when his household stood along with him.

No one spoke while the lord walked toward them. He was a man of her father's age. He had as little hair as a keg and resembled its rounded shape. Displaying his wealth and power with his scarlet cloak, he wore a smile that looked fake. He did not reach out to take Christian's arm in a warrior's grip.

"We seek shelter." Christian's face was taut.

"All are welcome at Castle Orxted, Lovell," the lord said, his words sounding as if he had repeated them so many times he could not imagine saying anything else. "All of you." His smile warmed as he looked at Avisa. "Including your loveliest companion."

She kept her face serene when the lord appraised her as if she were a mare for sale at a market day. She had measured his appearance closely too, but she was unnerved because every person in the hall was staring at her. Reminding herself of how the sisters were curious about any newcomer to the Abbey, she maintained her outward composure.

Inwardly, she was losing the struggle. Christian's hand was sliding along her waist, and her skin awaited his touch. She tried to subdue the anticipation rippling through her, but her body refused to heed her.

She was so focused on that battle that she stumbled when Christian drew her forward to greet Lord de l'Isle. Noticing heads bowed together in whispers, she straightened her spine. Even if nobody else knew the truth, she was representing the Abbey and the queen at Castle Orxted. She must not do anything to shame them.

Or Christian. She did not silence that thought, because it was one she needed to remember. If her actions reflected poorly on him, he might refuse to go any farther with her.

She heard no hint of embarrassment in his voice as he said, "De l'Isle, this is Lady Avisa—"

"We are deeply grateful for your hospitality," Avisa said before Christian could speak the rest of her name. Only now did she realize she should have given him a fake one. Christian had not connected her with her family, but Lord de l'Isle might. Then her hastily built tale would tumble down like a wall beneath the might of a siege machine.

"Come and join us for the late meal, milady," Lord de l'Isle said with a smile for her.

"Guy is wounded," she said, "and his bandage should be checked." She hated using Christian's brother's injury as an excuse to escape the curious eyes, but she had to find a place where she could repair her shredding composure.

"Wounded?" The baron lost his broad smile, and his hand went to the dagger he wore on his belt. "Where? By whom?"

She started to answer, but Christian squeezed her waist, silencing her.

"Not on your lands, de l'Isle," he said. "It happened a day's journey from here, but we need shelter."

"Any man of the king's is welcome here, and it is said the king accepted your pledge of fealty."

"Yes."

Avisa was amazed how cold Christian's voice became on that single word. Nothing in his face revealed why Lord de l'Isle's words had angered him. Her hope that the baron's answer would divulge the truth was dashed when Lord de l'Isle called for help to get Guy to a room where he could be tended.

Baldwin stepped back with a relieved sigh. Guilt spread across his face, and she patted his arm. The boy turned his head away. Was he ashamed that he was glad to be done with taking care of Guy? That made no sense.

"He wants to show his courage has not faltered while doing such a sapping chore," Christian said beneath his brother's curses as two men came to help him.

"It has not. He would have supported Guy as long as necessary." She stepped away from him. "As I would."

"There is no question of *your* courage, Avisa."

"And there is of Baldwin's?" She was astonished. The page had not lost his head while they crept through the woods. The boy had removed the arrow from Guy's thigh last night and all day had tolerated Guy's unending search to find someone else to blame for his pain.

"I do not wish to speak of that here."

She understood his good sense. When the two men helping Guy moved toward a door at the far end of the hall, she followed. Halfway to the door, she turned to discover Christian had, too. She wanted to ask if he trusted anyone but himself to oversee every little matter of their travels.

"You need not come, Christian." She saw Lord de l'Isle was behind Christian. What an odd parade through the hall! "I am sure, after our day's travels, you would enjoy chatting with our host while you quaff something potent."

"Nonsense. Guy is my responsibility, and he must be hungry as well."

"It is important that the wound be kept clean," she said.

From the doorway, Guy called, "I have endured enough of Baldwin's rough touch." He gave a groan that resonated through the hall as he watched them through one barely opened eye. "Do let me enjoy a gentler hand, brother."

In a low voice, Christian said, "Avisa, arguing with Guy will gain us nothing."

"Go and sit with Lord de l'Isle while I tend to him."

"I should—"

"You must tell him about the attack on us, because outlaws obey no boundaries. His tenants may be in danger."

She thought he would argue with her, but he nodded with obvious reluctance. "It should not take long."

"Good. After you have given our host the details *and* washed the road's dust from your throat, bring supper for us."

"You give orders easily, Avisa."

"When I know *I* know what is best."

A smile played along his lips. "Your order is the second-best idea I have heard in a long time."

"And the first?"

His fingers curved along her cheek. The fires she had seen when he held her by the stream last night burst forth in his eyes. "Don't ask unless you really want me to tell you."

Tell me! She swallowed hard, keeping the words from her lips as she hurried after Guy and Baldwin. She had never let anyone daunt her, not with a sword and not with a staff, but his eager eyes created sensations that she had never experienced before.

One of them was fear.

Chapter 5

"Will this do?" asked Lord de l'Isle's burly man as he swung open a heavy wood door.

Avisa peeked in and nodded. Unlike the previous room they had been brought to, the stone floors here were swept. It was a smaller chamber than the first, but it would be more comfortable. Someone had lit the fire, and the shutter on the room's only window, set back far within the extensive wall, was closed to keep out the cold air. Until now, she had not been certain if Lord de l'Isle's hospitality was genuine, for he had not welcomed the Lovells as she had expected. She was puzzled by the baron's chilly greeting. She would learn nothing from his men—they were sworn not to reveal their lord's secrets—so she knew she must wait to ask Christian.

Swallowing her exasperation, she turned her attention to the room. It was furnished with an empty chest and a simple bed without curtains. Two other doors opened from it. One, she guessed by the odors emanating from that direction, opened into a garderobe. After what she had seen in the hall, she was amazed to discover such a chamber here.

The other door led into an even smaller room. A pallet was tossed into the corner. A prie-dieu barely peeked out of the shadows, and she wondered if they were taking the household's priest's rooms.

She almost told the men to find another place, but paused

when Guy let out another groan, as he had during the slow journey up the keep's curving stairs.

She had used the time climbing those narrow risers to gather the shreds of her composure. Fear? She had nothing to fear from Christian, save that he would find out the truth.

Avisa stepped aside as de l'Isle's men tried to help Guy through the door. It would have been funny to see them bump their shoulders and heads if she had not been so exhausted and aching from the long hours of riding. Worse, Guy was in such a vile mood that she half expected the men to drop him on the floor and walk away.

"Thank you," she said sincerely to the two men. "Baldwin, help Guy."

The page set the bow and quiver by the hearth, then aimed a smile at her before going to help his master's brother. She was unsure what the boy meant by his smile, but she hoped it was that he shared her elation to be where they could sit on something without moving.

As Guy grumbled that he should have been offered food and ale immediately upon arrival, Avisa sent Baldwin to bring water to heat on the hearth. She ran her hand along the mattress on the bed and heard the crackle of fresh straw.

"I doubt anyone has slept here before you, so you need not fret about lice." She shrugged off her cloak and, closing the chest's lid, set it on top. Unhooking her sword, she leaned it against the hearth's outer stones. She was unaccustomed to wearing it all day, and it was glorious to have its weight gone from her waist.

Guy scowled. "Must you always be so cheerful?"

She took one of the buckets Baldwin and a serving maid were bringing into the room. "I can assure you that I am not always so cheerful. I am simply thankful that we do not have to sleep under the stars again tonight."

"And it is far more private." He limped toward her, and she wondered how much of his whining had been to obtain pity.

Avisa silenced that unworthy thought as she edged away. She should be thankful he was doing better.

"You and Christian must be eager for privacy," Guy continued.

"Actually I wanted a chance to talk with you."

"With me?" He doffed an imaginary cap and grinned. "I am honored."

"Why did that old man upset you?"

His easy smile vanished.

When he did not answer, she said, "I saw how upset you were when you noticed him sitting alone. Why?"

"Are you going to poke your adorable nose into all our matters?"

"No, I have no interest in doing that. I was asking because I am concerned about anything that might keep you and Christian from helping me rescue my sister."

He reached beneath one side of his tunic. Drawing out a ring, he held it up. The glass bead set into silver had a trio of linked blue spirals at its center.

"What is it?" she whispered, fascinated when the colors seemed to swirl as he tilted it to capture the firelight.

"A simple ring. I won it from the old man before we met you."

"If you won it, why did the sight of him trouble you?"

He shrugged as he tossed the ring into the air and caught it. "I was astonished to see him here. I did not know he was part of de l'Isle's household."

"He sat alone. He may be simply another traveler seeking shelter."

"True." He pressed the ring into her palm. "Take it. The blue matches your eyes, and it is too small for me."

"I cannot accept such a gift."

"You accepted our help to free your sister from Moorburgh. This is small in comparison." He closed her fingers over the ring. "Take it."

Avisa frowned when his hand trembled against hers. Something was not right about him giving her this ring, but she was unsure what.

She began, "I—"

"The water is ready." Baldwin's call from the hearth halted her answer.

"Already?" Guy frowned.

"It was boiling on the kitchen hearth, and it did not lose much heat on the way up the stairs."

Avisa pointed to the bed. "Please lie down, Guy."

He chuckled, once more the varlet. "An order I am eager to obey. I am yours to command, fair Avisa, so ask of me what you will."

"Just lie down." She heard a smothered sound from behind her and glanced at Baldwin.

A laugh? The page's hair had fallen forward, concealing his expression, as he took his leather pouch from his belt, opened it, and handed it to her.

She balanced the ring in one hand and the pouch in the other. "What do you have in there?"

"I keep a thread and a needle as well as linen for bandages," the boy said.

"You are well prepared."

"As a page should be." He bounced to his feet.

Avisa gave him a smile, and the boy grinned with pride. He was like a puppy, eager to please and thrilled when he did something right.

Her smile wavered when she turned to the bed where Guy was drawing the maid, who had brought water, down beside him. He had his other hand on the girl's breast as he whispered something in her ear. The girl giggled.

Avisa grabbed the maid's arm and pulled her up. "Go!" she ordered, as sharply as she did to a student who pretended to have practiced but had failed to sharpen her skills for the next lesson.

The maid's smile vanished. "Milady, if I took your place, I am—"

"Go!"

The maid rushed out of the room.

Your place? Avisa had no interest in being pawed by Guy Lovell. He was a handsome man, resembling his brother, but there was a cold slyness in his eyes that bothered her. It was as if he were evaluating each of them in order to obtain his will the quickest and easiest way possible.

She dropped the ring beside him. "You should keep this to give to a wench in hopes she will give you what you want."

"I did."

"Then it was wasted."

He grasped her left hand and jammed the ring on her middle finger. "That is yet to be seen."

Avisa tried to pull off the ring, but her efforts only gained her a reddened and swelling finger.

"Well?" Guy murmured as he lifted his knee-length tunic. His leggings reached only as high as his knees, then were held up by a string she knew fastened to the top of his breeches. "You will need to loosen my leggings." He grasped her hand and shoved it under his tunic.

She yanked her hand back before he could press it over his groin. Her fingers closed into a fist as she turned away from his knowing smile. What a beast!

"I thought you were a bigger man than that." Avisa was proud her voice did not quiver.

"Bigger?" His easy smile disappeared as an angry flush climbed his cheeks. "You barely touched—"

"A grown man knows he should curb his carnal desires during Advent."

He sputtered, and she bent over his leg to hide her smile. She might be unworldly in the ways between men and women, but she was not witless. During the time she traveled with Christian and his companions, she must make use of *all* the lessons she had been taught.

In the same even tone, she said, "You need not remove your breeches. The hole made by the arrow allows me to examine your wound quite easily."

"Oh." He frowned. "I will have to have Baldwin repair that rent."

"It might be embarrassing to appear among Lord de l'Isle's household with such a tear."

"There is that reason also."

Avisa glanced at his face and quickly away. In spite of her efforts, his bold smile unsettled her. It brought to mind Christian's smile in the moment before he had kissed her. Yet it was not the same. Christian's eyes had burned with eager fire, but his brother's were calculating.

"Here, milady," Baldwin said, "is a wet cloth to help you ease the bandaging off."

"Thank you," she said, wondering if the page had any idea that she was speaking not only of the cloth he offered her.

When his eyes shifted toward Guy and his mouth tightened, she realized Baldwin was quite aware of the meaning of Guy's veiled words. She wanted to tell the boy she could deal with Guy, but she refrained. A single unthinking word might mean the two men would decide not to continue on the journey with her to Lord de Sommeville's castle.

"Be gentle with me, fair Avisa," murmured Guy when she bent over his wounded hip.

"I have no intention of causing you more pain."

"But you are the cause of an ache deep within me."

She ignored him as she set the pouch on the mattress beside him and concentrated on peeling the stiff bandage away. With care, she dampened the edges where the blood had matted the strips of linen together.

Guy grunted a curse, then shouted, "Are you trying to rip my skin more?"

"I have not touched your skin yet."

"Then maybe you should. It would be better than you picking at my wound."

Again Avisa paid him no mind. Motioning Baldwin to raise Guy's leg and unroll the bandage from beneath it, she gasped when her hand was grabbed.

"You could make this much more entertaining," Guy said, running his thumb across her palm.

"An excellent suggestion."

His eyes widened. "Really?"

"Really. Why don't we try a game?" She lowered her voice

to a breathy whisper, copying the tone of a maid at the inn where she had stopped. "Do you want to play a game, Guy?"

"As long as you are playing it as well, fair Avisa."

"Most certainly."

"What is this game?"

"It starts with you saying nothing for as long as possible." She hoped her smile looked inviting. "A pleasure delayed is a pleasure doubled."

"Why deny myself any pleasure with you, fair Avisa?" He reached for her, but fell back on his elbows. "Take care, fool!"

Baldwin did not stop unrolling the bandage.

Avisa guessed the page was well accustomed to Guy's swaggering. She hoped Guy had not noticed the boy's twinkling eyes. She again dampened the bandage where it was glued to itself with dried blood.

Guy shrieked.

Avisa silently prayed for patience, not just for Guy but for herself. There had to be another way to get the bandage off without him screeching. She put her right foot on the bed and reached for her hem. She paused when Guy shifted, and she realized he wanted to get a good view as she raised her gown.

Turning away, she lifted the fabric enough to pull out the dagger she wore strapped to her right leg. It never felt as comfortable in her hand as her sword, although its hilt was carved in the same simple design. Maybe it was the difference in the weapon's balance. Her sword required her to use her whole body to offset its weight when she swung it. The knife needed only her arm, and that seemed too little protection when she faced an adversary.

She smoothed down her dress. Motioning Baldwin away, she began to cut carefully through the remaining bandage.

"What other surprises do you have hidden beneath your skirt?" asked Guy.

"I thought you were going to be silent." She set the knife beside the pouch on the bed. When she peeled back the sliced bandage, she gasped.

The uncauterized skin around the wound was red, and

there was some bruising from the arrow's impact. Baldwin pointed to another smaller wound, where the point of the arrow had poked all the way through Guy's skin. None of that surprised her, but she was astonished to see the wound lying wide open.

"You did not sew the edges of the gash closed," Avisa said.

"No." Baldwin tossed the bandages onto the fire.

"Why not? You have plenty of thread to tend to that wound and many others."

"I hope we have no need for the rest," said Christian from behind her.

She whirled to discover he stood so close that she almost knocked the plates he was carrying out of his hands. Taking a step back, she bumped into the page, who hurried out of the way.

"By God's feet, brother!" moaned Guy as he shoved himself up to his elbows. "What are you doing here *now*?"

"I came to see how you fare and to bring some food for our supper." Handing the plates to Baldwin to put by the hearth, he did not move so Avisa could slip past him. "Tell me, Avisa."

Even though she despised the tone he assumed when he spoke to her as if she had no more experience than young Baldwin, she was glad to see him. She would not have to endure more of Guy's suggestive comments when his brother was present. Or so she hoped.

That was the reason her heart pounded against her chest like a prisoner demanding freedom from a cell. She was certain of it, but as Christian's gaze swept across her face, she could not keep from recalling his lips doing the same. Her fingers trembled as she fought to keep them from slipping up his broad chest.

You belong to St. Jude's Abbey. You must never forget that. You must not. Maybe if she repeated that scold each time she was tempted by his strong arms and beguiling mouth she could resist.

"Guy is—" Baldwin began.

"I asked Avisa to tell me." Christian's voice remained clipped. "Why are you suddenly mute?"

Furious that he seemed immune to the sensations that were flooding her, making every rational thought a labor, Avisa put her hands up to his chest and pushed him aside. She guessed that feat was possible only because he tried to keep his weight off his right foot.

"He will live." She scowled at the brothers. "He will live *if* he learns to heed the wisdom of those wiser than he is."

Guy began to bluster, but she walked to the bucket of water by the hearth. Kneeling and washing her hands clean of the bits of dried blood, she realized there was no cloth to dry them. She wiped them on her skirt. The abbess had chided her for doing that many times, but the abbess was not here having to deal with these troublesome men.

As she started to rise, a hand settled on her arm. Christian's hand. If he intended to help her to her feet, his touch was having just the opposite effect. Her knees suddenly had no more strength than the water in the bucket. She wobbled, and his arm clamped around her waist.

"Maybe," he said, his voice ruffling her hair, "you should refrain from tending to Guy. The sight of blood clearly undoes you."

"No, it does not." She tried to step away, but he refused to release her. Or maybe she was not trying very hard, because she had been able to break Guy's hold on her with one of the simplest motions Nariko had taught her.

"You almost swooned last night in the clearing, and now you are as unsteady as a newborn colt. Both times you had just viewed his wound."

"I am fine. Please let me go."

"Not by the hearth. You might tumble into the fire." He drew her toward the chest and sat her on it.

From the other side of the room came his brother's grumbles as Baldwin checked the wound. Avisa paid the sounds no mind. She needed to focus on getting her traitorous body under control. Just the thought of Christian's touch sent renewed quivers along her.

"How is my brother?"

Avisa was startled by the sudden question, then told herself she should not be. Christian was concerned about his brother. Simply because her thoughts refused to linger on anything but his touch, his smile, his eyes, she could not assume his would be the same.

Making sure that her voice was steady, she answered, "From the wounds, I would say the arrow hit him as he was turning."

"So it struck him sideways rather than straight on?"

"Yes. It was good that we fled when we did."

His mouth became a straight line as if he were fighting to keep what he wanted to say behind his lips. He squeezed out through clenched teeth, "I would prefer you to use another word than *fled*."

"There is nothing wrong in retreating from a large assembly of one's enemies."

"There is nothing right about it either."

She nodded. "I agree, but you must admit that dying needlessly is no sign of courage."

"Must I?" He leaned one hand on the chest, tilting toward her.

She would not allow his unbridled masculinity to befuddle her again. Raising her chin, she met his eyes squarely. "Unless you want to be labeled as foolish."

"Something I doubt anyone has ever called you, Avisa."

"Not in my hearing."

The strain left his face as he laughed. "I will take that as a warning."

"Wise of you."

"And you should be as wise," he said, cupping her chin, "to recall that you agreed to follow my lead on this expedition to reach de Sommeville and save your sister."

"Threatening me is a waste of time."

"Because you think you can best me with your little sword?"

She was tempted to tell him that she was sure of it, but she had to recall her role as a helpless woman seeking a brave knight to assist her. Although the words were bitter, she said, "Because I would never forget what I pledged in order to save my—"

"What *is* your sister's name?"

"Mavise." She gave the name of the sister from St. Jude's Abbey who would be playing the role of her abducted sister.

"Mavise and Avisa? The names are very similar."

"Both names," she said quietly, hating to have to add another layer to the lies, "came from our great-grandmother's name, and we feel privileged to share the name of such a respected woman. It is that respect Lord Wain wishes to destroy. He has proven he would do anything to shame our family. Even murdering my father's men and abducting an innocent maiden."

His fingers curled up her cheek, stroking it gently. "He will pay for his crimes, Avisa. You believe that, don't you?"

"I believe good fortune was with me when I encountered you." She grasped his wrist. Instead of drawing his hand away as she had planned, her fingers savored the tickle of the hair along his arm. She let herself become lost in his heated gaze, breathing in rhythm with him.

"This is yours," he said in little more than a whisper.

"This?" She wanted to ask if he meant his arm or his eyes or his breath. She needed the last because she seemed to have forgotten how to draw one of her own.

He handed the dagger to her. "It does not belong to any of us. Therefore, I must assume it is yours. You are so well armed, Avisa, that I am beginning to understand how you escaped when others in your family did not."

A curse from the other side of the room shattered the connection. Christian released her and limped back to the bed. Avisa came to her feet and slipped the blade into its sheath under her skirt.

Putting her hand over her thudding heart, she said nothing as Christian questioned both Guy and Baldwin about what was wrong. Baldwin pointed out how he was trying to rebandage the wound.

"He is clumsy," Guy said. "I prefer Avisa's tender ministrations." He hooked a finger at her. "Come here, fair Avisa, and heal me with your sweet caresses."

"You will have to depend on Baldwin." Christian held out a hand. "Avisa, let us leave him to that task."

"Leave? To go where?" she asked. "You should be resting your ankle. Why don't you sit by the hearth and—"

"You said you would obey my orders."

Hoping this would be the only time she would regret that promise, she put her right hand on his outstretched palm. His fingers closed around hers. She would be able to free them if necessary with another of the motions Nariko had made her practice over and over, but once she revealed that skill, she could never again surprise him. For now, she would acquiesce.

"Thank you," Christian said quietly.

"For what?"

"For acknowledging that you need me now."

Avisa had no idea how to reply, so she chose to say nothing. She went with him toward the door. She saw his mouth was taut with pain.

Guy called, "You are wasting your time, brother. Fair Avisa believes that men should heed the church's counsel during Advent to restrain from their . . . what did you call it? Ah, yes—carnal desires."

Her back stiffened, and she saw Christian's mouth work. Was he again fighting to keep from giving voice to his thoughts? Whatever he wanted to spit out went unsaid, for he was silent as he steered her through the door.

Chapter 6

Many of the lamps along the narrow corridor were unlit. Light from the few remaining ones flickered across the arched ceiling that was less than a hand's breadth above Christian's head. Something moved in the shadows, and Avisa's hand went to her waist. She breathed in sharply when she realized she had left her sword in the room.

"No need to worry." Christian chuckled as a large dog stood up and shook its head before trotting away. "Jumping at shadows will gain you nothing, Avisa. Panic is your enemy's ally."

"So I have heard." She added nothing else as he opened a door. What could she have said? That he was repeating the very words she had heard from her earliest lessons at the Abbey?

The chamber behind the door was almost a twin of the one where they had left his brother and Baldwin. The fire on the hearth must have been very recently lit, because a chill clung to the air.

She knew she should wait for him to speak, but she could not keep from saying, "Sit and remove your right boot. Your ankle must be tended to."

"It is nothing."

"If that is so, why are you limping?"

He gave her a disarming smile. "You have too many wits for a woman, Avisa."

"I trust that insult was meant to be a compliment."

"It was meant to be a fact." He lowered himself with care to the hearth. Drawing off his boot, he set it to one side.

As Avisa reached out cautious fingers to explore the swelling around his ankle, he caught her left hand, drawing it away.

"Where did you get that ring?" he asked.

"Guy insisted I take it." She tugged at it again, but the ring seemed attached to her finger.

"My brother is a generous man."

At his clipped tone, she raised her eyes to his taut face. "Be that as it may, I am not so generous."

"I am glad to hear that."

Looking away because she did not want to get sucked into the vortex of emotions in his eyes, she probed the swollen area across the top of his foot. She had not guessed it was so bad. Other than his limp and an occasional tightening of his lips, she had seen no sign of his injury.

"I assume I shall survive." His chuckle was whetted with pain.

"You should not be standing."

"I was sitting most of the day, as you recall."

She did recall. The day's light had been short-lived, but the time had passed so slowly she would have been willing to swear the sunshine had lasted as long as on the summer solstice. With every motion of the horse, she had been pushed back against his strong chest. His thighs, pressed against the horse, had moved beneath her with a rhythm that sent the oddest, most uncontrollable sensations through her. His arms when she had grasped them while they forded a stream had been as unyielding as the trees edging the water. She could remember as well the odors of the wintry day mixed with his warm, musky aroma when he drew her within his cloak to protect her from the wind.

Pushing herself to her feet, she went to the bedframe. She took care to keep her back to him when she drew out the dagger and sliced through the fabric covering the straw.

Once she had several strips as long as her arm, she replaced the knife and carried the material back to where Christian still sat. He must be hurting even more than she had guessed if he was not pelting her with questions or comments about everything she said or did.

She knelt and balanced his heel just above her knee. With the pattern she had been taught by Sister Helvige, who ruled over the stillroom and tended to anyone who became ill or injured, she wove the strips around his ankle. They must be tight enough to give support while he healed, but not so restrictive that his toes whitened from lack of blood.

When he drew her barbette down off her head, her hair fell forward to brush against his leg. She tried to push it out of her face.

"Why did you do that?" she asked sharply.

"Your lovely locks should not be restrained."

She grabbed a handful of the hair that had escaped her braid and threw it over her shoulder. "You should be thinking of your ankle, not my hair."

"Thinking of something else helps me forget the pain."

"Is that so?" She looked up at him. A mistake, she realized, for he caught her chin between his thumb and forefinger.

"Or it may be your touch that eases the torment." Lifting her other hand, he pressed his mouth against her palm.

She pulled back as a lightning-hot bolt rushed up her arm. He would not release her fingers.

"Your hand," he murmured as he traced the length of her finger with his, "shows you are accustomed to harder work than most ladies."

"I cannot argue about something that I have far less expertise in than you."

He chuckled. "You always have an answer, I see."

To spite him, she did not reply. She drew her chin out of his grasp and bent to her task. Once she was done, she set his foot carefully on the floor and came to her feet.

"How does that feel?" she asked.

He wiggled his toes, then pushed himself up. He took a careful step and another and another. "Much better. Is there anything you *cannot* do, Avisa?"

"Many things." She watched as he reached for his boot and drew it on slowly. "I cannot understand why Lord de l'Isle was so hesitant at offering us shelter. He should be honored."

"He should." He walked with studied steps to the hearth and poked at the fire with a stick, stirring the flames higher. It had not been necessary, and she wondered if he was trying to keep her from observing his expression.

"Didn't he say something about you having the king's favor?" She knew Christian had the queen's. It was well known throughout England, even at the Abbey, that the queen and the king often disagreed vehemently.

She flinched, glad that Christian was still looking at the fire. Was that lack of marital accord another reason Queen Eleanor had established St. Jude's Abbey? The queen could seek sanctuary there, guarded by the sisters, if life became too intolerable with Henry. What a bizarre thought! And an unworthy one, for judging the royal couple suggested disloyalty. She hoped the Abbey would never have to choose between the king and the queen.

Christian's voice shook her out of her dreary thoughts. "It is true that I recently pledged my fealty to the king in Bayeux. While I was there, the king offered me welcome. Others were not hypocritical."

"Why shouldn't anyone welcome you warmly?"

"Because my father has been banished from the king's sight."

Avisa choked. "Why?"

"In 1147, my father served on the king's expedition against Stephen, who had wrongly claimed England's throne. Most of the men who came to England with Henry in that year were mercenaries, but my father believed that the Duke of Normandy, as Henry was known then, was the rightful heir to the English throne. My father abandoned the king on the battlefield, and Henry had to admit defeat."

She gasped, unable to envision Christian leaving any fight. If he had not wanted to protect her, he would have fought the outlaws in the wood until he defeated them.

"Henry had no choice," he continued, "but to accept Stephen's benevolence that paid for him to return across the Channel." He slammed his fist on the hearth stones. "If my father had not run away like a coward, England would have been spared more years of Stephen's rule, and Henry would have taken the throne in 1147 instead of seven years later."

"But the king trusted your father."

"Foolishly."

"Henry must have had a reason to put that trust in your father."

He gave a terse laugh. "He did. No Lovell had ever failed his liege lord until my father chose his own life over Henry's claim as king of England."

"Why did he make that decision?"

"He never has said."

"But the king accepted *your* offer of fealty."

"I am fortunate that King Henry does not blame the son for the mistakes of his father."

"As others do."

He did not answer, nor did she expect him to.

Clasping her hands behind her, she did not reach out to offer him the sympathy she was certain he would reject as he wallowed in frustration. "Do you believe your father is a coward?"

"He is labeled a coward. That is all that matters."

"Is it?"

He faced her, his hands locked behind his back as well. The pose emphasized his chest's breadth beneath his cloak. "Yes."

She recognized that tone, which she had heard too often since she had first encountered him barely a day ago. He would not be moved from his decision to change the subject, no matter what she said or did. So she would not try.

With a sigh, she asked, "What do you want to ask me that you do not wish your brother to hear?"

"Why don't you want de l'Isle to know your surname?"

She was prepared now. "I want nothing to connect me to my family. If Lord Wain of Moorburgh discovers I live and am attempting to rescue my sister, he may become desperate."

"But you told me your name."

"A mistake, I know now."

He sat again on the edge of the hearth and drew her down beside him. "I had no idea that you made mistakes."

"On that *you* would be mistaken. I have made many mistakes. One cannot learn without making mistakes." She paused, dampened her abruptly arid lips, and asked, "You will keep my name a secret, won't you?"

He did not answer, and she realized he was staring at her mouth. She held her breath as his finger traced her lips, taking the same path her tongue had. When he picked up her hand, she was unsure what he planned. She watched, puzzled, as he wiped his forefinger onto hers. He raised her finger to his lips. Her breath burst out of her when his tongue dampened her fingertip.

"Nothing about your family's name will pass these lips," he said without lowering her hand.

"Thank you." The two words shook, as her finger did against his mouth.

"What other secrets can I keep for you?"

She stared at him. How had she betrayed herself? "What do you mean?"

"I pledged that I will say nothing of your name." He turned her hand palm up and ran his finger along the lines etched into it. "But there must be other secrets you conceal. Secrets of the yearnings within your heart for some daring knight in your father's service or a tryst with one of his serving lads."

She pulled her hand out of his. As she drew her feet under her to stand, she warned herself to act as he assumed she would. "How dare you!"

He smiled. "I dare because, while we travel together, Avisa, you cannot allow silly girlish affection for some passing champion to divert you."

"I would not." Her eyes narrowed as she gave him her iciest smile. "Or are you accusing me of something you yourself are guilty of? Did you see some lass in the hall you wish to give a quick tumble?"

"You have seen through my pretense."

"Really?" She regretted the word as soon as she spoke it.

His smile broadened. "You are very insightful." He lifted a strand from her shoulder. "And very beautiful. So beautiful that every man in the hall could not keep from watching you as you left."

"You are exaggerating."

"Yes, but not by much. Our host sent a servingman to bring some wine, and that task kept him from watching you."

"Save your compliments for a woman who desires them."

"Speaking candidly, I see." He stood and held out his hand as he had in the other room.

Raising a trembling hand, she put it on his. He brought her to her feet, but did not release her fingers. They were standing so close she could see none of the room beyond his broad shoulders.

Her stomach growled, and she put her hand over it as heat flared up her face.

"Supper is waiting in the other room," he said with a laugh. "It seems you are as hungry as I."

"Yes, I am, if you are thinking that even your horse would be tasty right now." She was glad to let humor shred the tension that wove between them each time her gaze was caught by his. "If you have nothing else to say now, then—"

He put out an arm to block her way. His other one slid along her waist. His hand moved in a sinuous path along her, drawing her nearer. Trembling with the need to touch him, her fingers grazed his cheek, which was dark with whiskers and scoured by the day's wind. She pulled them back, amazed by the fire leaping from his skin to hers.

He took her hand and pressed it against his cheek. Her fingers slipped into his hair's ebony silk as his lips descended toward hers. Gently, his mouth brushed hers. The lightning-quick caress twisted through her, searing away all pretense.

With a groan, he tugged her against him. His mouth captured hers, demanding as much delight as he offered. When his fingers combed through her windblown hair, he lured her mouth into softening. His tongue darted between her lips, unwilling to be denied any of the succulent secrets.

Slowly her hands glided up his arms. She wanted to explore each hard muscle along them while his tongue invited hers to join it in a wild dance that seemed to have no rules.

When his mouth swept across her face, tasting her skin and setting it ablaze with lustrous fire, her breath raced. He tilted her head back, and the rough skin of his face grazed her cheek. Stroking his strong back, she softened against him as his feverish mouth pelted her with kisses. Wherever he touched her, her skin came alive. She guided his mouth back to hers. His husky laugh warmed her lips in the moment before his tongue slid along them again. She shivered beneath the eager assault, and her soft moan drifted into his mouth.

When Christian drew back, Avisa clutched his arms. Her knees were betraying her again, and she locked them in place. Taking a deep breath, she knew she needed to put an end to his kisses while she still could.

"I should check Baldwin's handiwork with the bandage," she whispered.

"Yes." Was it desire or amusement that made his voice

unsteady? Without looking at his face, she could not be sure. Her head snapped up when he added, "Forgive me."

"For what?"

"For kissing you. Guy said you hold to the strict rules of restraint during Advent." He grinned. "Although I shall not say I am sorry I tempted you, for you are most tempting."

"I told you to save your empty compliments for others, for I have no need of them."

"Very well. Then I shall tell you the truth. You asked me if I saw a lass in the hall I would like to give a quick tumble." His eyes darkened with the powerful emotions in his voice. "The answer is that I *did* see a lass I would like to have in my bed, Avisa. But it would not be quick. It would take as long as necessary for you and me to savor every bit of the ecstasy we could share."

"You should not say such things." She was losing control of everything between them. She must regain it.

"You asked me to be truthful," he said.

"Maybe not quite that honest."

"Is there someone else who holds your heart?"

The Abbey! she wanted to shout. "I am promised to someone else."

"Something I will try to remember when I am enticed by your soft mouth." He took her hand and ran her finger along his lips again as he said, "But, if you change your mind about that promise, these are waiting for you whenever you wish, Avisa. Don't forget that."

Chapter 7

Guy's complaints woke Christian. It was a familiar sound, but on this morn his brother had a reason for cursing.

"Hold down your voice," Christian muttered as he pushed himself up to sit on the floor. The room was filled with the gray twilight of the hour before dawn. Shadows still held claim to the corners where neither the light nor the warmth from the hearth reached. "You will wake everyone else."

Guy swung his feet over the side of the bed and leaned toward Christian. "Do you mean our fair Avisa?"

"I mean everyone else." By God's breath, he did not want to talk about Avisa before he had shaken the remnants of his dreams from his head. She had been part of each one, always elusive and incredibly desirable. Just as she was during the waking hours.

"I thought you wished to make an early start."

"There is no sense in leaving before the sun rises to let us see the road."

"And make sure there are no other surprises."

He gave his brother a scowl and stood. He winced as he put weight on his right ankle, but the pain was less than the night before. Every other joint protested the hours on the cold stone floor. He had tossed from side to side all night. The hard stones had not been as disagreeable as having whichever part of him nearest to the fire too hot while the rest of him froze. Even that he would have abided if his dreams had not obsessed him.

Hobbling to one of the buckets, he tapped the ice on top. The water beneath was the cold splash he needed to free himself from the images in his dreams. He quickly shaved, wincing when he nicked his face. His knife needed to be sharpened before they left.

Christian stepped aside as his brother limped to the garderobe. On the floor, Baldwin was stretching and scratching his chin, which was still as smooth as a girl's. The lad mumbled something as Christian walked past him to pick up his cloak.

He settled it about his shoulders and pinned it in place. Reaching for his sword, he paused. He looked toward the narrow doorway that opened onto the room where Avisa must still be asleep.

She had not wanted to use the smaller chamber and the pallet there, saying she had done nothing the previous day but be toted along like a bag of oats. She said Christian should use the pallet and she the floor. The woman could argue about anything, although she should know a knight would never allow a lady to suffer more discomfort than he did. That she was often correct added to his exasperation.

He took a single step toward the door, which was so low even Baldwin had to dip his head. A groan rose from deep within him as he imagined what he would see inside the room. Even his aggravation with Avisa could not halt his mind from forming a picture of her lying on a pallet. Her golden tresses would be draped over her breasts, swaying with each breath she took, and in waves along the enticing curve of her hips. Her amazing eyes would be hidden beneath lowered lids, but her inviting lips parted in sleep would be waiting for his as he gathered her close and showed her how they should linger in bed together on the wintry morning.

"What are you looking for?" asked Baldwin as the boy sat up and rubbed his eyes.

Christian shook himself as the boy's words shattered the fantasy of drawing Avisa into his arms and teaching her the pleasures he suspected she had not yet discovered. "Get ready to depart. Make sure we leave nothing behind."

As Baldwin nodded, clearly baffled—the only thing they had taken from their bags was the medical pouch—Christian went with cautious steps to the door. He peered in at the stripe of weak sunlight from a gap at one side of the shutter. A chill came from the chamber. It matched the cold inside him when he saw the room was empty.

"Do you think Lady Avisa left without us?" Baldwin asked from right behind him.

"No." He was puzzled about many things concerning Avisa de Vere, but he had no doubts about how desperately she wanted his help to reach de Sommeville.

"Maybe she went in search of something to eat." Guy patted his stomach as he walked toward them. "Why don't we do the same? My thoughts are always clearer when I have a full belly."

Christian did not move. "Impossible."

"I assure you that it is quite possible. My stomach and my thoughts seem intimately intertwined."

"It is impossible that she slipped out of the room without any of us taking note."

His brother chuckled as he swept out his hand. "Then fair Avisa must have climbed out the window."

When Baldwin ran to the narrow window and threw open the shutter, Guy laughed again. The page hunched his shoulders as his face reddened.

Tempted to remind his brother that Baldwin was not *his* page, Christian motioned for the boy to close the shutter.

"Bring everything with you," he ordered as he went to get his sword. Buckling it in place, he strode out of the room. He paid the twinge in his ankle no attention. He heard Guy's uneven footsteps behind him. By the time he had reached the steep staircase at the end of the corridor, Baldwin was running to catch up.

"Maybe she flew away," Guy said. "There are stories about—"

"Keep your nonsense to yourself."

"But if she could not sneak past without waking you, a fact that you aver wholeheartedly, there must be some other explanation." His brother laughed.

Christian did not answer. Any response would encourage Guy to keep making ridiculous comments.

Somehow, Avisa had crept from the room without waking them. Other sounds had disturbed him during the night, so she must have slipped out like an ethereal spirit.

Noise burst outward from the hall. Dozens of voices all wanting to be heard at once. Guessing their host would be at his table, Christian strode into the hall. He halted in midstep. His ankle stung at the sudden motion.

Directly in front of them was the old man Christian had noticed sitting alone last night. He still was on the same bench, picking at what appeared to be the same piece of dry bread. His rheumy eyes focused on them in a piercing stare.

"He looks exactly like that old fellow we saw the night before we saved Lady Avisa," Baldwin murmured.

"He does," Christian said.

"Why are you worrying about an oldster when our fair Avisa has apparently found a new champion?" Guy asked in his most snide tone as he pointed to the high table.

There, sitting next to de l'Isle, was Avisa. Her face was jeweled with sweat, and she drank from a tankard as if she had run the perimeter of the curtain wall a score of times. Her hair, although drawn back in braids, clung in wisps to her face. As she laughed at something de l'Isle said, the baron slanted toward her and refilled her tankard.

The laughter should have drawn many curious eyes, but no one looked toward the upper table.

"De l'Isle has his household well trained to pay no mind to his most private matters." Guy chuckled. "I doubt he will have such an easy time with taming our fair Avisa, although he appears to be enjoying the attempt."

Christian snarled an oath. He crossed the room and leaped up onto the raised platform before a single thought could form. His hand was on his sword's hilt, starting to draw it from its sheath when his gaze locked with Avisa's.

She blinked quickly, but her voice was serene. "Good morning, Christian."

Her serenity was like a blow across his face, snapping him out of his madness. He jerked his hand away from his sword.

De l'Isle grinned. "Lovell, Lady Avisa was telling me of your brave defense when you were set upon by outlaws. How you bested those fools by using bushes to conceal you makes for an amusing story! I had no idea you were so cunning."

"The lady is giving credit where it is undeserved. The idea to use the bushes was hers." His voice was more rigid than he had intended.

De l'Isle smiled at Avisa. "I should have expected as much from such a lovely lady."

Avisa returned their host's smile, but glanced at Christian as he sat next to her while his brother sat on their host's far side. Christian looked as grim as the low skies outside the keep. He motioned for Baldwin, whispering some instructions that sent the boy hurrying across the hall and out through one of the arches. When she started to speak, Christian cut her off by leaning forward to ask Lord de l'Isle a question.

What arrogance! He did not even ask permission before stabbing a slice of meat on the trencher in front of her. She backed away to avoid the dripping meat and the sharp blade. The abbess had informed her that food and dishes were shared at tables in the world beyond the Abbey, but Christian could have been courteous enough to let her know he was going to slash his knife in front of her.

"De Sommeville's castle?" asked their host, scratching a

scar on his cheek. "You should be able to reach that in a seven-day or less, as long as the weather remains fair." He winked at Avisa. "Things seem quite fair for you already."

"That is good to hear," Christian replied. "If all goes well, I soon will be able to continue on my interrupted journey." He scowled when he cut at the meat, his knife making no more than a dent on it.

"If you need to have it sharpened," the baron said, "you are welcome to use my armory."

He pushed the trencher to his left, away from Avisa. Resting his elbow almost in front of her, he said, "First tell me if you have heard of anything that would slow our journey." His broad shoulder wedged between her and the table.

"It is said," Lord de l'Isle replied, his face abruptly bleak, "that Becket was greeted with enthusiasm upon his return to Canterbury. A king's man would be wise to avoid the city now."

"We are not bound for Canterbury. We are headed west. I have something I must do there."

"Something you must do for you and the lovely Avisa?" His smile returned as he looked at her.

"Speak of what has transpired in Canterbury," Christian ordered.

Their host nodded, once again somber. She listened as Lord de l'Isle outlined the news a messenger had brought to the castle as quickly as he could ride from Canterbury. The archbishop had reclaimed his place in the cathedral.

"Every bell in the cathedral was rung," Lord de l'Isle said, his voice growing thick with anger. "Even the organ was put to the task of welcoming Becket."

"That is to be expected," Avisa said.

Turning his head, Christian aimed a fierce frown at her.

She ignored him. "The archbishop's brothers at the priory have been praying for his safe return for years."

"Not the prior." Lord de l'Isle looked at her, then past her as if she had disappeared.

"Prior Odo," Avisa answered, not accepting the silent dis-

missal, "needs to be reconfirmed to his post by the archbishop. He should be grateful Thomas à Becket can now do
so."

"England may," the baron said as if she had not spoken,
"soon have to choose between the archbishop and King
Henry."

"That is silly. Nobody—" She yelped more in surprise
than pain as Christian elbowed her aside, pushing her back
as he again slanted toward their host.

If Avisa leaned back any farther, she would topple off the
bench. Whatever was bothering Christian—and she guessed
it was more than the news from Canterbury—was something *he* needed to handle; she would not allow him to push
her ignominiously onto her rear end. Putting her hand on his
shoulder, making sure her long sleeve hid her arm from
view, she gave it a shove. She might as well have tried to
move the castle's wall.

"Milady, are you uncomfortable?" asked Lord de l'Isle.

"Yes." She frowned at Christian.

"Patience, Avisa," Christian said. "Is there a bridge at the
next river we must cross?"

"Once there was," de l'Isle replied.

"What happened to it?"

As their host began a rambling tale of the bridge, reput-
edly raised by the Romans more than a millennium ago,
Christian angled even more toward the baron. Avisa struggled to keep her seat, losing space with each subtle motion
Christian made. She gripped the bench, and fury swelled inside her.

Christian was trying to humiliate her. When his elbow
struck his knife, sending it spinning off the table, she ducked
under his arm and slipped beneath the table, glad for the excuse to put an end to whatever game he was playing.

She reached for the knife, but halted when she heard
Lord de l'Isle say, "I wish my wife were so compliant.
Lovell, I salute you!"

Grasping the knife as she heard Christian laugh in agreement, Avisa was tempted to drive the knife into one of his boots. Instead, she shoved the dagger out onto the lower floor and followed it.

The room was silent as everyone stared at her. She could almost hear their thoughts. *No lady wears a broadsword. No lady clambers headfirst from under a table.* To perdition's fires with them! She was a lady of St. Jude's Abbey, and she would not be held to the standards that constrained other women. If they—*if Christian*—did not like that, it was his misfortune.

No, it was hers. Through her head ran the abbess's voice warning her not to call undue attention to herself. As hard as it was to lie to Christian, playing a weak-minded woman who must answer for every moment of her life to a man was an even greater trial.

"Lady Avisa?" called Lord de l'Isle. "Are you all right?"

Before she could answer, Christian stood. He set his hands on the table and frowned. "What absurd thing are you doing *now*?"

She bit back the words that boiled in her. She had been sitting with their host, garnering information they needed for the journey, when Christian had arrived to start shoving her aside like a jealous child wanting its parent's attention.

In her sweetest tones she said, "Why, I was only seeking to *serve* you by retrieving your knife. *Serving* you is what you expect, isn't it?"

"Avisa—"

"Here is your knife!" She picked up the blade and drove it into the front edge of the table. Gasps came from every direction, but nobody spoke as she strode toward the closest arch.

Christian heard a snicker and refocused his scowl on his brother, who had a serving lass on his lap. Guy was paying no attention to anyone but the young woman who was kissing his cheek. Just once, he wished his brother would concentrate on something other than his next seduction.

So Christian could think of *his* . . . of Avisa. With a curse, he silenced that thought. Only a man with no wits would contemplate bedding such a woman. She could be soft in his arms, but as prickly as a briar the rest of the time. He should be thinking solely of rescuing her sister, reuniting her with Avisa, and bidding them both farewell.

When Baldwin ran to the table and asked if he should follow Avisa, Christian waved him to silence. He would not condemn his page to the task of confronting Avisa when she was in such a fearsome temper.

"Do as I told you," he ordered the boy.

Baldwin nodded, deflated, as he went to stand where he could observe the old man who seemed to watch each thing they did. Maybe the boy could discover why.

De l'Isle stared wide-eyed. "What a firecat! Maybe you do not have her as firmly in hand as I had thought, Lovell."

"Fair Avisa," Guy said with another laugh as he lifted the maid off his lap and patted her backside, "seems prone to the oddest actions at the most peculiar times. When we were on our way here—"

Christian did not wait to hear what tale his brother was about to spin. Pushing aside the trencher, he leaped over the table. His ankle twinged. He ignored it and yanked his still quivering knife from the wood. When Baldwin started again to follow, he motioned more vehemently for his page to obey his orders.

"I shall not be gone long," he said, more to calm the boy than to excuse himself from the high table.

"Take care she does not drive that dagger into you," de l'Isle said with a chuckle. He turned to Guy to hear more of what he had to say.

Christian went after Avisa. More laughter followed him out of the hall, and he cursed under his breath. Would he never get the better of her in this battle that had begun almost from the first moment they met? He snorted. He usually was not mistaken in his first impressions, but he had been completely wrong about Avisa. When she had bemoaned that she had been set upon by outlaws, she had seemed fragile and eager for his help and whatever else he might wish to offer her. Not until she gave the order for him to turn his horse into the wood had the battle truly begun.

It was time to end it. It was time for her to admit that she needed him.

He plowed through the corridor beyond the hall, paying no attention to those who jumped aside to keep from being knocked down. He was so focused on catching up with Avisa that he almost went past where she was talking to a servingwoman by an unshuttered window.

"I would speak with you now, Avisa," he said.

She faced him as the maid rushed away, looking back anxiously. "About what? Your rude behavior or your demeaning remarks? Or maybe you wish to ask my forgiveness for trying to push me off the bench for no reason I can fathom."

"You showed a lack of respect for our host by acting as you did."

"Me?" She appeared almost speechless with shock.

He took advantage of that momentary lapse to say, "He granted you the boon of sitting at his table, and you took that as a sign you should act like a man and participate in our discussion."

"I can assure you that Lord de l'Isle is quite aware that I am a woman, and he treated me accordingly." Stepping toward him, she jabbed a finger into his chest. "*You* were the one who forgot his manners."

He seized her finger. She did not try to pull away as she regarded him with a cool stare. He could break her finger in one easy motion, and she knew it. She must know as well that he would never harm a woman who had sought his protection.

"Avisa, how did you sneak out of our chambers?" he asked in lieu of replying to her accusation, which was not totally untrue.

She smiled. "Very carefully and on the tips of my toes."

"I heard nothing."

"I know. When one sleeps among many, one learns to slip out without waking anyone, even when there are rushes scattered on the floor. I shall be glad to show you the tricks I have learned, if you wish."

He knew she meant only what she had said, but his body tightened at the thought of letting him teach her very private lessons in a chamber where no one else would intrude. He hoped no sign of his thoughts seeped into his voice as he asked, "Where did you go?"

"Outside into the inner ward for some exercise."

"Exercise?" He reached past her to set his dagger on the deep windowsill. Slowly he drew her finger toward him, and she stepped closer. How could every word she spoke excite him?

"I was stiff from the long ride yesterday, so I thought I would loosen those tight muscles before our day's travels."

The scent of the day's cold air still clung to her hair, begging him to loosen it and bury his face in it. His hands imagined massaging her lithe body, molding it like clay against him. Every inch of him reacted again. He needed to put some space between them before he could not resist the temptation she offered.

When he released her, she took a step back. Had her thoughts wandered in the same direction as his? If so, she hid them well.

"If you will give me your knife, Christian, I shall take it to the armorer's to have it sharpened." A hint of a smile tugged at her tight lips. "Apparently you believe I have done something to tarnish your honor. Although I disagree, I would be glad to do this errand as a penance."

"Baldwin can take it to the armory." He did not want her hurrying away again so quickly.

"I wish to have my sword examined as well."

Her calm words were a bucket of ice water dumped over him. "You have no need to worry about the sharpness of your sword while you ride with us."

"Before you knocked your knife onto the floor, you had

questions about our route. If you attend to getting those answers and allow me to go to the armory, we will be able to leave before the morning is over. Isn't that sensible?"

"Yes." Again her words were logical; again he was aggravated that she seemed to see everything clearly.

"You need not sound reluctant to admit that it is a good idea."

"I did not realize I sounded reluctant."

"You seem to believe I am incapable of constructing the simplest thought." Her brow ruffled as her eyes widened. "Are the women in your life incompetent?"

"Quite to the contrary. They are quite competent."

"But they know their place and would never, ever, ever offer to go to the armory?"

He could not keep from smiling. How had she learned that her expression of baffled innocence stripped away his irritation?

"I cannot say for certain, Avisa, that no female has never—"

She held up a finger. "Never, ever, ever."

"Never, ever, ever offered to have a knife honed on a man's behalf." He laughed. "As you have persuaded me to admit to that, I assume you shall ask me next to hand over my knife so you may complete that errand."

"Yes."

He brushed the wisps of hair back from her cheeks, and the pink there deepened. Pleasure lit her eyes. Tracing the firm line of her jaw, he murmured, "And what will you try to convince me to do next, Avisa?"

"Not to give up the attempt to save my sister."

"You have already won me over to your side on that." He let his finger trail along her shoulder. "So if you have nothing more to ask of me, shall I try to beguile you into doing something for me?" He tilted her closer to him. "For us?"

Her fingers curved up his chest over his thudding heart as she offered her lips. He did not hesitate to accept. Holding her tightly, he savored her swift breaths pressing her breasts against his chest. She moaned when he held her hips to his, and he dipped his head to taste the salty skin along her neck where she had perspired during her exercise. The flavor was exhilarating, for he wanted her sleek and steamy beneath him as she opened herself to him.

Her hands slid down his back, clenching when he placed a gentle nibble on her earlobe. Slowly they glided back up his spine, sending a whirlwind of craving through him. When her fingers curved along his nape, they dipped beneath the top of his tunic. She pulled them back sharply, and he wondered if she had been seared by the same flame blazing across his skin.

"Don't be so scared," he whispered against her ear.

She quivered against him. "I am not scared."

He smiled. That was exactly what he had expected her to say. "You should be."

"Why?"

"Because these feelings created between us are more powerful than a flood."

She slipped her fingers beneath the top of his tunic again. "Then we should be careful."

"You are never careful." He teased the corner of her lips with his tongue, and they parted with a breathy, eager sigh. Her fingers splayed on his back. Even though her touch was not as silken as a lady's should be, her caress was exhilarating.

"It seems you two have settled your differences." Guy's laugh sliced between them.

When Avisa tore herself from his arms, Christian did not try to keep her against him. Her face was flushed, but her head remained high as his brother chuckled again. Was she embarrassed or angry—as he was at the interruption—or was her bright color from the heat that had surged between them?

"De l'Isle is curious what has delayed you, brother." Guy arched a brow and squeezed the shoulders of the woman be-

side him. It was, Christian assumed, the same maid he had
been toying with at the high table.

"Since when have you been willing to serve as someone
else's eyes?" Christian asked.

"Since de l'Isle is going to owe me for losing a wager."

"Wager?" asked Avisa.

Christian aimed a warning glare at his brother.

Guy either did not see it or chose to ignore it because he
was staring at Avisa. She was a luscious sight with her hair
soft around her face and her lips swollen from Christian's
greedy kisses. "That you, fair Avisa, would have already for-
given my brother. It appears you have." Releasing the serving lass, he patted Avisa's cheek, his thumb lingering a
moment too long against her face.

"Go," Christian said, grasping his brother's shoulder and
pulling him back from Avisa, "and collect your winnings."

"While you continue to collect your reward for calming
our fair Avisa's peevishness?"

"Enough, Guy! Go!"

"If you wish to lose your temper with me, fair Avisa, you
are welcome to anytime," he drawled before walking toward
the hall. He motioned for the servingwoman to hurry to his
side. She did, letting him drape his arm around her once
more.

"Cur!" Avisa snarled. Her eyes grew round with dismay.
"Christian, I should not have spoken so of your brother. Forgive me."

"There is no reason to ask forgiveness. He was loutish."
He reached for his knife on the sill and put it in the sheath at
his waist. "Why do you ask for my forgiveness *now* when
you did not before?"

"Because *I* had done nothing wrong."

Christian smiled and shook his head. "You are an exasperating woman."

"And you are keeping our host waiting. You should—"

"Be holding you."

"Return to obtain what information you can about the

road ahead of us. I will go to the armory. It should not take long to have the two blades sharpened." She held out her hand for his knife.

Seeing a flash of red, he grasped her arm and drew up her sleeve. She winced as the fabric brushed the scarlet mark just above her wrist. Blood was barely congealed on a long incision.

"How did this happen?" he asked.

"I was not careful." She lowered her sleeve over the wound. "It is nothing."

"How did you cut yourself?"

"I told you. I was not paying attention to what I was doing."

"This wound is not more than an hour old. You should have Baldwin tend it. Such an odd place for a lady to cut herself. What were you doing when you were not paying attention?"

She took his knife and stuck it in her belt. "Christian, we can stay here all day while you ask me the same questions over and over and I give you the same answers over and over, or we can be on our way to save my sister."

"How many times must I say it? You *are* the most vexing woman I have ever met."

"Because I speak plainly?"

"For many other reasons." He released her arm as she shifted it. Trying to hold her captive would risk injuring her further.

He thought she would say something else, but she spun on her heel and hurried along the narrow corridor. As she disappeared down the stairs to the inner ward, he was left to try to decipher her puzzling comments. He realized he had no explanation of why she was as guileless as a child one moment and as crafty as a necromancer the next.

He had no explanation . . . yet.

Chapter 8

Avisa's steps were light as she walked into the inner ward. Visiting the fief's armory in the outer ward had been a treat, for it brought memories of the hours she had spent within St. Jude's armory. She appreciated an armorer's single-mindedness. Focused on what he was creating at his anvil, he had not even looked in her direction when she asked if she could sharpen blades on his stone amidst the odors from the fire and heated metals as well as the sharp clang of the armorer's tools. He had nodded, and she had gone to work. Now Christian's knife was so sharp she handled it with extreme care.

She had already cut herself once today. While practicing with her sword in a hidden corner, she had heard footsteps. Her concentration had wavered, and she had ended up striking a stone. Her sword had ricocheted to cut her.

She closed her eyes and sighed as she bent her head into the cold wind. Her injury seemed insignificant in comparison with the news of the archbishop's welcome in Canterbury. That could signal that the stalemate between the king and his archbishop was coming to an end.

Somehow, she must persuade Christian to remain at Lord de Sommeville's castle even after he delivered her to the man who he believed would save her and her sister. Or . . . Her smile returned. She needed only to lead him on an indirect route.

At a shriek, Avisa reached for her sword. A child! Who was hurting a child? Realizing she still had Christian's knife, she gripped it more tightly as she ran.

A little girl was lying on the ground. The dark-haired child could not be more than two or three years old.

"Who hurt you?" Avisa asked as she knelt, wondering why the little girl was in the nearly deserted ward.

The child held up her hand. "Hurts."

"Who?"

"Hurts."

She must try something else, although she was unsure what. In her work at the Abbey, she taught the older girls. Other sisters tended to the infants and youngest girls.

"What happened?" she asked.

"Hurts." Tears rolled down chubby cheeks. "Make better."

She faltered. Should she offer the child the comfort she would one of her students? A pat on the arm and a warning to take more care.

The child let out another wail as she looked at Avisa. Not at her, beyond her.

Avisa was amazed when Christian scooped up the little girl, who looked even smaller against his chest. He murmured some words Avisa could not hear.

The child looked up at him. Tears still raced down her cheeks, but her sobs diminished.

"Where did you get hurt?" he asked.

The little girl held up her right hand as she had before, but turned it so Avisa could see, as she came to her feet, a bright line across her palm. The red was not blood. It was a bruise from sliding over the uneven stones.

"Does it hurt?" he asked.

She nodded.

He lifted her hand to his lips and kissed it loudly. The little girl began to giggle.

"All better?" he asked.

She nodded.

Setting the child on her feet, he gave her a gentle pat on the rear end to send her on her way. She toddled toward the keep.

Christian put his hand on Avisa's shoulder. "That little girl's barely scratched hand almost undid you. Why?"

She almost blurted out the truth as the warmth from his fingers urged her to soften against him. Instead, she stepped away. "She reminded me of someone."

His face clouded with barely suppressed rage, and she wondered how she had betrayed herself with so few words. With his fingers reaching for his sword and his cloak snapping in the wind, he could have been an avenging angel. Or maybe one of the devil's minions, for she could not imagine him turning the other cheek to any enemy. He was a warrior, a man willing to die to prove he had the heart of a wolf. He would not suffer lightly, she assumed, being made to look like a fool.

She was worrying needlessly, she discovered, when he said, "You must be anxious for more than your sister's fate. Others must have been lost in the attack."

"Yes." The word tasted like sour milk. Until she had stepped past the Abbey's gate, she had always been honest, even if the truth brought punishment. To lie now—to lie to *Christian*—was growing more appalling.

His voice became as taut as the lines carved into his forehead. "So many things must remind you of what you have lost."

"I try not to think of that. I try to focus only on what I must do." *That*, at least, was not a lie, although she meant for him to mistake the words' meaning.

He did, and another pulse of guilt cut its serrated edge through her. "I doubt many women would have the courage you have."

"Courage is important to you, isn't it?"

"As it is to any man sworn to serve our king." His mouth twisted. "However, for anyone born with Lovell blood, it is doubly important to show that courage has not been banished completely from our line."

"Your father—"

"Do not speak of him now, Avisa."

She fought not to recoil from the venom in his warning. Scanning the courtyard, she saw few people. None of them were close enough to overhear their conversation, but that did not seem to matter to him. Being ashamed of her family was something she could not conceive. The parents who had given her life she barely remembered. Her family consisted of those within the walls of St. Jude's Abbey, and each one there had found some skill to perfect. Striving toward that perfection brought pride and honor to the Abbey, even though pride was a sin.

"What is funny?" Christian demanded in the same rigid voice.

"Funny?"

"You are smiling. I did not think you would see my family's dishonor as amusing."

"I don't!" She wished—again—that she could be honest.

"You have learned much about my father in our short time together." He cupped her chin and tilted it toward him. "Have you learned as much about me?"

"I thought I had."

"But?"

She moved away from him slightly and handed him his dagger. As he put it in its sheath, she asked, "When you stormed toward the raised table in the hall, were you drawing your sword against Lord de l'Isle or against me?"

Christian had no intention of answering that question. He did not want to recall how the very sight of pretty Avisa beguiling de l'Isle had blinded him with rage.

Motioning to the other side of the inner ward, he said, "We are wasting time."

"It is no waste of time to discover what you intended to do."

He caught her by the shoulders. She stiffened, but he did not release her. Tugging her closer, he said, "Know this, Avisa. I have pledged to help you find your sister, and I will gladly sacrifice my life to save her from your family's enemy, but my thoughts are my own."

"I must know that I can trust you not to do something stupid because you are upset."

"You need not worry about that." He gritted his teeth as exasperation raced through him with every heartbeat. How did she know the exact words that threatened to flay him to his soul?

She put both hands on his chest and shoved. He did not let her push out of his hold, and her eyes grew round—not with dismay, but with a fury aimed at intimidating him. He refused to be daunted.

"If you are finished," he said coolly, "it is long past time when we should be on our way."

"You are eager to prove your courage, I see." Her eyes grew even wider. "Christian, I am sorry. I did not mean those words."

"No? If you want to know the truth, I am eager to be done with a woman who fails to be grateful for the help she has been offered." He let go of her and turned away. "Come along."

He strained his ears for the sound of her soft footsteps and smiled coldly when he heard the faint rustle of her skirt against the sword sheath she wore. Not looking back, he continued to walk toward the stable, measuring each step to protect his right ankle. The few members of de l'Isle's household scattered about the inner ward seemed so intent on their duties that he knew they were watching him and Avisa.

"Christian?"

He did not answer. If he faced her, he could lose himself in her blue eyes, which suggested a softness she seldom showed. Her gown would be pulled by the wind against her enticing curves. When the very sight of her put him at a disadvantage, he was wise to look away.

"Christian," she said, closer now, "I truly am sorry for what I said. I was upset."

"If you are distressed so easily, I would be a fool to trust *you*."

"Oh." Her voice was soft and almost broke on the single word. She rushed past to stand in his way. She called his name when he edged around her.

He kept walking. "We do not have time to argue this, nor do I have time to search for you when you wander off to do only heaven knows what."

"I told you I was going to the armory."

Knowing what he risked, he stopped and faced her. The wind had pulled her hair around the barbette, flinging it into her face. The strands accented each curve that invited his fingers to explore her.

Christian locked his hands behind him before he could surrender to that temptation. "I was speaking of when you slipped out of our rooms without telling anyone where you were bound."

"Are you furious because I was able to do so without waking any of you?"

"Yes."

"Oh," she said again, and he knew that he had startled her.

"Avisa, if you want to rescue your sister, you must grant us the courtesy of telling us where you are going."

"And each of you will grant me the same courtesy?"

"I cannot speak for Guy."

"It might be better if we do not know what he is doing when he wishes some privacy."

Chuckling, he offered his arm. Staying angry at Avisa was impossible. She was infuriating, but she also challenged him. And she was sensible . . . when she had no other choice.

Baldwin came toward them, leading their horses. Guy

stood by his own horse, his quiver flung casually over his shoulder. He was talking to a pair of women vying for his attention. Neither looked like the woman he had been with earlier. Christian suddenly envied his brother his polished way with women. Maybe if Christian had some of those skills, he would be able to handle Avisa more easily.

He doubted that, for she was unlike the simpering women who sought to gain a man's favor in exchange for their own sweet ones. He suspected she would welcome a man into her bed on her terms. He wondered what they were.

"Three horses?" asked Avisa.

"I arranged with de l'Isle for a steed for you," Christian answered, knowing he should be grateful that her question halted thoughts that could lead to trouble. The very terms to let a man into her bed might be the very terms that castrated him. "The gray is for you."

"Thank you."

He was startled by how much pleasure soared through him at her heartfelt words. His hand was stroking her face before he even realized what he was doing. Yanking it back, he said, "Help Avisa onto her horse, Baldwin."

"I will." The boy could not hide his eagerness to leave.

"And I shall be back as soon as I bid our host farewell." He looked at where de l'Isle was crossing the inner ward.

He took a steadying breath as he went to meet the baron. Each time he was near Avisa, every function in his body went berserk. He lost all hold over the emotions that he restrained with ease other times.

"We thank you for shelter and food, de l'Isle," he said, his voice once more serene. "The weather looks fair, and our destination should be a journey of only a few days hence. With good fortune on our side, the rest of our travels will be as uneventful as our visit here."

"With *her*?" De l'Isle laughed. "Lady Avisa is the sort of woman who keeps any situation from being tranquil."

"True, but I can deal with her."

"Then you are a better man than I." He grew abruptly serious. "There are tales that sift into Castle Orxted of those who prey on travelers."

"We are not frightened of common outlaws."

"I do not speak of common outlaws." He lowered his voice. "I speak of those who say they follow the old ways."

"The Saxons—"

"I do not speak of the English ways that were here before Duke William claimed the island's throne following his victory at Hastings. I speak of the ways that were old when the Romans claimed England. There are those among them who wish to see Becket dead."

Christian let the wind whip back his hood so he could better see de l'Isle's face. "You speak of the king's men. I am now counted among them."

"No, I speak of others. They want the Normans gone from England. Even the Saxons are outlanders to them."

"Are you talking about ancient Celts?"

"Yes."

Christian laughed. "You almost had me believing your tale."

"I am not jesting. There are stories of travelers who have vanished. If their bodies are found, they have been torn to pieces."

"Beasts of the forest," Avisa said from behind him.

"Beasts of the forest do not have knives, milady." De l'Isle's discomfort deepened. "This is not a topic for your ears."

"I am traveling the very roads you say are dangerous." Her hand went to her sword.

Christian rolled his eyes. Why hadn't Avisa waited on the horse as he had requested? The baron was uncomfortable—as any man would be—discussing such matters with a woman. "This conversation is between de l'Isle and me, Avisa."

"What makes you think a cult based on old beliefs is nearby, Lord de l'Isle?" she asked, ignoring him.

"There have been threats made to those who inquire into

what has been happening." De L'Isle shot a frown at Christian.

Avisa either did not see it or chose to pay it no mind. "This is not Wales, where the princes use the old ways to claim their lands. What have you done to halt them?"

"Lovell, you need to teach your lady her place," growled the baron.

"Have any of them been captured and questioned?" she asked.

"Lovell, *her place*."

Christian seized Avisa's arm and pulled her away from de l'Isle, whose face was becoming as ruddy as his cloak. "Thank you, de l'Isle, for the warning and for your hospitality."

"Be wary," he replied.

"It would be easier," Avisa said, "to know the danger if you could give us more information."

"Lovell . . ."

Christian tugged on Avisa's arm. For a moment she did not move, and he considered flipping her over his shoulder to carry her to the gray horse. That accursed sword she wore would most likely strike him in a place where no man wished to be hit.

He yanked on her arm again, harder, and this time she went with him toward where Guy and Baldwin sat with varying degrees of forbearance on their horses. He tossed Avisa up into the saddle. Her breast brushed against his arm, and he could not silence his groan.

"Are you all right?" she asked.

"I am fine!" Accursed woman! She had bewitched him with her beauty, but he would not lose himself again in her spell. "Stay there until I give you permission to dismount!" At his order, he heard giggles—not from Avisa, for she was regarding him with rage, but from young women loitering near the well house.

He strode to Blackthorn and swung up into the saddle. Damn all of them! Damn their laughter! And most of all, damn Avisa, for humiliating him in front of de l'Isle's household. Glancing at his brother, he motioned with his head toward the gate.

For once, his brother's thoughts must have matched his, for Guy was scowling. They had suffered too many insults because of their father. That the king had accepted Christian's pledge of fealty should have made a difference, but Avisa's antics were destroying any hope of that.

It must not happen again.

Chapter 9

Christian was angry. At her. He had been angry at her since they left Castle Orxted. Avisa had tried several times to begin a conversation. He had answered, but his crisp words curtailed any further discussion.

Baldwin rode beside him, a worried expression on his young face. The page had not been bothered by Guy's blustering fury, but Christian's quiet rage distressed him.

And her.

Avisa wanted to apologize. She should have silenced her questions, but Lord de l'Isle's warnings about the outlaws had been unsettling. She had tried, after they left the castle, to apologize but had been rebuffed by Christian's silence.

At sunset the wind strengthened. It was as cold as if coming from the North Sea. The horses bent their heads, and Avisa hunched into her cloak. Overhead, clouds thickened, warning of a coming storm.

From the left something rustled. She reached for her sword, then lowered her hand when she saw a pair of rabbits bounce across the road.

Christian glanced at her, but said nothing. Shame filled her at her reaction to nothing.

Guy rode more closely to her. "I am beginning to see why Moorburgh was able to overrun your family's fief."

"Why do you say that?"

"You were about to leap to our defense. A woman!" His

lips curled in a sneer. "If the men in your father's manor house were willing to let their women involve themselves in matters beyond the manor's wards, they may have allowed themselves to neglect their warrior skills, too."

Her fingers tightened on the reins, and she struggled to keep her voice serene. "What does one have to do with the other?"

"A woman's world should be focused on her home, her family, and her husband."

"So I have heard, even though I fail to understand why that must be true of all women." She gave him a feigned smile. "It is not true of me."

"On that," Christian said in the same cold voice he had used each time he had spoken to her since leaving Castle Orxted, "there can be no disagreement. I am curious. How did you persuade your father's armorer to make you a weapon?"

She wished Christian had stayed out of this conversation. Arguing with Guy was simple, because he responded with emotion, not with rational thought.

"It was my father's wish." The truth was as refreshing as a gentle breeze after a heated summer day. "I was happy to accede and learn a knight's skills."

"So you *do* yield your will to a man's on occasion?"

"When the request is reasonable." She should have remained silent, she realized when his lips straightened again. Continuing to vex him would not ease the tension between them.

"I hope you will think that stopping at yon cottage for the night is reasonable."

"Christian, I did not—"

"Be silent, Avisa!" He held up his hand. "Follow me slowly."

She admired his caution when approaching the cottage set behind a stone wall that reached as high as her fingers could stretch over her head. Most likely the residents were farmers, taking the short days to rest after long hours of bringing in the harvest. But until they knew the truth, they must be wary.

The long, narrow cottage was in better condition than the outbuildings. Its timbers were covered with straw and mud, but in a few spots sticks peeked through.

The yard had frozen into odd shapes along ruts where some wheeled cart must have recently passed. Avisa guessed it had not traveled far. During their day's journey, shortened by the quick passage of the sun into the thickening clouds, they had encountered only one other person on the road. Even the village they had passed through had appeared abandoned. With the day's chill, nobody moved far from a fire. Byres were empty; the animals had been brought within the houses for the heat coming from their furred bodies.

Thin fingers of smoke sifted through the thatched roof, signaling a welcome fire. Light shone past shutters that were not set well within the windows.

"If we had continued on to Canterbury instead of turning back, we would be sitting by de Boisvert's fire now," Guy said as he edged his horse next to Christian's. Snow began to swirl between them.

Christian scanned the yard again. He was pleased Avisa had heeded his order . . . for once. "I have thought about that."

His brother shivered. "Then give thought as well to those of us who do not have a fair Avisa to keep us warm."

Before he could answer, Avisa's laugh tinkled like ice-coated branches in a breeze. She crossed her arms on her saddle and gave his brother a smile. Christian considered warning Guy to take care, for her wit was more biting than the wind. Doing so would only anger both of them, however, and his brother should know by now that he was no match for Avisa in parrying words.

"A fair Avisa?" She tucked the fabric covering her face back beneath her hood. "I thought I was the only one."

Guy's mouth grew round before he stammered out, "I-I-I did not m-m-mean to—to suggest—"

"No?"

"I would not speak any words that you might deem less than esteem, fair Avisa." His brother had regained his equanimity more swiftly than Christian had expected. Maybe his brother was maturing . . . finally. That hope withered when Guy continued, "I only meant to suggest that you possess a sweet warmth."

"I am quite aware of what you were suggesting." She swung down from her horse with the same grace she brought to all her motions. "If warmth is what you seek, you might inquire of the farmer coming toward us whether he has a goat or a cow you might cuddle up to during the night."

Guy sputtered on his answer.

"Conceal your face, Avisa," Christian ordered in a rough whisper.

"What?"

"Don't argue with me!"

Christian hid his amazement when she obeyed again. Then he saw her fingers brush her sword's pommel as she drew one side of her cloak over her face, and he knew she had not acquiesced. She was preparing for battle. Did she see everything as peril? She must not overreact. She could reveal her intentions too soon to a foe.

And Christian's intention was to obtain them a place to spend the night. If the farmer knew they traveled with a woman, the price for such hospitality would become much higher. Although any man should be honored to welcome a king's man beneath his roof, the reality of a hard winter to come could make the farmer parsimonious.

The farmer was a man eroded by hard work and little reward for his labor. Even though his hair remained a rich brown, his face was dried from hours in sun and storm. Dirt encrusted his hands, and the unmistakable odor of manure emanated from his clothes. Yet there was a pride in his steps that implied he believed the low cottage was as magnificent as a baron's castle.

"You are welcome, milord," the man said, bowing his head.

"I am no lord. I am Christian Lovell, knight sworn to the service of King Henry Curtmantle. I travel with three companions."

The man relaxed. "You are welcome, sir. Our roof is your roof for as long as you wish to stay."

"We accept your offer of hospitality." He pulled a small pouch from beneath his cloak and shook it so the man could hear the clink of the two coins within it. He tossed it to the farmer, who smiled as he caught it.

"There is a place for your horses in the room against the back of the cottage. While you tend to them, I will have a sup prepared for you."

"Thank you—"

"Ralph." The farmer rushed back toward the house.

Christian turned to his companions. Motioning for the horses to be brought, he did not move as Guy, grumbling, walked ahead of Baldwin. Avisa stepped toward him, and he put his hand out to halt her.

"What have I done wrong now?" she asked, her irritation flaying him.

"Not you, but I."

She lowered the fabric in front of her face, and he wondered if the sun had decided to rise again to banish the storm. Her eyes were shadowed, but, even in the darkness, he could visualize her expressive lips and her cheekbones where a strand of hair curled against her soft skin.

"I had no idea you made any mistakes," she said. "What did you say to me? 'I know *I* know what is best.'"

"Must you always throw my words back into my face?"

She did not answer right away as the wind buffeted the yard, driving sharp bits of ice into his skin. He was astonished, because she usually had a quick response to anything he said.

"I am not sure about always," she finally said, "for our time together will be far shorter than that."

It was his turn to be speechless. He had not intended the commonplace words as other than a jest.

When she took his gloved hand and raised it between them, he hoped it was not quivering as the rest of him was. He wanted her touching him. Every part of him, with no cloth or leather between her skin and his. He wanted to discover every bit of her as he unlaced the back of her gown and drew it down over her shoulders, her breasts, her hips, which had pressed against his thighs during the ride yesterday.

"Avisa . . ." So many things he wanted to say, but none more than how he wanted to hear her whisper his name in ecstasy as he became part of her. He was succumbing to her enchantment once more. He did not care. He did not want to escape. He wanted *her*.

She turned his hand palm up. Putting her hand over his much broader palm, she placed something on it and closed his fingers over it.

Before he could ask what it was, she said softly, "Please return this ring to your brother. I do not want to be further in debt to him than I already am for his offer to help me free my sister."

"And to me, Avisa?" He dropped the ring into a pouch on his belt. "Do you consider yourself in my debt, too?"

"No." She smiled, and his heart pounded like a galloping horse. "You owe me a debt for saving you from your brother's errant arrow."

He put his hands on either side of her face and drew her within the shelter of his rippling cloak. "Guy will not accept your answer with grace. He will continue to press you to give him the answer he wants."

"I am aware of that."

He tilted her face beneath his. "In many ways, my brother and I are not alike. But you will find that we are much the same in wanting you."

"Christian, I have obligations to my family. I should think of nothing but that."

He pressed his lips to her right cheek. Her skin was cool but enticing. He did not resist. He was not sure he could as he laved her ear with the tip of his tongue. Slowly, deliberately, he traced each whorl. She gripped his arms as she slanted toward him.

"What are you thinking of now?" he whispered.

She drew back, panting as if she had raced from one end of England to the other. "That is unfair."

"Why?"

"It is cold. Can we discuss this inside?"

He took her hands and folded them against his chest. "We can discuss anything wherever you wish, Avisa."

"Don't try to confuse me with pretty words."

"I am trying to *woo* you with pretty words."

"So does Guy."

He released her hands. Her answer was like a blow to his gut. Maybe he was more like his brother than he wished to admit. His brother used honeyed words to lure women into his bed. Now Christian was doing the same with Avisa. Did she think he was as indiscriminate as Guy?

"Forgive me, Avisa," he said. "You have put yourself under my protection. I should not have spoken so to you."

"I want you to be honest with me."

"At times, too much honesty can be as dangerous as too little."

Avisa laughed at his grim tone. She could not halt herself. Christian was a proud man, and being humble fit him as poorly as a cloak on a cow.

Boldly she put her arm around him. "Another topic we can discuss where it is not so cold."

He drew her back beneath his cloak as they walked toward the cottage. "You are single-minded."

"In that, your brother and I are much alike."

His roar of laughter challenged the wind's clamor. She rested her head against his shoulder, delighting in the rumble of the sound both from within him and from outside. He had such a wondrous laugh, genuine and free of the burden of shame he believed he had inherited from his father.

They stepped into a smaller yard by the cottage's door. The wind swirled, lifting the snowflakes in a maddened dance. She wanted to rush inside, but she paused, knowing she must ask her question where no one else would overhear.

"What did you call the king?" she asked.

"Curtmantle. Have you never heard him named so?"

"No."

"He is well known by that name because he favors short cloaks. Odd that you are unfamiliar with it."

The wind slicing through the yard saved her from having to reply. She pulled her cloak to her face as the storm's howl rose like the cry of a pained beast.

It was not simply the wind. She heard a wolf issuing a challenge to the storm. Christian reached for his sword, then took her hand and told her to follow. She went most willingly. Let the wolves have the inclement night.

The cottage's interior was simple. People huddled by the round firepit in the middle of the room. Another room must be beyond because she saw a curtained door on the far wall. Low rafters brushed the top of Christian's head as he walked around a table. Pelts were stacked on the floor beside two bedframes covered with straw and more furs. A single woven blanket was folded in a place of honor atop the room's only other piece of furniture—a chest.

Four men sat on one side of the pit, and their women and children were clumped together on the other side. All of the men were of a similar age and build, so Avisa guessed they were brothers. The air was thick with smoke, and she wondered what was keeping it from escaping through the thatch overhead.

"It is about time you came in," Guy called, motioning for them to come closer to the fire.

Avisa threw back her hood and shrugged off her cloak. The wool was laced with cold, holding it to her. The cottage was not much warmer than the air outside, but most of the wind had been banished.

All eyes focused on her, the women's narrowed in frosty appraisal and the men's appraising as well. But there was nothing cool in their expressions. One man licked his lips and smiled. When Christian stepped between the men's lustful gazes and her, she was grateful.

He put his hand on Avisa's arm. "Avisa, this is our host, Ralph Farmer."

"Thank you for welcoming us into your home." She gave the thick man a warm smile, which he returned even though the household's women were watching him closely.

"It is an honor to have such a beautiful woman in our home," the farmer said. "If you wish—"

"Lady Avisa," Christian said quietly.

The man's smile wavered.

Avisa added, "You honor me with your compliments as well as your hospitality. However, do not take it as an insult that I appreciate the latter far more on a night like this."

The farmer stared at her, then chuckled. It must have been a signal, because the rest of his household began to laugh. The laughter was forced, but it allowed Avisa to have time to sit next to Guy.

When Christian dropped to the floor beside her, food was brought. It was better than she had anticipated. The rye bread was served with cheese and a cup of ale. She ate, grateful that the bread had not been made of acorns. The harvest must have been as good at this farm as in the fields of St. Jude's Abbey.

The men asked Christian, with deference, about any news he had heard. The women spoke only to hush the children. None of the household seemed interested in the archbishop's return, and Avisa guessed such matters had little impact on the lives of peasants beyond Canterbury.

They were far more intrigued by how Guy was trying to charm a woman younger than the others. She seemed overwhelmed by his attention and replied to him in a voice too low for Avisa to hear. A man who could have been the girl's father watched intently. If the girl did not reply to Guy's barely cloaked suggestions, the man elbowed her to respond.

Avisa looked down at the wooden trencher she was sharing with Christian. She knew fathers used their daughters to obtain favors from those of higher rank and prestige. Yet, to view such obvious tactics made her uneasy.

Christian patted her hand, and she gave him a slight smile. Only then did she note how he, too, was watching everything his brother did. As heir, Christian would be responsible for keeping his brother from making foolish promises that could place an obligation on their family.

She was finishing the last bites of supper when Ralph Farmer said, "You must take care as you continue west. Travelers have disappeared along the road."

"We were told by Lord de l'Isle of people who have foolishly returned to the ancient ways," Christian replied with a nonchalance she did not believe.

Neither did their host, who spat toward the firepit. "Lord de l'Isle hides behind the walls of his castle while these outlaws reign over wood and river."

Avisa bit back the question burning on her tongue. She would not embarrass Christian again by speaking when the other women were silent.

"Outlaws?" Christian asked as he reached for another chunk of bread. "Do you believe they are common outlaws?"

She waited for Ralph's answer, for Christian had posed the very question she had wanted to ask.

Ralph glanced at the other men. Some silent message must have passed among them because he said, "We have nothing to do with them, and so far they have left us alone."

"You are wise."

Christian's answer pleased the men, who offered him more ale.

While the men continued to talk, Avisa struggled not to

yawn. The women rose and led the children through the curtained doorway. They returned and spread pelts on the floor. Soon the children were asleep. The women busied themselves near the pelts. One held a spindle and spun fibers with an ease Avisa had never been able to master. She looked away when the motion became too spellbinding, giving her no choice but to surrender to sleep.

Despite all her efforts, the yawn escaped. She tried to hide it behind her fingers, but Christian came to his feet and held out his hand.

As he drew her up, he said, "Lady Avisa is fatigued. If you will take us to where she may sleep, I know she will appreciate your kindness."

Ralph Farmer jumped to his feet and made a great show of leading them to the doorway the women and children had used earlier. His wooden soles hammered the floor, but not one of the children stirred.

He drew aside the curtain and bowed them into the space. Avisa nodded her thanks as she entered a tiny room that stank of mildew. The storm must be past, because moonlight flowed across the dirt floor. An oily lamp offered barely more light. There was no place for a fire. Yet, she preferred the damp and chill to the smothering smoke.

As their host dropped the curtain back into place, Christian pushed on the bedframe topped with hay. It wobbled, but did not collapse.

"Avisa, this will hold you. The rest of us will find the floor more comfortable."

Baldwin spread his cloak over the hay and bowed toward Avisa. The page obviously wanted to be chivalrous.

Guy did not feel the same. "More comfortable? On the dirt floor? I think I will find somewhere else to sleep."

"You will sleep here tonight," Christian said.

Guy's chin jutted. "I am a man grown, and I shall sleep where I wish."

"No. You will sleep here. The girl is the wrong age."

"She is a pleasing age."

Christian sniffed in derision. "She is a peasant, and these peasant lasses give away their maidenheads at an early age. Isn't that right, Avisa?"

She saw his eye close in a conspiratorial wink, and she hurried to say, "By this time, she probably has spent hours beneath some bush with a lusty farmer."

"All the more reason not to pursue her," Christian said, slapping his brother on the back. "Why not wait? De Sommeville may have very appealing daughters."

"But he would insist on marriage." Guy pouted like a child.

"How do you know that is not the girl's intention?" Avisa whispered a silent prayer for forgiveness for what she was about to say. She hated speaking poorly of the lass caught between her father's ambitions and Guy's desires. "She must consider herself lucky to have caught the eye of a knight's brother. Who knows? She may be eager to foist some other man's son off on you."

"She acted virginal," Guy argued.

"Acted," his brother repeated.

Guy snarled a vile oath before stamping over to the bed and sitting on it.

Avisa kept her back to him because she could not mask her smile. She wanted to offer Christian her sympathies. His brother required more overseeing than his page.

As if she had spoken his name aloud, Baldwin said from the doorway, "I shall sleep on the other side of the curtain. There is not room for all of us in here."

"There is plenty of room," Christian said. "Do not let tales of outlaws unnerve you, lad."

Baldwin's flush was visible even in the faint light. "I would prefer, sir, to keep watch. Who knows who else might seek shelter here?"

Christian clapped him on the shoulder with less force than he had his brother. "Remember we have far to ride on the morrow."

"I do."

When Guy stood and walked toward the door, Christian frowned.

"Step aside, brother," Guy ordered. "Unless you wish me to relieve myself in front of our fair Avisa." He flashed her a smile.

Christian nodded. "Do not take long."

"I told you that I would not bed the lass."

"Or any of the other women." He seized his brother's arm. "I do not want to have to fight off a farmer's pitchfork because you tried to seduce his wife."

Guy shook off his hand. "Nor do I. All I want is to find somewhere where I don't have to sleep on the ground all alone." He scowled at Christian and pushed his way through the curtain without adding another word.

Chapter 10

"Not the finest place you have ever slept, I surmise, Avisa," Christian said as he surveyed the cottage's small room. Banging on the wall, he arched a brow at the hollow sound. "I believe the animals are on the other side."

"The room is fine." She wished she could tell him about the wintry nights when she had slept in the open as part of her training. "Baldwin did not take his cloak." Lifting it off the bed, she shouldered aside the curtain.

The lad was curled up like a pup, the muted sound of his snores concealing the low rumble of voices beyond. She spread the cloak over him. Letting the curtain fall back into place, she chuckled.

When she explained, Christian smiled. "The boy has the makings of a fine man-at-arms." Without a pause, he added, "You did well tonight, Avisa. Surprisingly well."

"At what?"

"Behaving as a woman should."

She was certain he meant his words as a compliment. "I never do anything else. I could not do anything else, because I am a woman, so that is how I must behave."

"You know that is not true." He tossed his cloak onto the floor. It settled like a broken-winged bird. Not bothering to smooth the dark wool, he stretched out.

As she sat on the bed, she cooed and batted her eyelashes.

"Would you prefer me draping myself over you as women do over your brother?"

"There are other ways for a woman to get what she needs."

"By acting helpless?" She wrinkled her nose.

"By knowing when she can use her uniquely feminine wiles to obtain whatever she wishes." He shifted on the cloak, rising up on his elbows. "God's teeth, every stone in the ground is cutting into me!"

"If you would rather sleep on the bed, you may. I can sleep on the floor. My cloak is thicker than yours."

"You will need that thicker cloak to keep the vermin away."

She leaned over the side of the bed and laughed. "So *that* is the reason you offered me the bed? You did not want to share it?"

He wrapped an arm around her shoulders, keeping her tilted toward him. "I never said anything about *not* wanting to share my bed."

She lost herself in his heated gaze. Within his eyes was the promise of the passion his kisses had hinted they could share. She needed only to let him bring her down beside him and . . . She drew back hastily. She had been sent to protect his life, not to sleep beside him. She was a sister at St. Jude's Abbey. Her vow to serve the queen and the Abbey must take precedence over anything else.

"And I said nothing about wanting to share mine," she replied.

Christian stood. "If you are going to be in a foul mood, go to sleep." He walked toward the curtain. As he opened it to peer out, he murmured, "Make a single peep, and I swear I shall gag you."

"You are the one in a foul mood." She laughed shortly as he dropped the curtain back into place. "Or should I say a fouler mood than usual? Do not fault me because you are upset with Guy."

"He is not the only one who infuriates me. If I had not run

into you, I would be spending Advent with good friends who provide an excellent table and comfortable beds."

Hoping he would not guess she was bluffing, she gestured toward the curtain. "Go! If you are unwilling to suffer a few nights of discomfort, how can I hope you shall be willing to face a sly foe like Wain of Moorburgh? Do you always mewl like a suckling?"

"Your father would have been wise to teach his daughter to hold her tongue. Was it your serpent's tongue that angered Moorburgh into attacking your family?"

She rose and went to where he stood. When she lifted her hand as if to slap his face, he grasped her wrist. She winced as his fingers dug into her skin. Her ploy had enraged him more than she had anticipated.

"Let me go!" she commanded.

"So you can hit me?" He laughed, but there was no humor in the sound. "Do you think me a fool?"

"I never said that. Rather, I would say you are arrogant and impatient and furious that you cannot order me about as you do everyone else in your life."

"But you agreed to obey me."

"I shall."

"When? You argue each time I give you an order."

"Only a fool would comply with every dictate you speak."

He pulled her closer. "Then you should be a fool, Avisa, if you want to save your sister's life."

His stormy eyes suggested a far greater peril than winds or wolves. Yet, she understood how a mariner felt when staring out into a wild sea. Such fury would be dangerous, but the possible discovery was so alluring that no hazard seemed too great.

She had to say something. Something that he would guess she would say. Something to vex him enough so he would release her and she could pretend she was glad.

"Is witlessness what you prefer in women, Christian?" she whispered. If she spoke more loudly, he might hear her lips' trembling anticipation of his upon them.

"No."

"Yet, you have bid me to be a fool. Why?" She tried to step back, but his arm enfolded her to his hard chest.

"Because I wish to learn what you hide behind honed words aimed at lashing a man to pieces."

"That is not my aim."

"Then what is it?"

This time when she drew back, he released her. She was tempted to fling herself back into his arms, but she had to hold on to whatever small shreds of composure she had left. Walking toward the window, she kept her back to him as she struggled to compose her expression. She must spin him another tale, another *lie*. The very thought was appalling.

"I do not want you to like me," she said.

"You need not worry about that."

She whirled to face him, even as her mind was warning her to put an end to the conversation. "You don't like me?"

"What is there to like about you, Avisa?" He moved toward her as he counted on his fingers. "First of all, you are pigheaded. Second, you show no gratitude for what we have done for you."

"That is not true! I am very grateful."

"Third," he went on, as if she had not spoken, "you find every possible way to dishonor me." He held up the three raised fingers to halt her protest. "Your actions in the hall at Castle Orxted are the perfect example. Fourth, you bring forth the worst emotions in everyone we meet."

"What do you mean?" She should end this conversation. She should walk out and leave him here. She should, but the shock of hearing him say he did not like her had pierced her like a spear.

"You saw those men out there." He motioned toward the closed curtain. "They are now in trouble with their wives because they could not conceal their lust for you."

She slapped the wall. Bits of dried mud drifted to the floor. "You cannot fault me for my appearance. I had nothing to say about that."

"But you could have remained cloaked until we were beyond their eyes."

"All during the meal?"

"Yes."

"You are being absurd. Are you going to blame the weather and the early sunset and the trouble between the king and the archbishop on me as well?"

He grasped her shoulders. When she arched them to try to break his hold, he tugged her closer. His hands slid down her arms slowly. Her body pleaded for her mind to put aside her outrage and soften against him. Her fingers quivered in anticipation of caressing his firm muscles. A sigh strayed past her lips that craved his mouth upon them.

As his arm curved around her waist, he bent toward her. She waited for his kiss, desperately wanting it and hating herself for wanting it. He did not kiss her. Instead he paused so close to her that his lips brushed hers as he spoke.

"I would never blame you for the storm outside, Avisa." His fingers slipped into the plait falling down her back. Loosening it, he murmured, "I blame you for the one within me, the firestorm that engulfs me each time I look at you, touch you, smell your sun-washed hair." He lifted a handful and held it to his nose.

"That is your problem, not mine." She struggled to keep him from banishing her anger as she drew her hair out of his hand. "You need to curb your lusts."

"Not your problem, you say?" His lips caressed her neck where her heartbeat throbbed the strongest.

"Christian—"

His mouth slanted across hers, and he pressed her against the wall. His tongue parried, quick as a sword, with hers as he explored her mouth. She must pull away. She must tell him to stop. She must . . .

She chased his tongue back into his mouth and slipped her arms up his back. Each brawny muscle responded to her touch. She could please him as he was pleasing her. A heady sense of power soared within her. It vanished into an explosion of sensation when his hand cupped her left breast. Quivers raced through her, and she gasped his name. She was losing control of her own body, which was moving wildly against him, begging him not to stop.

Stop this. You are of St. Jude's Abbey. You are here only to protect him. You must not fall in love with him.

Love? Where had that thought come from? He had just told her that he did not like her. How could she be thinking of love?

"Open your eyes," he whispered.

She *should* open them and see the situation for what it was. She had a chore to complete. Entangling her life with his was wrong. She must not let her longings rule her, or she might stumble and reveal the truth of how she was manipulating him into believing her lies.

"Open your eyes, please." His breath against her face brought the scents of ale and a warmth she wanted to capture and hold close to her heart.

She did as he asked, instantly wondering if obeying that simple order had been her greatest mistake. Whatever he had unleashed within her glowed in his eyes. They narrowed very slightly when his thumb slid up her breast to toy with its tip.

She moaned as tingles coursed down her to set off a trembling deep inside her. Her head sagged back against the wall, and he trailed gentle nibbles along her shoulder. As he raised his other hand to seek its way along her right breast, he pushed one leg between hers. It moved up against the very place where the vibrations were focused, and she gripped his shoulders. Could he feel the tremors, too? Could he ease the ache throbbing inside her?

He stepped away, and she rocked on her feet. She clutched the bedframe beside her and stared in disbelief at him.

"So lust is not your problem, milady?" he asked, his voice empty of emotion.

"You braying ass!" She wrapped her arms in front of her as she fought down the longing to reach out to him. How could she want him when he had been frank about not liking

her and then had lured her to a feverish pitch only to taunt
her?

"Does that mean that you have changed your mind about
the desire that rages like a storm between us?" A cold smile
curved along the lips that had been so fiery against her.

"Be silent!"

"As you wish." He bowed his head. "Sleep well, milady."

The curtain rustled, and Guy walked in. He muttered
something. Tossing his cloak on the floor, he sat heavily on
it. He continued to grumble as he pulled off his boots and
leaned back.

"Sleep well, brother," Christian said.

"I could have," Guy replied.

Avisa looked away before either man could discover that,
for once, she empathized with Guy. From the corner of her
eye, she saw Christian lie down on his cloak again. He folded
his hands beneath his head and closed his eyes. Before either
she or Guy could say another word, he was asleep.

She tried to get comfortable on the straw on the bedframe. Curse Christian! He must know that she could not
sleep when her body was on fire with craving for him. It had
been stupid to let his kisses and wild caresses beguile her
until she forgot the promises she had made to the queen and
to the Abbey. She must stay out of his embrace. She hoped
she could summon the willpower to resist him.

She wondered if there was that much self-restraint in the
whole world. She could not halt herself from looking over
the side of the bed.

He slept easily.

With another curse she should not have known, she
dropped back into the straw. She pulled her cloak around her
and wondered why she had hoped he was awake. To talk
more? She had nothing to tell him except that, in spite of her
vow to St. Jude's Abbey, in spite of her vow to Queen
Eleanor, in spite of her assertions otherwise, all she wanted
right now was to sleep in his arms.

Chapter 11

Avisa lowered her sword and wiped her sweaty face against her left sleeve. Frowning at the material attached to her sleeve and falling almost to her feet, she wished she had the more practical gown she wore at St. Jude's Abbey. No wonder it was uncommon for women to wear a sword. The very thought of fighting off an attack in a gown with such absurd sleeves would be enough to daunt the most stalwart of heart.

How had the Abbey diverged so greatly from the world beyond its walls in the few years since its founding? Common sense ruled behind its walls, but she could not say the same of the people she had encountered on her journey.

She had counted Christian as one of the rare ones with a sensible head—until last night. She wondered if his bizarre manner was the reason Queen Eleanor had sent Avisa to make sure he did not get himself in trouble.

She stabbed the sword into the stack of hay. The cur! The son of a cur! He had known exactly what he was doing when he began to seduce her. Everything he had done had been deliberate, and she had been feebleminded enough to fall for his arousing scheme. She drove the sword into the hay again, pulling it out and shaking the bits of grass from the blade. Damn him!

She flinched. No one from St. Jude's Abbey should be cursing a soul to damnation. But no one within those walls had ever met Christian Lovell. The arrogant, self-serving ass!

Whirling, she slashed the sword onto a branch blown down by the wind. It shattered beneath her blow. Pieces flew in every direction, clattering on the hard earth.

Avisa paused and took a steadying breath. She was letting rage gain control over her. Fury was swinging her weapon, not calm thoughts. One of her first lessons had been aimed at keeping her emotions in check. She taught the same to her students, reminding them how Saxon King Harold's men had let a hint of victory at Hastings lure them into defeat at the hands of the Normans. The fools had given in to emotion. She could not do the same.

She raised her sword to hip level, hoping more practice would rid her of frustration. Staying any longer might mean Christian noticing that she had again slipped out while he slept.

Slept! She had not been able to garner even a moment of slumber last night while he . . .

"Calm yourself," she said. Maybe her own voice would ease the tension scattering her thoughts in myriad directions.

She needed to practice and be back in the cottage before Christian was the wiser. He had accepted her explanation without too many questions at Castle Orxted, but she doubted he would swallow her lies a second time.

Pointing the sword's tip toward the ground, she focused her eyes on an invisible enemy. She swung upward in a semicircle to block that enemy's blow. Her sword rose as if to mirror the unseen sword. Taking a step back, she blocked the invisible sword before driving her own into the right arm of the enemy.

"Where did you learn to do *that*?" whispered a soft voice from beside the wall.

Avisa had thought she could be alone before dawn's light touched the cottage. Crooking a finger, she called for the girl, who appeared to be younger than of Christian's page, to come out of the shadows.

The girl's dark hair hung limply, and her clothes were covered with stains. Her eyes, however, were bright with curiosity.

"A friend taught me to use a sword," Avisa replied with a smile. She was amazed she *could* smile. Pushing thoughts of Christian from her head, she rested the sword's tip against the ground. "I practice to keep my skills ready."

"You are a lady, and ladies do not fight. That is a knight's duty." The girl crept closer and stared at the sword.

"If there is no knight nearby, a woman, be she wellborn or peasant, must be prepared to defend herself and her home."

"Could I learn?"

Her smile widened. The child was not ready to accept the place forced upon her by her peasant state or her feminine one. Several of the women at St. Jude's Abbey were not highborn, but their minds were as sharp as those whose fathers held the king's favor.

"Most certainly you can learn," she answered as she sheathed her sword, "but it takes many hours of hard work before you can master even the most basic moves."

"Will you teach me?"

"I need to continue my journey. If you sincerely wish to learn such skills, go to the gate of St. Jude's Abbey and speak my name and your wish to find a teacher." She faltered, realizing she had almost spoken the truth. Her smile returned when she added, "The gatekeeper at the Abbey shall direct you to where you can be taught."

"Is it far?"

She pointed toward the rising sun. "If you walk in that direction for a fortnight, you will be nearly there. You can ask for directions at any church or holy house."

"I have never traveled beyond the crossroads."

"It is for you to decide if the journey is one you wish to undertake." She held out her hand, and the girl put hers on it. "The first lesson you must learn is to think about everything thoroughly. Only then should you take any action. If finding a teacher is what you truly wish to do, consider the best way to journey there. Can you join with others traveling in that direction to give you protection against outlaws and unscrupulous innkeepers? Do you have some skill to barter for food along the way?"

"It sounds dangerous." Her eyes grew big in her thin face.

"It is." She smiled. "But I can tell you that what you will learn is more than worth what you risk."

"Even my life?"

Avisa patted the girl's hand. "I am not suggesting you risk your life. I am suggesting you seek a way to obtain what your heart desires. Learning that will allow you to open yourself to what else my teachers have taught me."

"And I will be taught to use a sword?"

"You will be taught many things, including how to wield a sword." She released the girl's hand and ran her fingers along her sword's hilt. "But first you must go to the Abbey and speak my name to the sister waiting at the gate. She will know where to send you. Once you reach your teacher, you must be willing to give all of yourself to each lesson. What is within you is as important as anything else."

"Each lesson? You mean there are others?" Her voice became hushed, and she glanced around the yard as if expecting someone to be eavesdropping. "Have you learned to read and write?"

"Yes."

"Even our parish priest does not know how to write. He claims he can read, but he pretends. I know this because he uses the same verses from the Bible over and over."

Avisa laughed. "How surprised he would be if you returned with the ability to read! I warn you. Do not make your decision quickly. Once you set upon this course, you cannot go back to what you were before. You are committing your life to your studies and the wishes of your teachers. Consider every aspect of the journey."

"I will." She turned, then threw her arms around Avisa in a strenuous hug. "Thank you, milady."

"You are welcome . . ."

"Fayre." The girl squared her shoulders. "I am Fayre de Beaumont, daughter of Orvis de Beaumont."

Avisa smiled at the girl's grand introduction. "You are welcome, Fayre de Beaumont. You have an aristocratic name. Why are you living in this cottage?"

"I am an orphan, and these farmers gave me a home. I owe them my life."

"But now you pine for more."

"Yes." She ran a finger along the sheath holding Avisa's sword.

"If you decide to seek a teacher by going to St. Jude's Abbey, I wish you all the best."

"I will seek a teacher, and I will be the best." The girl started to add more, but the call of her name sent her running back toward the cottage.

"I would not be surprised."

"What would not surprise you?" asked Christian from behind her.

Avisa looked over her shoulder to see him leading the horses from around the back of the cottage. The bags holding their supplies were tied in place. Guy and Baldwin were not in sight.

"If we get an earlier start than normal today," she answered with her best smile. While talking to young Fayre, she had almost been able to imagine herself behind the walls of St. Jude's Abbey. There, her greatest concern was if she could learn Nariko's next lesson. The sight of Christian reminded her that her life was no longer that simple.

He was walking with no hint of a limp, but she knew it would be several more days before the pain left his ankle. She wished she could not care about his suffering. He certainly had turned away from hers last night.

"What does getting an early start have to do with St. Jude's Abbey?" he asked.

"Nothing." She bent to check the gray horse's saddle, try-ing to compose herself. She should have guessed his keen ears would allow him to hear a conversation before he came into sight.

"I heard you mention St. Jude's Abbey to the young girl scurrying back into the cottage."

"She expressed an interest in a cloistered life, and I told her of St. Jude's Abbey, which my family has supported since it was founded." It was heavenly to be able to speak the truth, but she must not allow herself to become so lax again and ruin the Abbey in the queen's eyes.

His nose wrinkled. "A cloistered life is no life for anyone with an ounce of soul within them."

"You have it backward. A cloistered life is good for one's soul."

"Do not misunderstand me, Avisa. I admire those willing to put away earthly pleasures and tribulations for a life of unending sameness and study. However, it is not a vocation I would choose."

She had no chance to reply before Guy, still complaining about sleeping alone, and Baldwin joined them. As they swung up into their saddles and bid the farm families a farewell, she looked to the east and the sun that was turning the sky a deeper blue. Just beyond the horizon was St. Jude's Abbey. When the king returned to England and made peace with his cantankerous archbishop, Avisa would return to the Abbey. It was where she belonged, the place where she could learn new skills and instruct others in what she had mastered, the place where she served the queen, the place where she would no longer be tempted to forsake every vow for Christian's touch.

Could it be that Christian had done her a great favor by showing her how easy it was to fall prey to her desires? Instead of being furious that he left her aflame with the need for him, she should be grateful that she had been alerted to how easily she could betray everything she truly loved. *Truly loved!* She truly loved the Abbey. She did not truly love Christian. How could she love a man who treated her so?

She repeated that to herself as they rode out of the cottage's yard and farther west. Maybe if she said it enough, she would come to believe it.

"How much farther?" asked Guy as he ducked under branches stretching across the road. He cursed when his unstrung bow caught on a branch and both struck him in the back of the head.

"Does he ever tire of asking that?" Avisa was glad her hood hid her face so she could grimace, as each step the horse took added to the pain trailing down her legs. She had not ridden much in recent years, and she had paid the price with various aches during the past fortnight.

"Apparently no."

She smiled at Christian's answer. More than once, she had been tempted to ask him why he had brought his brother with him. Guy had no interest in attending the wedding, for he loathed missing the Christmas holidays at the Lovells' manor house. If their father had not planned on attending the wedding, too, Guy would have remained at Lovell Mote.

She could now smile in response to something Christian said. For the first week after they left Ralph Farmer's cottage and traveled every meandering road she could lead them along without rousing their suspicions that she was making the trip far longer than it needed to be, she had spoken to him only when essential. She had thought, when the news spread through the countryside that Archbishop Thomas was bound for London and beyond to visit the younger king, that her obligation to keep Christian away from Canterbury was coming to an end. Further news revealed how wrong that expectation had been.

The archbishop had been denied entrance into London, and the younger king had not welcomed Thomas à Becket to his court not far from St. Albans Abbey. Even the archbishop's envoy had been turned away. Avisa was amazed that the archbishop had tried to petition King Henry the Younger, because Archbishop Thomas had been vocal in his disgust that King Henry had held a coronation without the Archbishop of Canterbury to preside. It had become another wedge between onetime friends.

Rumors were discussed wherever they halted, most centering around whether the archbishop would dare to excommunicate the king or if the king would have the bothersome Becket killed. The queen's words at St. Jude's Abbey were echoed around fires at inns or fortified houses.

The uneasiness permeating the countryside had made her quarrel with Christian seem insignificant. She guessed he felt the same because he had begun to talk with her, but with the gentle, careful coolness shared by strangers. He had not touched her since the night at the cottage. If she needed help mounting her horse, Baldwin gave her a hand up.

"How much farther?" called Guy again as he drew his horse even with theirs.

Avisa frowned and pulled back on her horse's reins. There was not enough room for three horses abreast on the narrow road, and Guy knew that. Was he jealous that Christian had been talking with her? She pushed that thought aside. Guy did not want his brother's attention. He wanted all of them to take note of whatever he said or did or wanted.

"Avisa?" asked Christian with more patience than she believed she could muster.

"I am not exactly sure," she replied. "I have not traveled these roads often."

Guy's tone became more petulant. "That is more than we have traveled them."

"We are not lost, if that is what you fear."

Guy looked over his shoulder, regarding her past the feathers on his arrows. "Assuming *you* know the way."

"Don't *you* know your way home?" she asked sweetly.

Beside her, Baldwin stifled a giggle. She smiled at the

boy, making sure her smile could not be seen by Guy, whose own face was becoming an unhealthy shade of red.

No one must guess that she had picked the previous turn because Guy had been gloating about how much stamina his horse had. The rolling hills ahead of them would offer a chance for him to prove that. She had no idea where this road led, other than that it wandered north and west and away from Canterbury. Lord de Sommeville's estate should be only a day's journey beyond where they were now, but she must take care that they did not reach the castle too quickly.

Avisa scanned the open field edged by a trio of copses. The puffs of clouds in the sky overhead were mirrored by white spots on some of the closer hills. Sheep grazing on common land, she guessed.

The sun was not far from touching the hills' tops. Winter's shortest days had been a blessing when she had sat within the comfort of the Abbey's walls and enjoyed the hours of storytelling and singing. She treasured those evenings, but never as much as she did now.

"You look pensive," said Christian.

She was astonished to discover that he had moved back beside her. Baldwin had gone ahead to keep up with Guy, whose shoulders were hunched against the cold.

"I was thinking of a warm fire." She was always pleased to speak the truth to him. "Gathering by it with dear ones on a night after a chilly day like this one has always been one of my favorite things to do."

"Especially during the Yuletide."

She nodded, then realized he might not have been able to see her action, for his own hood concealed his head. "The holiday's traditions are welcome during short days and cold nights."

"It is good that your memories give you comfort now."

"Yes, and I cannot wait until the hour when I can enjoy the warmth of that hearth again."

"You sound confident it will be possible."

Avisa hastily recalled the story she had spun for him. No woman whose home had been overrun by a rogue baron could assume that she would ever be able to return to that hearth.

"I must be," she said. "If I surrender myself to doubts, I am already defeated. Wouldn't you feel the same?"

"I would like to think I would." He brought his horse closer to hers.

Something rustled in the bushes along the road. Avisa drew in her horse and strained her ears to hear a repetition of the sound. Her hand went to her sword when she saw a motion in the field near where wheat sheaves were stacked. A broader hand covered her gloved one, and she jerked her fingers away as the luscious fire surged through the leather and up her arm.

"What is wrong, Avisa?" Christian asked.

That I cannot stop reacting to your touch, she wanted to say. She could not. There was no time for anything but being alert.

"Stay silent," she hissed, dropping her voice to a whisper. "There is someone watching us."

He edged his horse around hers, blocking her view. With his hand shading his eyes, he scanned the field. Shadows were emerging from the wood as the daylight waned. "I see nothing."

"There is someone near those sheaves."

"I see no one."

"But that does not mean no one is there."

He faced her. "Avisa, you cannot let the wind sifting through wheat frighten you. I know you have every reason for being scared, but we have vowed to protect you."

And I have vowed to protect you, Christian Lovell. She swallowed the words. The satisfaction of seeing his face when she threw the truth at him was not worth breaking her vow to the queen.

"I am not frightened," she said with as much serenity as

she could muster. "I am concerned, because someone is watching us."

A baa came from the field, and Christian chuckled. "There is your *someone*, Avisa. A lost sheep seeking its flock."

She saw the dirty white head of a sheep looking at them with a witless lack of curiosity before bending once more to graze. "I did not see a sheep. I saw someone."

"I see only a sheep."

"Did you consider that the sheep may have wandered toward us to get away from whoever is . . ." She looked past him and scowled. "Whoever *was* in the field?"

"If there was someone there, whoever it was is not there any longer."

Avisa nodded reluctantly, unable to dispute that. "All right. Let's go."

"We have been keeping a close watch in every direction." He patted her gloved hand. "You are safe with us."

"We are safe together."

"Yes." He reached across her and pulled her sword from its sheath. "And I intend for us to stay that way."

"Christian! Give me my sword."

"I told you that *I* would protect you." He slid her sword into a leather loop hooked to his saddle. "Let's go." Slapping his boots against his horse, he rode away.

Avisa did not hesitate. Reaching beneath her skirt, she drew her dagger. She held it in one hand as she struck the reins against her horse. She held on tightly as she raced after Christian.

He turned in his saddle as she neared. With a smile, he dug his heels into the horse. It whinnied as it sped along the road. His cloak flew out behind him, snapping against the trees along the road.

She smiled as she matched his speed. Yells came from Guy and Baldwin behind them, but she concentrated on Christian's cloak and the trees. With a shout, she ordered her horse to go even faster. She was a lighter load, and her horse was strong. The distance decreased between the two horses. She bent over her horse, all pain from riding forgotten, as they drew even with Christian. She spat dust out of her mouth.

"I am not giving back your sword, Avisa." He laughed.

"I do not need you to give it back. I am taking it."

"Don't be foolish."

"I have never been less foolish." She gave him a challenging smile.

He put out an arm to block her from reaching across him to get her sword. She ignored it as she slapped the reins against her horse. Edging away from Christian, she heard him laugh in triumph. She wanted to tell him that the race was not over, but she must give him no warning, just as he had given her none. She leaned over the horse as they advanced slowly past Christian.

"What are you doing?" he called after her.

"Teaching you a lesson," she said too quietly for him to hear.

The horse beneath her fought for every inch it was gaining. She did not raise her head, keeping so low that her nose was less than a finger's breadth from the horse's mane. Looking back, she watched as more and more of Christian's horse was behind her.

She needed to be patient. If she moved too quickly, they could be hurt. If she waited too long, he could slip out of her trap. Gauging the distance between his horse's nose and the tail of her horse, she counted to ten.

Yanking on her horse's reins, she turned him directly into Christian's path. Christian shouted. His horse reared. She raised her dagger.

"Are you out of your mind?" he shouted.

She threw the knife. It caught his cloak before it came to a stop in the trunk of a tree behind him. He turned to stare at the quivering dagger. With a shout, she jumped down from her horse and ran to pluck her sword from his saddle. Just as she drew it, he clamped his hand over her wrist.

"You are a madwoman as well as a maddening one," he growled. "If—"

"Christian!" came a shriek of terror. "Help!"

"Baldwin!" she gasped.

The page was facing two men, both more than a head taller than he, with only his knife. Beside him Guy began slashing wildly with his sword. He was not striking anyone, because the attackers moved beyond his reach. One raised an old-style axe.

Avisa tugged the dagger out of the tree. The moment his cloak was free, Christian wheeled his horse at a nearly impossible angle and raced back to his page and brother.

She took a single step to follow, then whirled as more men appeared from behind the trees. They faltered when she drove her knife back into the tree and raised her sword. The fading sunlight danced along its honed edge. With the tree and bushes behind her, nobody else could sneak up on her, and the knife was there if she needed it.

A bearded man laughed and moved toward her. She watched him closely. A large man with a protruding stomach, he wore a simple smock and, around his neck, a leather strap holding several glass beads. Two were clear, but one had a circular design cut into it. Like the three men with him, he carried a leather-covered shield.

Shouts and cries of pain came from where Christian had ridden, but she could not allow herself to be distracted. She kept her sword between her and the bearded man.

He said something in words that were neither Norman nor English. Even so, she understood their meaning from the way his lips curled beneath his thick mustache in a condescending smile.

She balanced on her feet lightly, trying to be ready for whatever move he made. Every lesson she had ever had played through her mind as she watched his eyes. It did not matter what weapon he held behind his shield. Anything could be used to kill her if she was unprepared.

He reached out and tapped the tip of her sword with a

long knife. He repeated his comment. The other men laughed.

She did not move.

He hit her sword again, this time harder.

She did not move.

His smile faded as he swung the knife against her sword.

She met the blow with a twist of her sword. His knife flipped out of his hand.

Raising his shield, he snarled a curse. She understood the Norman words, as he intended.

"I do not plan to meet Satan today," she said with a smile. "Nor do I intend to bend my knee to his leeches."

He spat, "Bitch!"

"Do not speak so of your mother." She slashed her sword toward him.

His long beard fell down the front of him, leaving only a finger's length beneath his chin. He groped at the hair on his smock, then stared openmouthed at her. Behind him, his companions murmured uneasily.

Her arm was grabbed from the left, and she was shoved aside. She started to swing her sword, but halted when she realized Christian now stood between her and the men.

"Stay there!" he ordered, raising his crimson-tipped sword. Blood came from a rent in his left sleeve. More was splattered on his tunic, but she could not tell if it was his.

The men took a step back. Their shields clanked as they made them into a wall in front of them as they retreated.

She said, "I can—"

"Stay there! Baldwin, make certain she does not leave this spot."

She tried again. "Christian, I can—"

"Stay there. Stay with Baldwin." He glanced at her for only a second.

She nodded, realizing he was focused on the boy's safety.

"Guy, with me!" he shouted, rushing toward the bearded man, who fled back along the road.

A spear struck the tree only inches from Baldwin's head. He cowered and let out a frightened cry.

Yanking her knife out of the tree and shoving her sword into its sheath, Avisa pulled the boy after her into the bushes. Briars tore at her clothes and skin, but she did not slow. Baldwin was not much more than a child, with a child's untested skills, and he would be in the way now.

An arrow flew over their heads, then another. She hunched down in the bushes. If Guy was using his bow again, his aim put all of them in danger.

"Are you hurt?" she asked.

Baldwin shook his head no.

"Good. Stay here." She edged around him.

"You cannot go."

She flinched when she heard the dull thump of a fist against flesh. Peering through the bare branches, she saw a man reel backward and collapse. Others shouted and leaped toward a man still on his feet. Laughter, cruel and intoxicated with perverted pleasure, reeled through the shadows as they swarmed on the man.

"Christian!" screamed Avisa.

When she started to jump up, Baldwin grabbed her arm. She broke his hold on her with a motion she had practiced with Nariko enough to make it instinctive. He stared at her in disbelief.

"You cannot go!" Baldwin cried.

"He needs my help."

"He said you were to stay here and I was not to let you leave this spot."

"But he needs my help!"

"He gave me that order."

She gripped the front of his tunic and shook him so the branches behind him rattled. "This is no time to be as pig-headed as Christian. Will you allow him to die so you can say that you followed his orders? What good will it do to speak those words over his grave?"

He stuttered an answer.

Avisa did not stay to listen. Telling him to remain where
he was, she crawled out of the bushes. She had no idea if he
would obey her. There was no time to worry about that.

Standing in the thickening shadows, she looked both
ways along the road. The horses had vanished. No surprise,
for they would be a fair prize for the outlaws. She winced.
If she had not been trying to repay Christian for taking her
sword, they might have been better prepared to fight off
their attackers.

Something moved to her left. Someone was on the road.
Someone was coming toward her. Her sword's song as she
drew it from its scabbard sent a pulse of strength through
her.

"Identify yourself!" she called.

"Shut up, Avisa."

She recognized that grumble. "Guy!" She ran to put her
arm under his and led him toward the bushes.

He fell to his knees. Through his fingers pressed to his
head, blood flowed. His bow was gone, and the quiver
empty. She wondered if he had hit anyone with the arrows.

"Where is Christian?" she asked as Baldwin peeked out
of the bushes.

"Doing battle."

"You left him to fight alone?" She stood. "Where?"

He pointed back along the road.

Through the dim light, Avisa saw two men trying to drag
another into the trees. He did not want to go. The outlaws
must be trying to abduct Christian. Her mind wanted to
know why, but she ignored questions she could not answer.
She ran toward them. From behind her she heard Baldwin's
pounding footsteps as he shouted for her to let him help.

The men had left the road by the time she reached the
spot. Blood soaked the blanket of leaves. She exchanged a
look with Baldwin, who held Guy's sword, before edging
into the shadows.

"Take care," she whispered. "They cannot have gotten
far."

"Avisa! To your right!"

At Baldwin's warning, she slashed upward at a sword. It flew from the outlaw's hands. He stared at her, his eyes as round as the beads on a thong tied around his neck. Before she could swing her sword again, he bolted away.

Steel clanged again. Through the trees, she saw Baldwin on his knees in front of another man. Blood was streaming down his face. The outlaw was toying with him, jabbing at the boy and mocking him.

She slipped behind the outlaw. With her sword's tip, she pricked the skin behind his right ear.

"Put down your sword," she ordered.

The sword fell into the leaves.

As the page picked it up, Avisa asked, "Where is Christian Lovell?"

The outlaw shrugged.

She tipped the sword, nicking his ear. "Tell me where he is unless you want to lose your ear."

"There." He pointed past Baldwin.

Not lowering the sword, she said, "Check to see if he is being honest, Baldwin."

The page wiped blood from his face as he obeyed. He bent toward the ground, then called, "He is here, milady! Senseless, but alive."

"Fortunately for you, outlaw." She lowered her sword to the middle of his back. "Get out of here!"

As the man ran away, Avisa hurried to where Baldwin was kneeling. The boy swayed, and she told him to sit against a tree. When he started to protest, she handed him her sword and ordered him to keep a lookout. She doubted he could see much through the blood, but at least he was alive.

She turned to Christian, who was lying facedown next to his sword and saddle sacks on the ground. The cowards had struck him from behind. Gritting her teeth, she exerted every muscle to push him onto his back. His head lolled to one side, but other than the tear in his left sleeve, there was no sign of injuries.

She put her lips close to his ear. "Christian, wake up."

He groaned, but did not open his eyes.

Lightly she tapped her fingers against his cheek.

Again he groaned.

Shouts came from beyond the trees in the direction of the road. The outlaws must be returning. Guy could not hold them off on his own.

She slapped Christian's cheek hard. When his eyes remained shut, she struck him a second time.

He seized her wrist as his eyes opened. "What in hell are you doing?"

"Guy!" she cried. "The outlaws!"

Pushing her aside, Christian struggled to his feet. She handed him his sword and ran to Baldwin. Helping the boy up, she led the way out onto the road. It was empty.

The outlaws were gone.

So was Guy.

Chapter 12

Avisa put the warm cloth on the bandage over the swelling on Baldwin's forehead. The boy gave her an unsteady smile.

She bent to dip another piece of fabric in the bucket on the hearth. She had cut off her cumbersome sleeves and found they made perfect strips for bandages. While she had been slicing the material, someone had brought water and laid the fire in a dirt pit at one side of the chamber.

The farmers who lived in the simple cottage across the yard from this byre had been eager to help them. They had suggested that Christian, Avisa, and Baldwin stay in the byre because it was hidden from the road and had a good view of the field beyond through the single window in the larger room. They had provided pallets and covers in addition to more food than the three of them could eat. She guessed they hoped to ask Christian to rout the outlaws from the wood. Then they would be able to stop worrying about having their families and their livestock stolen.

That battle had to wait. Baldwin and Christian needed to be tended to. Christian had insisted she clean the boy's wounds while he learned what he could from the eldest man in the household, a man whose name she could not remember. It had been that man who persuaded Christian to wait until daylight before trying to find his brother.

"Outlaws love the night," the farmer had said. "They

practice their demonic rites in the darkness. They are afraid of the light, so they will not go abroad in it. You can sneak up on them at dawn and retrieve Sir Guy."

Avisa doubted even that information would have halted Christian if the farmer had not gone on to say that the outlaws seldom killed their hostages. Instead they traded them for foodstuffs and supplies.

"Sometimes they do kill," the farmer had to admit, as he looked at Avisa. "But they kill virgins whose blood they believe appeases their wicked master. They did not take the lady, so that must not be their intention." His face had become ruddy. "Is your brother a virgin?"

She was not certain how Christian had answered because she had helped Baldwin into the other room. If she had stayed, she was certain she would not have been able to hold in her laughter. Guy Lovell a virgin? Not with his proclivity for women—any woman, anywhere.

"Is something funny?" Baldwin whispered from the thin pallet. "You are smiling as if you have just heard a jest."

"I am smiling because the bleeding has stopped." Another lie to compound the many she had already told, but she did not want to distress the youngster more.

"Will there be a scar?"

She was uncertain if he was worried or hopeful. "It is too soon to tell."

"I would—" He moaned as he shifted the cloth on his head. "I would like to say thank you, milady, for saving my life."

"You would do the same for me."

"Of course! You are a lady. It is my duty to offer up my life to protect yours."

She patted his arm gently. "I appreciate that, but let's hope there is no need for such a sacrifice."

"When we go to retrieve Sir Guy—"

"One problem at a time. You need to rest."

"I should not be resting when he has been captured by those bastards." He started to sit up.

Pushing him back with care, she said, "We will not be rescuing him tonight. You need to rest while Christian and I devise a way to get him back."

"I am glad you will be helping us." He grasped her hand. "Sir Christian does not like you drawing your sword in battle, but I saw you fight. You are very brave, milady."

"As you are, Baldwin."

His smile broadened before he winced again.

"Rest," she ordered again. "The morning will come all too quickly."

Avisa sat by the pallet until the boy drifted into sleep. His face was contorted, even in his sleep, and she hoped one of the farmers' wives had dried thyme. Boiled in water, it made a potion to ease an aching head. As she came to her feet, picking up the bloodstained cloths with one hand and the clean ones with the other, she knew she should make enough for Christian, too. He had been knocked hard in the head by those accursed outlaws.

She stepped over the raised sill and went into the other room. It was large only in comparison with the room where Baldwin was sleeping. The dirt floor was smooth from many feet.

By the window, Christian stood. His elbow was propped on the wall, and he leaned his head against his palm. His grimace was identical to his page's.

She wished she could offer him solace, but she had none. She had failed the queen, letting Guy be captured and both Christian and Baldwin be injured because she had been so determined to show Christian she was worthy of being one of the ladies of St. Jude's Abbey.

"I can bandage your head now," she said softly.

"It can wait." He turned to look at her. His features, even in the smoky lamplight, were not as gray as they had been among the trees. "How is Baldwin?"

"He is resting."

"Will he recover?"

"Yes, and be the wiser for his first real taste of battle."

Christian rubbed his hand against his chin, sharp with a day's whiskers. Trust Avisa to think first of honing the boy's skills in battle. Any other woman would have been prostrate with terror. She had jumped into battle with the outlaws, even though outnumbered.

He should be grateful that she had been ready to risk her life. She had saved them, and most amazingly of all, she seemed to think there was nothing out of the ordinary about her feat.

"Baldwin is young," Christian said, "so he could not be completely prepared for what awaited him."

She dropped the soiled cloths on the floor by the hearth. "No one can be completely ready for battle until one faces it the first time."

Picking up the cloths, he tossed them into the fire. He went back to the window and stared out at the night.

"Christian, I am sorry," she said.

"You did the best you could." He laughed tersely. "You did better than the rest of us put together. I will never forget the shock on that outlaw's face when you trimmed his beard. You are very skilled with that short sword, Avisa. If Guy was half as competent, he might not be a prisoner now."

"Any of us could have been taken."

"It should have been *me*!" He slammed his fist into the wall. Dirt tumbled around him, but he ignored it.

"Why are you blaming yourself? Blame Baldwin and me. We left Guy, wounded and alone, to chase the outlaws."

"To save me." He swore. "You had to save me, a knight in King Henry's service. A woman and a child had to save me."

"Is that why you are upset? Because you think you lost a chance to show you are as courageous as one of the king's favorites? What was his name? De Tracy?"

"Why are you babbling about him?"

"Because you are complaining that you are alive. Does that bother you more than your brother's fate?"

"Don't be ridiculous."

"Why not? You are."

A trio of steps took him to the firepit at the room's center. He sat on the edge of the hearth. "In the morning I shall ask Farmer John to gather his neighbors to assist in routing the outlaws."

"And that is it?" She knelt beside him and dropped the remaining strips from her ravaged sleeves on the hearth. Her fingers were careful as she wrapped a piece around his throbbing head.

"What more do you expect, Avisa? I assume you have some daring scheme to rescue my brother."

"No, I have no suggestions." She tied the cloth in place. Picking up another piece, she set it on her lap and grasped his sleeve. She tore back the blood-caked material. "Let me get some water."

"Why? I don't need you dripping icy water down my arm to add to my discomfort." He sounded petulant even to his own ears.

"How do you expect me to see the laceration with dried blood in the way?"

"Just bandage it and be done with it."

Standing, she put her hands on her hips, pulling her gown tight against her. He swallowed roughly as he stared at those curves he wanted to explore. When he had held her in the other cottage, her hips had pressed against him in an unspoken offer to release the cravings he fought to restrain.

"*I* am tending to your arm," she said icily. "*I* will decide what should or should not be done. *I* would appreciate you appreciating what I am doing for you."

He sighed. On the morrow, he would need her cooperation, and he would never get it if her eyes sparked like embers on a hearth.

"I do appreciate what you are doing for me," he replied. "But it is unnecessary."

"*I* will decide what is necessary. I was taught to clean a wound before tending it. It makes sense, and I see no reason to change what I learned at the Ab—" Her face became a bleached mask. "In our stillroom." She ran into the other room, her skirt flying out behind her to offer him a tantalizing glimpse of her slender legs.

What had upset her now? She was the most confounding woman he had ever met. He owed her a debt for saving his life and Baldwin's, a debt he had no idea how to repay. Among knights, such matters were easily understood, but she was no knight.

He started to come to his feet when she returned with the bucket, but she motioned for him to stay where he was. Setting the bucket beside him, she dipped a clean cloth in the water. She leaned his hand against her leg so his sliced sleeve was in front of her. Carefully she dabbed at the crusted blood and peeled the material away from his wound.

"Is there anything you cannot do?" he asked as gently as her touch.

She looked at him. The fury faded in her eyes, and he saw puzzlement. "Many things."

"It seems you are adept at everything you do."

"An illusion, I can assure you." A tired smile lightened her lips.

Suddenly he wanted nothing more than to pull her to him and finish what he had begun a fortnight ago when he tried to show her that she was as susceptible to desire as he was. Her hair glistened like royal gold in the fire's light and brushed his cheek while she bent to her task. Each flicker on the hearth flowed over her face, accenting the sassy curve of her cheek and her chin's defiant tilt. With his hand balanced on her knee, he needed only to splay his fingers across her leg as he leaned her back on the floor.

He looked in the opposite direction. She was a lord's daughter, and he owed her his life and the life of his page. Honor demanded that he protect her, even from himself.

"All done," she said. "Can you move, or is it too tight?"

He considered answering her honestly. The bandage could be no tighter than every muscle along him. Again he silenced his body's entreaties. "It is fine."

"I am glad."

"Thank you, Avisa." He could barely speak as he imagined holding her beneath him as he thrust into her.

"You are most welcome." As if she could sense his thoughts, she shivered, her soft body grazing him. God's breath, she was a treat for the eyes and every other sense!

She stood and stepped away.

He looked at her. He could not halt himself. His brows lowered when he saw her uncertainty, something he seldom had seen on her face.

"I want to say I am sorry," she whispered. "If I had not been trying to get my sword back, we might have been aware of the outlaws sneaking up on us."

"You were aware of them, but I discounted your observations."

"What I thought I saw might not have been the outlaws."

"You need not try to make me feel better by saying that."

You could make me feel better by lying down beside me.

Did his expression change to betray his thoughts? Or could it be that hers were identical? He was not sure because she avoided his eyes as she told him she should check on Baldwin. He nodded, and she wished him a good night.

He had no idea what could be good about it when she was not beside him.

The sound was hushed. On other nights Avisa might not have heard it. Tonight she was on edge as the events of the day played through her dreams, contorted and out of shape like a room reflected in a polished shield.

She opened her eyes to darkness. Beside her, on the thin pallet, Baldwin was snoring. The bandage was a dark swath against his pale skin. She envied the boy his ability to find an escape in sleep.

A scraping sound.

Where was it coming from?

Avisa slipped from between the pelts and drew her dagger. There was not enough room to use a sword.

Scrape.

It was outside the building, moving from the back toward the front. Pulling up her cloak's hood to prevent her hair from catching the moonlight, she strained her ears. Furtive footfalls. A single pair. Someone was sneaking around the building.

Staying low to the floor, she crept out of the small chamber and into the larger room. The window was shuttered, although the cold oozed around its edges. She bit her lower lip when she saw the silhouette of Christian lying by the hearth, his back to her. She could not wake him to help her. Not only was he hurt, but he would insist that she remain inside while he checked outside.

Or he might look at her as he had by the fire when she finished tending to his arm. Moving away from him had taken all her strength. She was unsure if she could again walk away from the craving that burned in his eyes and on his fingertips.

Stop thinking of that! Think about what you were sent here to do. To protect Christian and his companions. She had failed to keep Guy safe, and she could not be so careless again.

Groping for the outer door, Avisa found it after bumping into the wall's warped boards. She reached for the latch. It would not lift. She tried again. Her fingers slid off the wood, scorched by the friction. Holding her breath, she slowly stood.

Scrape.

The sound was closer to the door. She set her dagger on the floor before putting the heel of her palm against the latch. Gripping her wrist, she jammed her hand up to pop it open. It did not budge.

Scrape.

The sound was farther away now. What was happening? She pushed up. The latch gave up a bit of its hold. She shifted to try again. This time the door came open with an earsplitting squeal.

Grabbing her dagger's haft, she slipped out into the night's cold. Something erupted out of the dark. Her arm was seized, sending her knife flying. She was shoved back into the byre. She fell over the raised threshold. As she tried to get up, her shoulders were pinned to the floor. She tried to roll away and dug her nails into her captor's arms. With a yelp, he grabbed her wrists and, pulling her arms over her head, held them to the floor. She kicked at him. Her skirt tangled with her flailing feet.

"God's breath!" came a husky whisper next to her ear. "Enough, woman!"

"Christian!"

"Who else did you think it would be?" He shifted to lie beside her, but did not release her.

She tugged at his tunic, trying to get away. She paused when something clattered toward the corner.

"What was that?"

"What was what?"

"I heard something roll across the floor."

He glanced in the direction of the sound, then laughed. "A scurrying mouse, no doubt. Stay close, and I shall protect you from such a fearsome predator, Avisa."

"Let me up!" She wiggled, but his strong legs secured hers to the floor, bringing her body tight to his. "That may be a mouse, but I heard someone outside the byre."

His smile appeared diabolical as the light accented every plane on his face. "I know. That is why *I* went to check and startled one of the farmers on his way back from milking his cows. He was carrying an iron-tipped staff with him, wary of attack. He dragged it behind him when he brought the milk to the cottage."

"How did you get out there ahead of me? You were sleeping right over—" She strained her neck to look at the silhouette by the fire. A pile of pelts, she realized.

"You should not let the night fool you, Avisa."

She hoped darkness hid the blush coursing up her cheeks.

"And you have to stop thinking of everything as a battle." His thumbs stroked the skin on the inner side of her wrists. "You need to think as a woman should." He drew her beneath him again.

She stared up at him. She had been close to him often, sleeping not far away on the cold nights of their journey, tending to his injuries, laughing together, snarling at each other. They had shared every emotion, every reaction, every passion . . . but one.

"Christian, let me up!"

"You are in a strange position to be giving orders. It is time for you to start heeding sense. You ask for my help, and then you go off on your own again to do something stupid. Maybe I should let you go and prove how thick-skulled you truly are. But if I did, and you were killed, I would be dishonored for allowing you to die while under my protection. *That* is not going to happen." His smile was more threatening than his words. His dark brows lowered over his compelling storm-gray eyes. "So save your orders for others."

"Others who will see sense in them?" She tried to squirm away. "You are a fool as well as a tyrant."

He brought her face toward his. A raw yearning filled his whisper. "And you are the most splendid woman I have ever met."

She gasped in the moment before his mouth covered hers. As his hard body pressed her to the floor, she was surrounded by the longing she had fought futilely to escape. Her arms swept along his back. Each touch, each puff of his heated breath, demanded that she surrender to desire. As his leg brushed against hers, she arched toward him, wanting to feel him with all of her. The void within her had returned, aching for him to fill it. All she needed to do was give herself to him.

You belong to St. Jude's Abbey. You are a sister within the Abbey. It is not right for you to be here with him. The voice in her head was insistent.

"No, Christian," she whispered.

"No?" Incredulity filled his voice.

"No." She slid from beneath him, and the cold within the byre encased her. If she returned to his arms, the night would be wondrously warm. Her place was not in his arms. It was by his side, keeping him safe as she completed the vows she had made to the queen and the Abbey.

"Avisa . . ."

"Good night." No two words had ever been so difficult to speak.

"Don't go."

"I must." Pushing herself to her feet, she backed away. "I must." Maybe if she repeated the words enough times she would accept them herself.

Standing, he touched her cheek, then drew back his fingers. He said nothing as he went to the pelts clumped on the floor. Lying down, he pulled them over him and turned his back on her.

She had never felt so alone. Even knowing she had made the right choice was no comfort, because the right choice had never seemed so wrong.

Chapter 13

Christian settled his mail shirt in place. The loops of chain clanked with each motion.

Avisa watched in silence as he withdrew chain gauntlets from the sack he had carried on the back of his horse and placed them on the windowsill. The outlaws had foolishly left this sack behind when they fled with the horses. When he was dressed like this, no one could doubt that Christian Lovell was a brave and dangerous knight in the service of the king. Did he hope to daunt the outlaws with his appearance?

She fingered the links on the mail coif that would cover his head and neck. It was not as heavy as she had expected, and she wondered why the armorer at St. Jude's Abbey had not made mail for the sisters. She almost laughed at the thought. Until Queen Eleanor had come, no sister had ever expected to leave the Abbey.

"Thank you," Christian said as he took the coif and lifted her hand to his lips, kissing it gently.

When her fingers curled over his, she longed to bring him closer so he could kiss her mouth. She released his hand, aware of young Baldwin watching. The boy stood beside him, ready to assist in any way he could.

Christian drew the chain hood over his head and thanked his page when Baldwin handed him his dark cape. Swinging it around his shoulders, he hooked it in place. He settled the hood over the chain mail before taking his sheathed sword from Baldwin. After belting it on, he picked up his gauntlets.

"Wish me good hunting," he said.

"You?" Avisa came to her feet. "Don't you mean all of us?"

"You are staying here. Baldwin will make sure you are safe."

"I am going with you."

"You are staying here."

Why did he have to be so unreasonable?

"Christian, you need every blade you can find. There were at least a half dozen of them. Who knows how many compatriots they have among the trees? Do you think you can defeat them by yourself?"

"I appreciate your offer," he said, stroking her hair, "but I do not want your help."

"Because I am a woman, or is it because of what we almost did—" She glanced at Baldwin, who was making no effort to hide his dismay at being left behind.

"It is both, Avisa, as you should know. You are a lady. A knight's duty—"

"Means nothing if he is dead."

"It means everything, Avisa. You understand so much about Guy, but you do not understand much about me."

"I understand I do not want you to die."

"I agree with that." A smile eased his mouth's rigid lines. "And, if I were to survive while letting you be wounded or worse, I might as well die."

"Because you believe that your honor would be tarnished?"

"Because I could lose you, Avisa."

His mouth found hers with the zeal of a starving man facing a feast. When his arm swept around her, he pulled her so close she could not draw in a single breath. His own flowed into her mouth, luscious and dangerous. She should deny herself these kisses that haunted her, keeping her from sleep-

ing. She could not. As he lifted his head, his eyes burned
with the fires erupting through her.

"Don't ask me to choose," he said, "between you and my
brother."

"I would not do that!"

"But you are. I will not endanger you to save him, but I
must save him."

She drew in a deep breath and released it slowly. Arguing
was futile. If only she could be honest . . .

"You cannot go alone," she said, stroking his chest, trying not to think she might never see him again.

"If I find I need help," he said, "the men at this farm are
eager to put an end to the outlaws and their strange beliefs.
They have proven that by lending me their horse."

"But farmers do not know how to use a sword."

"A pitchfork or a scythe can make a fearsome weapon."

"I want to help you."

He bent toward her and whispered, "I know you do, but
I need you to stay with Baldwin. I fear he would not have a
chance when his head is still unsteady from being battered."

"But, Christian—"

"Vow to me that you will not allow Baldwin out of your
sight."

She started to retort, then said, "I pledge that."

"Good." He pulled on the gauntlets, then opened the
door. Raising his voice, he called, "Watch over her closely,
Baldwin. Remember, a lady's life has greater value than
ours."

"I will."

And I shall watch over both of you. Avisa went to the
door as soon as it closed behind Christian.

She opened it, paying no attention to the icy wind, and
watched him cross the narrow yard to where his borrowed
horse waited. He was the image of vengeance yet unfulfilled. The thin sunlight glistened off his mail shirt, but she
noticed the dark line of something that must be blood.
Where had he been fighting before?

She watched him mount and turn the horse out of the byre's yard. He raised his hand in her direction before riding onto the road and turning left at the nearby crossroad.

"Be safe," she whispered.

Closing the door, Avisa leaned back against it. She looked across the small room to where Baldwin was blinking back tears. The boy dashed them away, embarrassed.

She squared her shoulders and went to where her sheathed sword was leaning against the wall. As she buckled it in place around her waist, a twinkle caught her eye. She bent and picked up the ring Guy had insisted she take. It must have fallen out of Christian's pouch when he held her on the floor, tempting her to surrender to him. Lifting her skirt, she drew out her knife and dropped the ring into the sheath. She set the dagger's point in the middle of the ring, so it would not be lost. She would return the ring to Guy when he was safe.

Avisa turned to see Baldwin watching her. "Is everything set so we can leave?" She laughed sadly. "Of course, it is. We lost almost everything to the outlaws."

"You are to stay here, milady."

"Don't be absurd. We are not staying here while Christian rushes off to possible death."

"You promised—"

"I only agreed not to let you out of my sight." She smiled coolly. "I said nothing about not following Christian."

"He believes—"

"Baldwin, are *you* willing to wait here while he faces our enemies alone?"

"No, but I vowed to watch over you."

"Then you shall have to watch over me as we help Christian free Guy." She swung her cloak around her and pinned it in place. Shifting the heavy wool, she made sure her sword arm was free.

Baldwin did not hesitate. Pulling off the bloodstained bandage from around his head, he threw it into the fire. He grabbed his own cloak and rushed after her. Slinging his cloak over his shoulders, he caught up with her in the yard.

"Are you certain you can walk?" she asked.

"My head was struck, but my legs and arms still work. I will be able to walk." He held open the gate at the road. "And I can fight. I wish to make the one who hit me pay."

"I hope you get the opportunity." She led the way out of the yard and looked back once at the small building. She would complete her task for the queen. And then . . .

She was no longer sure what she would do then. Her plan to return to St. Jude's Abbey had seemed straightforward until Christian dared her to risk everything to find rapture in his arms. Now . . . now she needed to make sure he stayed alive. Everything else, even the pleas of her heart, must be set aside.

The sounds of battle came from directly in front of Avisa and Baldwin. Shouts and the clash of steel. After wandering for half the day in search of Christian, growing tired and discouraged and hungry, Avisa had despaired that they would find him before nightfall made searching impossible. She motioned to Baldwin, hoping he could see her in the gray light as snowflakes floated around them, and slipped among the trees. She drew her sword. Low bushes caught at her gown, and fabric tore when she yanked free. She did not slow.

She burst into a clearing. It was empty. All around were the signs of a recent fight. Bloody bodies and discarded weapons. Where had the fighters gone? It had been only seconds ago that the noise reached the road.

She went toward the far edge of the clearing. Ahead of her, she could see the signs of where the outlaws had scurried away like the rats they were. Some must have been injured—she saw blood on the fallen leaves. Wounded men could not move as swiftly as she. If she gave chase, she should be able to catch them before they reached their lair.

Savoring such a victory would have to wait. Outlaws

slowed by their wounds would not have Christian with them. He would be guarded by the strongest and swiftest. She must find those men.

"Milady!" called Baldwin. "Where are you going?"

Nowhere, she wanted to reply. Instead she said, "I will not go out of your sight."

He nodded. "Nor I from yours." His voice trembled. Not with fear, but with anger that he had not been by Christian's side.

Baldwin went to the corpses and looked down at them. One was lying facedown, and he struggled to turn the man over.

"What are you doing?" Avisa asked.

"Sir Christian taught me that no knight or his man should leave an enemy suffering near death on a battlefield. Giving his enemy a quick release from agony is his duty." The boy grunted as he shoved the man onto his back.

She nodded, not surprised at Christian's compassion. It was another aspect of his sense of honor and obligation. As she continued to scan the trees, hoping for any sign to tell her in which direction the outlaws had taken Christian, she heard the boy call to her, his voice shaking with emotion.

Running to his side, she saw the hilt of a sword protruding from beneath a corpse. She knew by the engraving that it was Christian's.

"Sainted Mary," the page cried as he bent to push the corpse aside. "He would not have left it here of his own accord."

"Nor would they have left it here if they had taken note of it."

The boy grinned. "He must have given them such a battle they did not think of anything but capturing him." His expression fell into dismay as he realized what he was saying.

Horror gnawed at her stomach as she looked around the clearing again. There were four bodies, but none of them was Christian's. Where was he?

"You have keen eyes, Baldwin," she said, putting her

hand on his shoulder to halt him from trying to shift the corpse. "Can you determine the route the outlaws took from this clearing?"

Pride glistened in his eyes as he jumped to his feet and began to circle the clearing, looking for any clue that had eluded Avisa.

Kneeling by a corpse but not touching it or the sword, she frowned. The blood from the man's fatal wounds had already dried to a crust on his head. He had been dead for several hours. But she had heard the sounds of fighting minutes ago. What was happening here?

She saw the dead man was wearing a leather strip with glass beads on it. Some were clear, but others had spirals of color inside them. Just like the outlaws who had attacked them yesterday. And just like . . . she began to pull out Guy's ring with the glass bead, then halted. If the outlaws still were nearby—and she suspected they were, for there was no other explanation for the noises that had brought her and Baldwin here—she did not want them to guess she had the ring. She was not sure what the similarity meant, but she did not believe in coincidences. There must be some connection.

"Lady Avisa!" Panic heightened Baldwin's voice.

Drawing her sword as she jumped to her feet, Avisa forced all emotion from her face. She saw a knife at the page's throat. A man, dressed in the simple clothes the outlaws wore, was behind him. She edged slightly to her left, so her gown covered the hilt of Christian's sword. As soon as they found him, he would want it to repay the outlaws for kidnapping his brother.

"You are Lady Avisa?" the man asked.

"Yes." She made sure her voice was as impassive as her expression. "And you are?"

"Someone with a message for you."

"I am listening."

"You will be able to listen better when you are not holding that sword."

Knowing she had no choice, Avisa slid her sword back into its scabbard. "I will also listen better if you release the boy," she replied, her head high.

The outlaw, a scrawny man of enough years to be her father, shoved the boy aside, revealing that he, like the dead men, wore a cord with the glass beads on it. Putting his sword into the sash closing his dark tunic, he smiled. His teeth were irregular and nearly the same yellow as his hair.

"You save me the chore of finding you, milady," he said.

"How can you say that when you must have made the noise that led us here?"

His eyes slitted. "You are clever, milady."

"Where are Christian Lovell and his brother?"

"They are our prisoners."

"Where *are* they?"

"Where they will stay until you come prepared to pay a ransom."

"They are alive?" choked Baldwin.

"What value would there be in killing them now?" Avisa answered before the outlaw could. She drew the boy slightly behind her, paying no attention to his protests. "Then they would get nothing for their pains but two corpses. Those have no value." She clasped her hands and met the outlaw's gaze evenly. She hoped he did not have the wits her father was reputed to possess. "What price do you ask for their freedom?"

"The price you are told."

"How can I have what you want available if you will not tell me what it is?"

"You will be told when you come to ransom them."

"Where and when will that be?"

"There is a village not far south of here. Through it runs a stream. Follow that stream one league to the west. You will see a clearing with a single tree in its very center. Wait there, and you will be contacted."

"Very well. When?"

"At the moment when the sun touches the western hills."

She shook her head. When the shadows were thick beneath the trees and it was impossible to see beyond a few feet in any direction, she and Baldwin would be at too great a disadvantage. She needed to persuade the outlaw to make the odds a bit more even.

But how?

"There are other ways for a woman to get what she needs," came Christian's voice from her memory.

"By acting helpless?" she had asked.

"By knowing when she can use her uniquely feminine wiles to obtain whatever she wishes."

She had not guessed she would come to understand Christian's words under such horrendous circumstances. She had depended on the skills from St. Jude's Abbey. Maybe she had become too dependent upon them.

Avisa lowered her eyes, but peered through her lashes, ready to gauge the results of her ploy. "You cannot expect me to go into these woods after dark." She gave what she hoped sounded like a genuine sob of fear. "These woods are filled with restless spirits."

"You believe such tales?"

"Don't you?" she shot back, hiding her face in her hands. She watched the outlaw through her fingers. "You cannot ask me to enter the forest once the sun is setting."

"At dawn—"

She squealed in dismay. "That is even more frightful, for the spirits that find no rest will not have returned yet to their unconsecrated graves." She shook her shoulders, hoping the dimming light would prevent the outlaw from seeing how feigned every motion and word was.

"Lady Avisa?" Baldwin sounded confused.

She could not fault him. Everything she was saying suggested she was witless and helpless.

"Oh, dear Baldwin! What would I do without you?" She put her arms around him and pressed her face to his shoulder, taking care not to move enough to reveal the hilt of Christian's sword.

The boy stood as motionless as a tree. "Milady?"

"Act as if you are comforting me," she whispered. "You are supposed to be *my* companion."

For a long moment, he did not speak. She wondered if he had heard her. Maybe he was too young and too frightened to comprehend what she was trying to do.

She breathed a nearly silent sigh of relief when he said, "You know I would die for you, milady."

"That should not be necessary," the outlaw grumbled. "All you must do is follow the instructions I have given you."

Avisa pushed herself away from Baldwin and dropped to her knees. Now her gown covered the hilt completely. Holding up her clasped hands, she pleaded, "Let me follow them at an hour when the sun banishes the shadows of the undead from beneath the trees. I beg of you, kind sir, to heed my request."

"I am not the one who can agree."

"Then I implore you to ask your master." She pressed her hands to her face again and forced her stiff shoulders to quiver. Making the hiccuping sounds he seemed to believe were sobs, she sat on her heels. "I cannot enter the wood when the dusk frees wandering spirits."

"The boy—"

"He is injured."

"I see no sign of an injury."

"His head was struck very hard when you first attacked us. Every word he speaks sounds as if it comes from a drunkard's tongue." She peeked again through her fingers, to see whether the outlaw would react as she hoped. "I want to ransom Christian Lovell. I truly wish to, but I cannot when I am taken away by the restless dead."

"Milady—"

"Please!" she cried.

A disgusted grunt came from the man, and Avisa dared to believe he was growing tired of the argument and would relent. When he muttered something, she looked up.

"Wait here. I shall come back," he said.

"Thank you, kind sir." She considered groveling at his feet, but that might be too outrageous. She wished she knew what a lady should do in such a situation. That most ladies probably would not find themselves in these circumstances was no help.

Avisa waited for the man to disappear among the trees. Slowly she came to her feet. She wanted to be sure that he was not loitering out of sight while he waited for her to reveal that she was playing him for a fool. Bemoaning the sad fate that led them to the clearing and her fear for Christian and her terror at entering the forest except at midday, she paused only when Baldwin gestured that the man was gone.

She gave him a smile. "You did well, Baldwin."

"He may not come back."

"He will." She reached for Christian's sword. Putting her foot against the corpse's shoulder, she yanked the blade from beneath the dead man. The blood still pooled under the corpse ran along it to drip on the ground. Kneeling, she wiped the sword against the dried leaves. As she came to her feet, lifting the sword that was longer than hers but so well balanced she could heft it easily, she looked at Baldwin.

The boy's gaze focused on Christian's sword. He fumbled for his own. Drawing it, he touched its tip to the blade.

"I swear I will not surrender to death," he said with a dignity too old for his years, "until my cousins are free."

"That is a vow I will help you keep." She slid the sword into her belt behind her own, looping the leather over the hilt to hold it in place, as an icy wind swirled through the clearing. Had the temperature dropped, or was the chill from within her heart?

She should have kept Christian from riding away on his own. If she had told him the truth, would he have listened or would he have been even more resolved to keep her from fighting by his side?

An hour passed and then another as they waited. Avisa dared not leave because anything she did might give the outlaws the very reason they needed to slay Christian. The sun moved toward the distant hills. The odors of death hung over the clearing.

She hated doing nothing. Why had she let the outlaw go alone? Maybe if she had insisted with more feigned tears, he would have allowed her to travel with him. She could have seen how Christian and his brother fared. She might even have been able to arrange their release. Now all she could do was peer through the trees, hoping one of the shadows would metamorphose into the outlaw.

"Looking for me, milady?"

She whirled at the taunting voice. The outlaw had finally returned. Not alone, for two other men were with him. She fought her instinct to reach for her sword. They must think of her as a helpless, hapless woman.

"You came back!" she cried, hoping she was showing them the reaction they expected. She kept her arms folded in front of her, one hand on each side of her cloak, holding it closed over the two swords.

"Our leader has graciously agreed to your meeting time, milady." He bowed his head, then straightened, his smile as icy as the wind. "But you must agree to his terms."

"Speak them, and I shall see—"

"He will not negotiate with a woman."

"The boy cannot handle the negotiations. He is too injured in the head." She glanced at the page, and Baldwin looked at the ground. To give credence to her lie or to hide his frustration?

"We thought so, too. That is why I offer you a champion, milady." The outlaw threw his head back and gave a laugh that echoed among the trees.

"A champion?" Her heart began a wild dance in her chest. Was he releasing Christian? That made no sense, but she could not keep the hope from bursting within her like notes of a joyous song. "Who?"

"See for yourself." He gestured past her. "Return to the road, and you will find your champion waiting there."

"And then?"

"And then you will have someone to deal with Pyt—"

"Who?"

His amusement vanished, and she knew he had not meant to speak the name. His hands trembled as he looked at his compatriots. Did he expect someone to slay him for speaking what must be their leader's name?

"Go to the road and collect your champion," he snarled. "You will ride east to a ford on the stream and then wait for further instructions at the inn on its far side."

Avisa nodded. Trying to obtain more information now would be unavailing. The outlaw was as scared as she had pretended to be. Another glance at Baldwin silenced the lad before he could speak.

She took a step away from the outlaws and grasped the page's arm. The slightest tug told him to match her paces as they backed away. The man did not move, nor did his smile return, as they left the clearing.

"Do you believe what he said?" Baldwin asked, barely loudly enough for her to hear.

"He has no reason to be false with us."

"But, milady, he is an outlaw!"

"An outlaw who wants whatever ransom he is going to ask for to share with his fellows."

"Why wouldn't he tell us what he wants?"

"Because he hopes that when we see Christian, we will be so happy we will be willing to pay whatever he wants."

Baldwin scanned the bushes. "How shall we pay it?"

"One problem at a time." She smiled and put her hand on his shoulder. "Let us find this champion he promised us."

Baldwin did not protest further. She wondered if her eyes glowed with hope as his did. Was he, too, imagining them finding Christian—unhurt and alive—by the road?

As they emerged onto the road, Avisa looked in both directions. She saw someone sitting, his head in his hands, to her left. Before she could move, Baldwin raced along the road.

"Guy!" came his shout. "Milady, 'tis Sir Guy!"

Avisa swallowed her despair as her hopes were smashed. She walked toward Guy. The outlaws could be watching even now and waiting to spring a trap. Until she was somewhere she knew was private, she must maintain her pretense as a terrified lady.

As she neared, Guy came slowly to his feet. He looked horrible. His hair was matted over the blood where his face had been cut. One sleeve of his tunic was connected only by a few threads. Bruises darkened his face, and crimson still dripped from one corner of his mouth. She guessed the outlaws had given him a parting blow.

She pulled off her cloak and held it out. Guy snatched it, wrapping the thick wool around his shoulders.

Baldwin tried to hide his dismay. "Would you like my cape, milady? You will become chilled."

"Why are you worried about her?" Guy wrapped it more tightly around him, as if he feared she would demand it back. "How about some sympathy for *me*? Those damned outlaws raised a lump on my skull."

"But they freed you." She scanned the bushes beneath the trees. "Why?"

"How in the devil's name am I to know what such fools are thinking?" He winced.

"Are you hurt badly?"

He grinned and took her hand. Drawing it to his cheek, he pressed her palm against his icy skin. His other arm swept around her waist and tugged her closer to him. "Why don't you kiss me and make it better, fair Avisa?"

"Nothing can make any of this situation better."

"I can think of a few things." When she started to storm away, his arm tightened around her. He ignored her order to release her. His fingers swept upward along her back, twisting in her loose hair. Her eyes widened as his mouth descended toward hers. She shoved out of his arms, blinking back tears. She wanted Christian kissing her, not his brother. She wanted Christian safe.

Guy reached for her again. Her reaction was instinctive. She grabbed his wrist and twisted his hand behind him. He yelped, and she quickly released the hold that Nariko had taught her.

"Where did you learn to do *that*?" Guy asked as Baldwin edged closer, his eyes wide.

"Why are you asking questions?" she fired back. "The only thing that matters is freeing Christian. We are to go to a ford and the inn on its far side. There we will find out what we need to know to ransom Christian. Do you know what they want, Guy?"

He shrugged, but did not meet her eyes. What was he hiding? She would find out when they reached the inn. Then they would rescue Christian. She had vowed on her life and her honor to keep him safe. And she would.

The inn was cramped with low ceilings. Spiders and other creatures lived among the rafters. Mud sprinkled down on to the stone floor and the rickety table. A single bench was set beside the table, and the hearth near the back wall was unlit. Oily lamps smoked, but could not cover up the scent of rotten meat and dog droppings.

The innkeeper, a woman with thick gray hair and a wrinkled face that was still beautiful, ushered Avisa and Guy through the common room and into a private room that was not in much better condition. She waited expectantly for their reaction to the crooked bedframe topped with straw and the window where the shutter had come loose.

Avisa said quietly, "It will do. Thank you."

She scowled at Guy, who was opening his mouth to make a comment that she guessed would be caustic. He had complained endlessly on the short journey to the inn. He wanted his horse. He was a baron's son, and a baron's son should not be walking. He was cold. He was thirsty. Why didn't they send Baldwin ahead of them to get horses? She had ignored his suggestion of what he and Avisa could do to spend the time until the boy returned, just as she had ignored his idea of making the page run all the way to the inn when Baldwin was showing the double strain of his injury and his fear for Christian.

"Lady Avisa is very gracious," Guy said before wandering back to the common room and calling for some ale.

"Lady?" The innkeeper's eyes widened. "We have never had a real lady beneath our roof. We are honored, milady. Tell me what you wish, and I will see it is brought."

Pulling off her gloves, Avisa dropped them onto the bedframe. "We are waiting for a message. If you could have the messenger brought to me immediately, I would appreciate it. He will be from Pyt."

"Pyt?" Her eyes got even wider. "Milady, you should not be having any dealings with such a man."

"I must." She was not going to explain further.

"Pyt and his followers are not mere outlaws, milady."

"So we have been told. They wear glass beads around their throats. Do you know if they have some meaning?" She thought of the silver ring Guy had given her. The bead with its swirls was like the ones the outlaws wore.

"Who knows what evil those beads represent? Those outlaws are an abomination, seeking to bring England back into darkness."

"We were also warned about that." She looked out the door to where Guy and Baldwin were in deep conversation. The page was frowning, so she guessed Guy was displeased about something the boy had said. "But we have no choice. We must wait to see if he contacts us."

"You need only wait, and Pyt shall contact you."

"You make such attacks sound common."

"King Henry the Senior is across the Channel, and King Henry the Younger is seen as having little authority." The innkeeper lowered her voice. "Now that Archbishop Thomas has returned to England, the church officials have no time for secular matters. They are gathered trying to decide if they will stand with the archbishop or with the king."

"Are you saying we must negotiate with Pyt and his fellow outlaws without assistance from the constable?"

The woman laughed sharply. "The constable knows better than to cross Pyt. The last constable boasted of putting an end to the outlaws. He was found in several pieces throughout the parish."

Avisa put her hand over her stomach, which was threatening to spew up everything within it. "Then we shall have to deal with these outlaws ourselves."

"Milady, you need to realize that nobody *deals* with Pyt. He states his terms, and he is paid."

"What does he usually ask for?"

The innkeeper shuddered. "What his victim wishes least to pay. If you hope to see your friend alive, you will do what he tells you to do. One mistake, and your companions—all of you—will be dead or wish you were."

Chapter 14

"We may have to wait to meet with Pyt, but that does not mean we have to sit and do nothing." Guy tilted back his tankard and drank. He dropped it onto the table.

"What do you suggest we do?" Avisa glanced past Baldwin, who sat beside her on the bench in the inn's common room. Word of Christian's abduction must have flown with hawk's speed through the shire.

More than a dozen men had arrived in the past hour. They brought pitchforks and scythes, the very tools Christian had said could be wielded as weapons. Each one had bowed his head to her before pledging to help her free Christian. None of them spoke of a reward for such bravery. She had nothing to offer them in return. Nor did Guy or Baldwin. She hoped that ending the outlaws' hold on the shire would be reward enough.

The men were gathered around the cask on the opposite side of the room. Ale had loosened their tongues and honed their courage, and they were now boasting about what they would do to make Pyt and his men rue their decision to attack the nearby farms.

Guy looked up from his tankard and grinned. "I can make a few suggestions, fair Avisa, if you will come with me to our private room."

"You have taken a greater knock to the head than we thought."

"But I am hale enough to—"

"That knock to your head may have damaged you more than you realize."

Baldwin turned away, and Avisa heard his muffled laugh. Guy must have heard it as well, because he stood and wobbled across the room to refill his mug with ale.

But Guy was right. They did not need to sit here and do nothing.

With a curse she was glad the abbess had not heard her speak, Avisa pulled up her skirt and climbed onto the bench, then the table. She drew her sword and struck the stone wall.

"Listen to me!" she called.

"Milady, you should not—"

"Silence, Baldwin!" She looked at his strained face. Resting her hand on his shoulder, she gave him a smile. He did not return it, and she knew she would not see him grin until Christian was found. "Silence, all of you!"

To her left, two men continued to argue. She tapped one on the head with the flat of her sword.

"Avisa, what are you doing?" yelped Guy as he faced her.

"Hold your tongue, Guy." She rested the sword's tip against the battered table and stared at the score of men around her. When she motioned for them to sit on the floor, only Guy did not obey. Then, when the men scowled at him, he complied. Good! Maybe he was finally seeing the sense of working together.

Avisa appraised the men. Not a single one looked as if he had any experience in battle. They wore the clothing of tenant farmers who depended on their liege lord to protect them from invaders. Yet they were the only help she had. Guy was useless in a fight, and Baldwin, in spite of his efforts to pretend otherwise, was greatly slowed by his injuries.

Fear welled in her throat, and she swallowed hard. No sign of weakness must betray her. She had vowed to protect Christian Lovell's life, and she would do that, no matter the cost.

As she looked at Baldwin's expectant face, she almost

faltered. She did not want to have his life ended before it had barely begun. He would not remain behind, and she would not ask him to. Like her, he had sworn a vow, and, like her, he would keep that pledge even if he had to give his life.

She wished she could believe the same of Guy. He was no coward, but he also was no warrior. Maybe he would stay at the inn if she asked him to. She could not ask that. Pyt expected Guy to negotiate Christian's release.

"I am Lady Avisa," she said when the men shifted restlessly. "You have each come forward and pledged your help in overcoming these outlaws who have been tormenting this shire. They attacked us on the road and hope to ransom the king's man, Christian Lovell. Together, we can stop these beasts who steal your property and prey on your family and travelers."

A cheer met her words.

"I can promise you the glory of a wondrous fight," she said, watching their faces. "I can promise you that your families and your beasts will be safe in the fields. I can promise you that the outlaws shall be sorry they ever started their treacherous work in this shire."

More cheers rumbled among the rafters.

"Make no mistake," she said. "Sir Christian will be returned to us, and these outlaws shall feel the full force of our fury."

Baldwin jumped to his feet, waving his hands in excitement. "They will regret the day they attacked us. When we have had our vengeance, those outlaws will rot in hell as their women sob with grief. Vengeance will be ours!"

Applause and huzzahs met his words. "Vengeance will be ours! Vengeance will be ours!" The words wove through the clang of steel as Baldwin and Guy beat their swords together.

Raising her broadsword over her head, Avisa drove it into the table. "Be ready to leave with the dawn."

Again cheers met her words. This was what the men

wanted. Action and a chance to repay the outlaws, wound for wound.

As Guy poured another round for the men before they found a place to sleep, Avisa pulled her sword out of the table and sheathed it. She smiled sadly as the bragging began anew. Each man wanted to be the one to slay Pyt. She wondered how many would falter once weapons were drawn and how many would not return. She could not think like that. She must think of freeing Christian before the outlaws murdered him.

Slipping out of the common room after telling Baldwin to get some rest, she went into the private room. The innkeeper had found a woven blanket to put over what looked like fresh straw on the bedframe. The lamp burned brightly, and a fire blazed in the pit. Starlight splattered on the rushes covering the stone floor and on Christian's sword leaning against the bed, but the moon must have set already. She wondered what the hour was. Cold and damp had been chased from the room. Winter was growing stronger, but it seemed the deepest chill was within her.

"How am I going to pay for this?" she mused aloud. She sank to the padded bench by a small table. Drawing up her skirt, she looked at the dagger on her leg. The weapon was well made, and the innkeeper might accept it as payment for a night's shelter.

"Sir Christian will see they are paid," said Baldwin as he came into the room, carrying a tray. The aroma of spices rose from the single cup on it.

"Baldwin, I thought you abed by now."

"First I wanted to bring the mulled cider the innkeeper made for you."

She smiled and took the cup. "A reward for my perform-ance out there?"

"You ignited the fire of righteous fury within them." He set the tray on the table.

"I hope it stays burning long enough so they do not flee

at the first sight of the outlaws. The three of us alone have proven less than worthy adversaries for Pyt's men."

Dismay lengthened his face. "Milady, you should not go to meet the outlaw leader. If I might suggest—"

"If you intend to talk me out of going to help rescue Christian, you need not bother. I will go. He depends on me." *And the queen relies on me.* Avisa would not fail in her duty.

"He depends on you to let us do what we should." He wrung his hands. "You are a lady. You should not negotiate with outlaws."

She sighed. "No one knows that better than I, but there is no one else."

"Let Sir Guy go. The outlaws released him so he could negotiate for Sir Christian's release."

"Baldwin," she said, amazed, "you must have guessed that Guy was released because Pyt and his men believe him incapable of doing anything but capitulating and giving them what they want."

The boy's toe dug at the edge of a stone along the firepit. "I have thought of that, milady, but Pyt will be expecting Sir Guy."

"And we shall do something unexpected. That puts our enemies at a disadvantage because they will be unsure what we might do next."

"But you are a lady. It is wrong for you to come with us when you could be endangering your life."

"Enough! I will not hear any more of this." *You might convince me to listen to sense, and I cannot in this time of madness.* "If you cannot accept that I will be leading this expedition—"

"No, no, milady! I will go with you. I will follow you, for I promised Sir Christian that I would not allow you out of my sight."

"Thank you, Baldwin." She patted his arm. "Get some sleep. I shall do the same once I have prepared myself for our meeting with Pyt."

He took her hands and bowed over them. "I know you will find the right words just as you found the right ones tonight, milady."

"Good night, Baldwin."

"Good night, milady," he said softly.

As he went out the door, her smile vanished. Yes, she would need to find the right words. The wrong ones could mean death for Christian.

"The hour is near."

Christian raised his head and fought the yawn tickling the back of his throat. He had remained awake the whole night, not trusting the outlaws. Cowards that they were, they might slay him before he could wake and fight them off.

He almost laughed at the thought. He had been unable to defeat them yesterday. The outlaws had swarmed out of the trees like maddened bees from their disturbed hive. He had held them off at first, seeing several fall. But eventually their numbers had proven overwhelming, and he had been captured. His first hope, that he would be able to contrive with Guy for a way to escape, came to naught when he discovered his brother had been released.

That made no sense—but nothing about the outlaws did. They had searched him and his bags, then left him tied to the tree still wearing his mail. As he looked around the bare clearing where he was sitting, he saw no sign of even the simplest hut. Food and refuse were piled together by a brook that edged the clearing. People wandered in and out of sight among the trees. They were dressed in common clothes, torn and dirty, yet each wore around his or her neck a thong with at least one glass bead on it. Few glanced in his direction. Quite the opposite, for they seemed anxious to avoid his eyes.

Except a muscular man who strode toward him. The man could have been a stonemason or a woodsman; his arms were lined with sinews. Pale hair hung around his shoulders, and a thick beard hid the lower half of his face. Nearly colorless eyes peered from beneath bushy brows.

He squatted in front of Christian and smiled, revealing an almost toothless mouth. "I hope you are comfortable, Lovell, for it appears you shall be our guest longer than either of us wished."

"Are you the one I hear called Pyt?"

"I am." He laughed, and heads turned in the clearing.

Christian saw fear on those faces before the people looked hastily away again. What hold did this man have on them?

"There seems to be a problem," Pyt continued. "The arrangement for your ransom is not going as planned."

"You released my brother to handle that. He—"

"Listens to the orders of a wench." Pyt picked at his two remaining teeth and chuckled. "Maybe she will give him better counsel than your father's advisors gave him when he fought with Henry of Anjou."

Christian's flush of exasperation at his brother's antics vanished as he gasped, "My father? You know my father?"

"Everyone knows about Robert Lovell and his cowardice." He laughed again. "I was glad he chose not to side with King Stephen."

Christian fought back the red haze of fury at the insults. He had heard the same before, and he had learned that losing his temper gained him nothing but more ridicule. The king had accepted his fealty, a sign that Henry believed the Lovell family's honor could be redeemed.

When Christian did not respond to the outlaw's contemptuous words, Pyt said, "If your father had helped Henry more, we could have Stephen's son on the throne now instead of that pretender."

"You were Stephen's man?"

Pyt flung out his hands. "Why do you think we hide amidst the trees? We refuse to pledge ourselves to a man who stole the throne and has coronated his son to ensure that his line is not tossed back across the Channel."

Shifting so his wrists did not burn against the rope, Christian wanted to ask what Pyt knew of the battle when his father was accused of abandoning the king. Such answers would come more easily when Pyt was *his* prisoner.

"So you refused to pledge your loyalty to King Henry, Pyt?" he asked. "Do you pledge it instead to some heathen god?"

"No!"

"You are not part of the cult rumored to be trying to bring back the old ways?"

Pyt's face became gray. "No, that evil is not here, but farther west in the Welsh hills."

"We have heard the cult is in this forest."

"We are not part of that. We are honest men who have been outlawed by a pretender king."

Either the outlaw was a great actor or he was genuinely fearful of the ones who claimed to worship ancient gods. An interesting fact, but nothing that would help Christian. "Where are we meeting my brother?"

"Not far from where you fell into our hands. I hope your brother is wiser than he appeared while with us. If he fails to bring your ransom . . ." He drew one finger across his throat.

"What ransom do you ask for the son of a dishonored man?" He ignored Pyt's motion. The outlaw would not kill him as long as he believed he had a chance of obtaining whatever it was he wanted.

"I will speak of it when we arrange for your release. If your brother has any sense, he will do what we wish."

"Guy knows what he needs to do."

"Does he? My man who has been watching your brother says he listens to a pretty wench."

Christian did not let his expression change. God's blood! Guy needed to think of getting Christian out of these bonds instead of trying to get between some woman's legs.

Pyt rested his left elbow on one knee. If he thought to confuse Christian with such a lackadaisical pose, he was wasting his time. The outlaw's fingers were twitching and his eyes darting about as if he feared an attack at any moment. But from whom? Were there rival outlaws in the wood?

"I am told it was quite a performance," Pyt said with a grin that did not lessen the uneasiness in his eyes.

"My brother has much experience with women, and he knows how to persuade them to do his bidding."

"Your brother?" Pyt shook his head, the matted blond strands falling across his face. "I do not speak of that fool. The tale I was told was of the woman." His laugh returned. "It seems she made an impression on those who witnessed her call to arms at the inn. She jumped up on a table with a broadsword and exhorted every man to follow her into battle against us." He slammed his fist into his knee and guffawed. "Silly woman! How many men did she think would pay attention to her request when her yellow hair falling over her shoulders and her bright blue eyes ignited their loins?"

Christian had to struggle not to let the outlaw see his reaction. Pyt was speaking of Avisa. His brother was stepping aside and letting Avisa arrange for the ransom? For the first time, Christian believed he had a chance of getting out alive.

But he did not want Avisa talking ransom terms with Pyt. She had a gentleness that the outlaw would quickly take advantage of. In her innocent attempt to free him, she could be hurt or worse.

"Is that so?" Christian asked, keeping his voice emotionless. He could not give Pyt any more of an advantage by letting the outlaw guess how unprepared Avisa was for such negotiations.

Pyt jabbed a finger in Christian's chest. If his hands had not been bound, Christian would have gladly broken that poking finger. The outlaw realized that, too, for the superior smile had returned to his face.

"Your brother has fewer wits than a child," Pyt said, "which he proves by heeding the entreaties of a woman afraid of old superstitions."

"Is that so?" If he kept the outlaw babbling, maybe he would learn something to help him escape before the meeting even began. That would be the best way to keep Avisa safe. "Which superstitions?"

"She wept like a babe at the thought of coming to the wood at sunset or dawn because she fears the unhallowed graves will open up and spew out their corpses to walk the wood." He threw back his head and laughed. "She believes the tales created by others before us who have used this wood for sanctuary."

Christian tried to imagine Avisa weeping in terror and could not. He hoped he would never see her cry.

"She is but a woman," he said with the same indifference.

"Who needs to be wise enough to bring your ransom."

"That is unlikely. Women are fools, their only thoughts of flirtations and getting a man to give his name in exchange for a place in her bed. The only person more foolish than a woman is a man who tries to do business with one." He arched a single brow and braced for the blow he knew would come.

Pyt's eyes widened just before his fist drove Christian's head back against the tree. Christian tasted the salty flavor of his own blood. Even as his tongue checked that none of his teeth had come loose, he was watching the outlaw rise and walk away. Pyt had come to gloat, but Christian had seen fury and uncertainty on the outlaw's face.

"Take care, young Lovell."

Christian looked to his left, then groaned. The motion sent agony through him, blurring his eyes. A piece of cloth dabbed at the blood rolling down his chin, and he muttered, "Thank you."

"Pyt will kill you if you become a bother." An elderly man dressed in a long tunic the same color as his gray hair sat in front of Christian. His motions suggested he was far younger than the many years chiseled into his face.

A familiar face. Christian recalled seeing it before, but where? His thoughts were as unsteady as his vision. He tried to concentrate, ignoring the pain riveting him. Recognition clapped through his head like thunder.

"I saw you at Castle Orxted," he said.

"Yes, you saw me there, as you had seen me a short time before."

"Before?"

"When you chided your brother for his lack of respect for an old man."

Christian growled a curse. "*You* are the old man he insulted?"

"Yes."

"But that makes no sense. Why would you be so far from where we first met you?"

He swept out his hands. "Because *this* is my home."

"You are one of Pyt's men?"

"I am my own man, but Pyt serves my purpose now."

"And what is that?"

The old man chuckled. "None of your concern. Your sole worry should be making sure you are alive when tomorrow dawns. Do not expect that Pyt will release you as he did your brother when that young fool became too troublesome."

"He released Guy to arrange my ransom."

The old man shook his head, and Christian's eyes blurred again as he tried to watch the old man's face. When the old man put his hand on Christian's shoulder, he said, "He was ready to kill your brother until you fell into his trap. Now he is in a rage because it is clear that your brother is incompetent even in arranging a ransom."

Christian wanted to argue, but he could not disagree with the truth. Guy would have intentions of helping—until he was distracted by some pretty wench.

"Release me, and I shall see you are rewarded," Christian said.

"Such a reward will do me no good if I am dead. If you think you can escape Pyt's wood, you are wrong. He will see you and your companions dead before the sun rises. Pyt hates anyone who helped bring about Henry Curtmantle's rule."

"Then he should not despise anyone of my blood." He did not try to keep the bitterness from his voice. His head was aching worse with each passing second.

"Your father fought well and with great valor during several forays against Stephen. Pyt will not forget that."

"He has not forgotten my father's cowardice."

"Heed my advice, young Lovell, so I may repay an old debt to your family. A debt older than King Henry's hold on his throne."

"My family? What debt would you have to my family that is older than . . . ?" His eyes widened. "What are you saying?"

"You know the truth, young Lovell. It is within you, flowing through you with each pulse of your heart. Do not doubt that what you know is true."

Christian clenched his bound hands in frustration. "Speak what you know."

"A vow once taken into the heart cannot be broken."

"Do you speak of my father?"

"A vow once taken into the heart cannot be broken."

He swore. "Stop talking in riddles, and speak the truth."

"I speak the truth when I say that a vow once taken into the heart cannot be broken." He stood. "And I speak the truth when I say you must take my words as a warning, young Lovell. Wait for the lady to pay Pyt what he demands."

"My brother will be arranging for the ransom, not Avisa. Pyt will not negotiate with a woman. He has said so himself."

"He will take your ransom from any hand."

"What does he want? Gold? More horses?" He did not add that he had neither.

"He wants something that you have and he does not." The old man's smile wavered. "He believes it will offer him a great and ancient power to force Henry from his throne."

"Great power?" Christian spat on the ground. "He disavowed any connection to the cult rumored to be in the wood. Does he believe in it after all?"

"He believes what will get him what he desires, and above all else, he desires to see the king banished across the sea as he was in 1147."

Christian lowered his eyes at the reminder of the campaign when the king had been shamed to have his rival pay to return him to his lands. If Lord Lovell had been courageous instead of deserting his king, that never would have happened. Now his son was bound to a tree and waiting for a woman to put her life in danger—again—to rescue him.

"I don't want Avisa to have any part in this ignominious situation." He wished he could take back the words. Maybe Avisa was right. He *was* mewling like a suckling.

"That choice is no longer yours, young Lovell," the old man said. "You must let the circumstances unfold as they shall if you wish to save her life."

He looked at the old man, forcing his eyes to focus. "Are you saying I must do nothing but wait for Guy to pay my ransom?"

"For *Lady Avisa* to pay it." The old man leaned toward him and whispered, "You must let her do this. Paying your ransom may be the sole way for you to keep her alive until you travel beyond Pyt's shadowy realm."

Chapter 15

"Where are they? Are you sure you have the right place?"

Instead of answering Guy's impatient questions, Avisa scowled in his direction. He was standing next to Baldwin and had been complaining since they left the inn. Either he was oblivious to the glances exchanged by the men who had come with them, or he did not care that his grumbling was adding to their anxiety as they prepared to come face-to-face with the outlaws. Whichever it was, she wished he would be silent.

Bushes rattled, and she heard a sharp, collective intake of breath behind her. She raised her chin as she tightened her hands on the reins of the horse she had borrowed from the innkeeper's neighbor. The idea of leaving without Christian was abhorrent, but she must be prepared to retreat in order to gain another chance to free him.

Men appeared from behind the trees. Their dark brown tunics blended well with the wintry wood. Each man carried either a bare sword or a dagger. Each wore glass beads, and she resisted checking to make sure the ring was still in the sheath. Seeing no bows, she was relieved until she reminded herself that the archers might be hidden in the shadows.

But where was Christian? She had assumed he would be brought to the meeting. Her hands clutched the reins so hard the leather cut into her palms. She forced her fingers to loosen. She must be ready for any surprises these criminals could devise.

No one spoke aloud as the men formed a half circle facing her and her allies. Hearing Guy's whispered curse, she wanted to warn him to silence. She refrained because he might start whining again that *he* should be riding the sole horse. No hint of discord must reveal any fractures in the strained coalition she had built at the inn.

One of the outlaws stepped forward. He wore mail, and she wondered from whom he had stolen it. For a moment, she thought it was Christian's, and fury turned her blood to fire. She calmed herself when she saw the rust and broken rings in the mail. Christian's had been in good repair.

The outlaw had an arrogant smile on his thin, lined face. He was not an old man, just one well worn by his hard life. "You are here, Sir Guy, and—"

"*I* will be negotiating Christian Lovell's release," Avisa said, moving the horse toward him. She stopped beyond his sword's reach. "You may address me as Lady Avisa."

The outlaw looked past her. "Sir Guy, if you wish to see your brother—"

She jerked back on the reins, and her horse rose to dance on his rear feet. The man who had spoken backpedaled, and the other outlaws cowered. As the horse put its hooves on the ground again, still far enough away from the outlaws that their swords were useless, she said, "You will speak to *me*."

The outlaw in mail took two paces forward again, his face red with either rage or humiliation. She guessed the latter because his fellows were chuckling as if they had stood their ground instead of cringing like the mangy beasts they were.

"Lady Avisa, did you say?" he asked.

"Yes," she answered. If he thought he would intimidate her with his dismissive tone, she must show him how mistaken he was. "Are you Pyt?"

"No. He awaits you elsewhere."

"Then lead us to him."

"On foot."

She smiled. "We will travel with you on foot, but I shall not leave my horse to be stolen, as our others were, by your fellow outlaws."

He nodded, his mouth straightening.

As she dismounted, Avisa motioned for Guy and Baldwin to step forward. The grousing she had expected from Guy did not come.

"You are to bring no weapons, by order of Pyt." His expression warned that Pyt intended to inflict insult for as long as possible.

"I will place my weapon in its sheath on my horse, and the others will comply with the order as long as that order includes safe passage for all of us to Pyt and for all of us, including Christian Lovell, safe passage past the borders of the lands Pyt terrorizes."

Avisa unbuckled her sword belt and hung it over the long sack tied to one side of her saddle. If the outlaws had any hint of her plan, they would try to slay her before she could draw another breath.

"No weapons is the order I was given."

"That I understand." She kept her head high. "We shall wait while you return to Pyt, so *you* may fully understand what I suspect was his complete order."

The man did not move. "That was his complete order, milady."

"Then you may convey to Pyt my regrets that we shall not be able to negotiate Christian Lovell's release today as he requested." She turned her back on him. "We are leaving!"

Baldwin protested, "Lady Avisa, we cannot—"

"Go in there without promise of safe passage out again!" she retorted. Holding out her hand to Guy to help her mount, she raised her voice. "We leave now."

"Do you think that would be wise?"

She turned to ask Baldwin why he continued to balk, but

her question became a gasp as she stared at another man who strode toward them. She yanked her broadsword off the back of her horse when she saw the glances exchanged by the outlaws. Eager, pleased glances. Who was he?

The brawny man also wore a rusted mail shirt. The sleeves reached only as far as his elbows, but the shirt dropped past his knees. Over it he wore a strand with the strange beads that matched the ones the other outlaws had. His eyes were as colorless as his hair and thick beard. He pulled a broadsword from behind his back. She fought to remain still as he stopped in front of her. If she moved her sword, he would cut into her before she could swing it.

"I am Lady Avisa," she said with quiet dignity. "I have come to speak with Pyt about arranging the release of Christian Lovell. You may take him that message, or you may impart to him that we have taken our leave. The choice of whether we speak today or some other time is his."

"All choices are his in this matter." He laughed as he gestured toward the trees beyond him. "Milady, if you will come with me . . ."

"I await Pyt here, along with his promise of safe passage."

"There is no need for you to wait any longer." A smile curved along his lips, and Avisa forced her fingers not to stiffen into a fist. He was amused by her! She would be a fool not to make these demands for their safety. *He* would be the fool if he underestimated her.

"Sir," she said coolly, "it is always wise to even the odds against one. If Pyt is too frightened"— she ignored the shocked gasps from both his men and hers at her forthright words—"to come here among us to greet a lady with due respect, then it behooves me to question what else a man of so little honor might do."

His smile remained steady. "Pyt of the Forest at your service, and I do not fear men who travel in the wake of a woman's skirt." He bowed, but his feigned smile vanished as he straightened. "Where is the ransom you were to bring with you? Or have you come to pay Lovell's ransom with nothing more than witless farmers and worthless pitchforks?"

"A specific ransom was never requested."

"But you should have brought gold or a pile of thick fleeces."

"Do you really believe I would be so imprudent?" She hoped he could not guess she was bluffing. "I have come to negotiate for Christian Lovell's release, as you requested."

"There shall be no negotiation. I know what I want, and you shall bring it to me."

She gave him her iciest smile. "We shall discuss the exact terms of our agreement once I have seen that Christian is still alive."

"He is."

"I wish to see that for myself."

"You do not trust me, milady."

"That is the first thing you have said that I can agree with. Where is he?"

"Alive. You need know nothing more, milady."

"Forgive me if I do not accept the word of an outlaw. Why are you afraid to show me that he lives?"

"I am not afraid, milady, but you should be." He waved his hand again toward the trees. "Let Lady Avisa see what she will be paying for."

Christian was pushed out from among the trees by two men who flanked him on each step. She was amazed to see he still wore his full suit of mail. His hands were lashed together in front of him. He was gagged, and a bright red mark on his face matched another darkening into a bruise. She gripped her sword's hilt tightly. How she longed to run it through Pyt! She heard Guy swear and Baldwin's anxious prayer. She said nothing. She must remain focused on the outlaw standing an arm's length from her.

"You see him, milady," Pyt said. "Now I wish to be paid."

"What do you want?"

"A ring," he replied.

She heard a buzz of surprise behind her, but he was saying just what she had expected, since she had seen that the glass bead on the silver ring was almost identical to the ones the outlaws wore.

"A ring?" she asked, letting puzzlement fill her voice. "All of this for a ring?"

"A very special ring." He lifted his beads. "It would look like these. We know you have it, for it was stolen by Guy Lovell. He did not have it, and neither did his brother. We have searched them and found nothing. That leaves you and the boy. Which of you shall we search first?"

As Pyt's fellow outlaws hooted in anticipation, Christian swore. He strained against his bonds, but it was useless. He could do nothing to stop what was about to happen. Even his worst nightmare of the meeting between Avisa and the outlaw paled before the reality. Every word she spoke, every motion she made, was intriguing Pyt. She seemed completely unaware of that as she folded her hands on top of her sword, whose point rested against the ground between her feet.

"Neither of us shall you search," she replied. "There will be no ransom paid today."

Baldwin rushed forward to grasp her arm, but she shrugged him off.

"*I* am handling the negotiations," she said in a fierce tone she had never used with the boy.

The page stared at her in disbelief, then looked to Christian. "Sir, please tell her to take care. For her life and yours."

"Yes," Pyt snarled, "do tell her."

The filthy cloth gagging Christian was untied and tossed aside. His dry lips yearned for a drink of cold water—or the warmth of her soft lips. He cursed silently again at the unbidden thought. He must not be distracted by thoughts of her eager kisses. But how could he not want her when she looked so proud and so indomitable as she faced the outlaw? She was not cowering before Pyt. If his brother had been half as brave, they would not be negotiating with an outlaw now. She kept her horse to her back, so she could not be attacked from behind, and she balanced lightly on her feet. If she had been a man, Christian's hopes would have been high. She was certainly not a man, and he hoped Pyt would not ask for both the ring—and her.

When she motioned again for Baldwin to move back, he saw how she glanced at the packet tied behind her saddle. Had she, in spite of her claims otherwise, brought something in that soiled cloth for his ransom? He had not guessed fleeces could be compressed into such a long, narrow packet.

"Avisa, you should leave," he said.

"I did not come all this way to leave without you," she answered calmly.

"I should have guessed you would not be wise enough to stay away."

"Fine words when we have come to negotiate your ransom."

"I told you, milady," Pyt said in his surly tone, "there would be no negotiation. You shall pay me what I ask, or yon knight will be shorter by a head."

"I told you I would be reasonable, Pyt, but I must insist on the same from you." Her unperturbed answer suggested she was doing nothing more exciting than arguing about the price of eggs in a marketplace.

Christian was awed by her serenity when she stood within reach of the outlaw's sword. Then he noticed the slightest quiver of her fingers on her own. So faint was the motion that he doubted he would have seen it if he had not been watching both Avisa and Pyt closely in hope of discovering a chance to put an end to these verbal jousts without injury to her.

"Very well, milady. I shall be completely reasonable." Pyt gave her a mocking bow, and her hand tensed on her sword.

Wanting to shout not to be so witless, Christian kept his

mouth shut when the outlaw straightened and her fingers relaxed again on the hilt. What was she planning? He prayed it would not end with them dead. He could imagine no more ignoble end than dying with his hands bound and a woman attempting to free him.

"What is your demand, Pyt?" Avisa asked.

"The ring. Silver with a glass bead containing blue swirls. You were told that already."

She pointed at Christian with her sword. "You ask me to exchange a fine piece of jewelry for a man who could not even defend his companions? Pyt, you must think me as great a fool as you."

When the outlaw growled again, Christian started to caution her. She frowned and jabbed her sword in his direction as she continued to deride his courage and the outlaw's brains.

He winced as her sword almost cut his hand. How could she be so careless? Idiotic woman! She— He swallowed his gasp of astonishment. She had, while arguing with Pyt, sliced into the ropes binding him. He wiggled his wrists, testing his bonds. He caught one section of the rope before it could fall to the ground and betray that she had freed him even as the outlaws watched.

"If you are unwilling to pay the ransom for Lovell," Pyt snarled, "I will have you searched right here, milady."

She laughed derisively as she rested the sword between her feet again. "What honor is there in searching a woman who has come in good faith to negotiate with you?"

"You forget, milady. I am an outlaw. I have no honor." He gave a shout.

His men swarmed toward her.

Christian tore his hands from the ropes. They were stiff, but he drove his fist into the face of a man beside him. Pain rippled across his knuckles, but the man fell to the ground. He put out his foot to trip up the other man who was rushing forward to jump him. The man's head struck a tree, and he dropped to his knees, barely conscious.

"Christian!" He heard Avisa call out.

When he looked toward her, praying he had not heard her death cry, she pulled his sword from the packet behind her saddle and tossed it to him. She had brought his sword with her and had it right under Pyt's nose!

He caught the hilt in time to swing it into the outlaw racing toward him. The man screeched before tumbling to the ground. Whirling, he snapped a thick branch in half before it could shatter his skull. He kicked aside the broken pieces and drove his sword into the man who had been about to use it.

Shouts came from all around him. His brother was surrounded by peasants using pitchforks to hold the outlaws back. Several of the farmers were chasing Pyt's men through the trees, their scythes taking deadly swings against them. He ran to where Baldwin was falling back under the attack of two outlaws. Driving his sword into one, he raised it toward the other man. The outlaw whirled and ran, but was stopped by one of the farmers. All around them, Pyt's men were dying. None were being allowed to escape.

"I . . . I . . . I am fine," Baldwin panted.

"Get the horse and take it back toward the road before these thieves make off with it. They have stolen enough from us already."

"Lady Avisa?"

"I will get her. Go!"

Slashing to clear a way through the few outlaws still in the clearing, he clenched and unclenched his left hand. He had to get more feeling back into it. Pyt was battle-hardened, so he would not be routed like the cowards disappearing among the trees.

Then there was no one in front of him. He raised his sword . . . and lowered it. He could only stare as Avisa faced Pyt across bare swords. She did not need his help or anyone else's. Her sword swung, halting her opponent's with an ease few men had mastered. Pyt was outmatched, but he seemed reluctant to acknowledge that by breaking off the fight. Maybe he could not believe a woman was beating him.

Her sword came down on his arm below the ragged rings on his mail, and blood splattered on the ground. The blow staggered him, and he fell to his knees. She put the point of her sword to his throat. When he slanted away, she kept the tip beneath his chin. He tumbled onto his back. She raised the sword high, and he shrieked in terror. She drove the sword through the links in the mail that pooled around him like a woman's skirt. He tried to pull away, but she had pinned him to the ground.

Pyt snarled a curse, but she smiled and said, "Our negotiations are at an end, Pyt of the Forest."

"Are they?" The outlaw laughed as another man leaped forward, dagger held high.

Knowing he could not reach her in time to save her from the knife, Christian ran forward. "Avisa, get your sword! Let Pyt go! Save your own life!"

She ignored him and Pyt, who was chortling with victorious, vicious delight. She leaned back as the outlaw swiped the knife at her. Raising her clenched fists, she stepped *toward* him. Was she mad? Her hands blocked his arm from another swing at her, hitting him so hard that he grunted with pain. She grabbed the man's arm and bent it back. At the same time, she pulled him toward her hip. The man soared over her, striking the ground. Bones cracked before she released his arm, now at an impossible angle.

The man was staring at her in shock and horror. Beside him, Pyt seemed to shrink against the earth, absolutely defeated.

Pyt and the man she had beaten with such ease were quickly surrounded by some of the farmers, who already were talking with excitement about the public execution to be held. The outlaws began to plead for their lives. The farmers promised Pyt and the other man as much compassion as the outlaws had offered to them and their families.

One of the peasants held out Avisa's sword to her with an

awed expression. Bowing his head, he said, "Thank you. You have done all you promised and more, milady."

She gripped the hilt in silence as she watched the men pull their captives to their feet and lead them away.

When Christian took a step toward her, she spun, raising her sword. Her eyes snapped with icy flames. Such emotions on her lovely face were terrifying to behold.

"They are defeated," he said.

The battle lust vanished from Avisa's eyes. Her face eased from its savage mask to the gentle lines he knew. She lowered her sword, and blood ran down it to mix with what was already on the ground. Her chest heaved, but she kept her head high as she drove her sword's tip into the crisp leaves.

"You are ransomed, Christian Lovell," she said quietly.

"Where did you learn to knock a man from his feet like that? Don't tell me that your father taught you. I have seen nothing like the moves you made against that man. What haven't you told me?"

"You are quite welcome." She started to turn away.

He caught her arm, but released it when she winced. "Forgive me, Avisa. I should have expressed my gratitude first, but you must admit that your skills are unexpected."

"Not to me. I worked hard to learn what I know."

"Tell me who taught you how to disarm an armed man so easily."

"There is nothing easy about it." Again she began to turn, but this time she halted herself. "How do you fare?"

"I am alive, thanks to you." He shook his left hand and took a cautious glance around them. The clearing was empty save for them and a few of the men who had accompanied Avisa. They were gathered together, cheering their victory. "My wrists are a bit stiff from being bound for so many hours."

She sheathed her sword before taking his hand. Turning it over, she ran her thumbs along his palm and down to his wrist. He yelped when she dug into his skin deeply.

"If you feel pain," she said, "the damage is not permanent."

"You can be a coldhearted woman, Avisa." He pulled his hand out of hers and, wrapping his arm around her waist, pulled her to him. "Yet you burn like a coal in my arms."

He gave her no chance to answer as he captured her lips. Her rapid breath grew even swifter, and his tongue chased its pulse into her mouth. As sweet as he recalled, each flavor within offered him another reason not to stop. Her arms arched up his back, and she quivered when he ran his tongue along her neck before drawing her earlobe into his mouth.

All thoughts of the outlaws evaporated from his heated mind as he pressed her back against a tree. When his hands at her waist rose to cup her breasts, her soft moan was as heady as a brimming glass of mead. Her fingers curling against his back were intoxicating and invigorating. He wanted to drink deeply of her untested passion. Hearing a groan of pain, he released her reluctantly as he looked to where his brother was limping toward them.

She leaned her head against the mail over his chest. "I feared I would never hear the sound of your heartbeat again."

"You feared something? After what I have seen, I would have sworn you feared nothing."

She tilted her head back and smiled. "One of my first lessons was that people will believe what they see. If they see fright on your face, they will press their attack. A determined expression may make an opponent wonder if the battle can be won."

"Who taught you all of this?"

"Milady!" someone shouted.

She was gone to answer the call before he could demand that she answer *his* question first. What was she hiding? He intended to find out.

Chapter 16

At the sound of voices, Avisa put her hand on her sword. She drew her fingers back when she recognized Guy's voice among them. He was standing by some briars, picking thorns out of his tunic and complaining as usual.

Guy had not shouted to her. The call had come from one of the men who had volunteered at the inn.

"This way, milady," the short man said, urgency deepening his voice.

Snow swirled through the air, and she drew up the hood on her cloak as she went with him through the thick brush laced with briars. Already the sun was heading toward the horizon, signaling the end to the short winter day. The air was growing colder with the passage of each minute. The wind was gaining strength, as if the outlaws had uttered some curse to drive them from the wood.

If she had guessed Christian would see her keep that man from cutting into her with his knife, she would have . . . she would have done nothing different. She had to keep herself alive to fulfill her obligations, but she remembered Queen Eleanor's warning.

You are to keep him far from Canterbury at the same time you allow nothing to connect you to St. Jude's Abbey. The value of the Abbey to me would be lessened if anyone else was to learn of my true intention in founding it and having young women trained to serve me in times of trouble.

Christian would not stop asking questions, so she had to find a way to answer them without revealing the truth about the Abbey. What lie could she tell him now?

A groan came from in front of her, and she forgot the queen's admonitions and Christian's curiosity.

"Baldwin!" She knelt beside the motionless boy. Fresh blood shone along his left side and puddled beneath him.

He opened his eyes only a slit. "Milady . . ." He struggled to sit.

"Don't move." She put her hands gently on his shoulders and lowered him to the ground. Pulling off her cloak, she spread it over him. The wind sliced through her gown, but she paid the cold no attention.

"Sir . . ." He winced.

"Both Christian and Guy are safe, thanks to you."

He opened his mouth to speak again. Only a moan emerged.

"I must examine your wound," Avisa said. "It will hurt worse when I do so, but I must see where to bandage it."

He nodded, then grimaced as he reached for the bloodiest spot on his tunic.

She kept his hand away and told the man to open the pouch she took from Baldwin's bloody belt. As he did, she asked, "What is your name?"

"Norman son of Norman son of Ethelbert son of—"

"Norman," she interrupted before he recited his family line back to the Garden of Eden, "there is a stream not far from here. Find something to carry water in and bring me back no less than what you can cup in your hands three times."

He looked down at his broad, work-worn hands. "I will return as fast as I can."

"Good!"

As Norman hurried away, she put her hand against Baldwin's forehead. No heat of fever burned there, but she knew it might be hours before that threat was past.

"How did you get hurt?" she asked. "I saw you leading the horse away."

"I left the horse with . . ." He grimaced, then gamely went on. "I left the horse with Sir Guy and returned to do battle at Sir Christian's side. I did not get far."

"You did your best." She kept her smile in place even as she seethed at the thought of Guy hiding with the horse while the boy went to fight.

"Pyt?" the boy asked.

"He is captured."

A ghost of a smile drifted across Baldwin's lips. "I knew once you freed Sir Christian, he would make that outlaw rue everything."

"It was a lovely sight." She saw no reason to tell the boy the truth. "Shall I tell you?"

"Yes!" he breathed as pain tightened his face.

As she bent to check his side, Avisa began telling him an embellished story about the battle. She quickly realized it was important to keep the story riveting so Baldwin did not drift off to sleep. He was losing so much blood. If he faded from consciousness, he might not regain his senses.

Christian pushed through the bushes just as Avisa finished sewing Baldwin's wound closed and binding it with pieces torn from Norman's shirt. She looked up to see the despair and rage mixing on Christian's face.

"How is Guy?" she asked.

"He is all right in spite of his complaints. Nothing but a few scratches to add to his earlier injuries."

"Baldwin is hurt."

"How? I sent him with the horse."

She wound the rest of the thread back into a ball and put it in the pouch, which she hooked to her own belt. "He left the horse with your brother and went back to help you."

"I told him to stay with the horse. He . . ." Christian shook his head and sighed. "No, I did not tell him to stay here. I thought he had enough sense in his young skull not to rush into the fight again."

"He is a Lovell."

"What do you mean by that?"

At his abruptly indignant question, she took a half step back. She halted herself. She had not let Pyt intimidate her. Nor would she allow Christian to.

"I mean," she said in the cold voice he had used, "that he worries more about his courage than his life. He is exactly like you, Christian. Not like your brother. If it bothers you that Guy sought to hide, then vent your frustration on him. Not me."

She walked away, even as he called her name. From the corner of her eye, she saw the other men's astonishment when she did not slow. Let them think what they wished.

Avisa stopped the horse in the castle's inner ward. As she brushed snow from her cloak, wincing as she moved her left arm, she saw anxiety in Christian's eyes. He stood with one hand balancing Baldwin across the saddle. Christian's cloak was draped over him, so she could not see if the boy was conscious or not.

Christian shouted to a group of men working on what appeared to be the base of a tower. Lighter stone marked where new towers and a long, three-story wing had been added to the keep recently. The tops were crenellated and guarded by warriors armed with bows. A stable was filled with horses, and she heard the lowing of cows.

Two men ran over.

One called, "Is the boy ill? We do not want sickness within these walls."

"He is wounded," Avisa answered. "We were attacked by outlaws. Do you have a healer?"

"Martha knows about healing herbs."

"Where can I find her?"

He pointed to the left. "The stillroom is beyond the kitchen."

Christian stepped forward. "Who is lord within these walls?"

"Lord de Sommeville," the man answered.

Avisa tensed. Quickly counting in her head, she let her shoulders sag with relief. She had kept Christian and the others wandering about in the countryside long enough to allow help to arrive from St. Jude's Abbey to confirm the tale of her sister being taken by a wicked lord. Her task had just become more difficult because, once Christian was sure the baron would grant her sanctuary, he would have every expectation that he could continue on his interrupted journey. She must find a way to make him stay.

There was a simple way. She could welcome him into her bed. A frisson of sensation that had nothing to do with the chill wind slid along her as she imagined him smiling down at her in the moment before their mouths met. To think of his skin against hers sent her head spinning, and a quiver ignited deep within her.

You belong to St. Jude's Abbey. You are a sister within the Abbey. It is not right for you to be with him. Even the relentless voice could not lessen the longing within her. She was reaching out to him before she could halt herself.

Christian gave her a questioning look when she ran her hand along his arm. He must think her mad for touching him when they stood in an unfamiliar castle in the midst of a snowstorm. But the familiar longing smoothed the rigid planes of his face.

"I am so glad we are finally here," she said, once again relieved to be able to speak the truth. "If you can get Baldwin off the horse, we can have him taken to where we can tend to his wounds."

His face hardened again, and she wanted to apologize for distracting him, even for a moment, from his concerns for his page. She said nothing as Christian signaled to the men, and the one who had not spoken came forward to help. Pulling his cloak off the boy, Christian spread it on the ground. The two lifted Baldwin from the horse while Guy watched, a wretched expression on his face.

"Who are you?" asked the other man, who still stood in front of her.

"I am Lady Avisa de Vere," she replied, using her formal title because she suspected he would be more willing to heed her if he knew it. "Please inform Lord de Sommeville that I am here."

She had guessed right. The man put his fingers to his forelock and bowed. "Right away, milady."

With help from the men who had been watching with curiosity, Baldwin was carried into the keep and up the stairs to a room where there was a real bed. He was placed on it near the headboard, which was carved with animal figures. The bed-curtains were embroidered with vines and flowers. His face was as colorless as the clean linen beneath him.

"Close the shutter on the window," Avisa ordered one man. She started to motion toward the window with her left hand, but paused as pain slashed across her shoulder. Silencing her groan, she said to another man, "Have the fire lit. Tell Martha in the stillroom that we need healing herbs and water brought. Hot water."

"Bring clean rags, too," Christian added as the man rushed to the door.

She tried to give Christian a bolstering smile because she knew how fearful he was for the boy. It was impossible, and she simply stroked his arm again with silent sympathy.

When he whirled her into his arms, she was shocked. His kiss was hard and deep, as if he hoped to find and share some hidden wells of strength within her. He released her just as suddenly, and she grasped the upright on the bed. He looked at her in disbelief. Had his abrupt loss of control, when his page lay wounded, astonished him?

He had restrained himself for so long with her. Could she curb her own need for him if he did not hold back? A shiver, both anxious and eager, riveted her.

A grumble from Guy, who was sitting on a bench she had not even noticed, released Avisa from the spell of Christian's kiss. She could not always depend on someone else to intrude. She needed to keep herself in check as she found some other way to persuade Christian to stay far from Canterbury. Toying with his emotions was not the way to convince him.

"Christian," she said, "go and speak with our host while I see to Baldwin's care. Tell him you travel with me, and you will be welcome."

She wanted to retract the words when she saw Christian's face tighten. He must have seen them as a suggestion that the sons of Lord Lovell might not be received by Lord de Sommeville. The baron had already agreed to act as their host as a favor to the queen, although Avisa doubted he knew why. She had to be careful. If Christian grew angry at her, he could depart as soon as Baldwin was well.

"Lord de Sommeville," she went on, "must know that I would seek him out to gain his assistance in rescuing my sister. Please ask him to consider offering it to me."

"Are we your pages now to run errands?" Guy asked, with another moan. When she glanced at him, he pressed his hand to his side and hunched as if in the greatest agony. He muttered, "The boy is not the only one suffering."

She swallowed the words she should not speak, even though she was well tired of Guy's complaints. He might not have been injured further if he had watched where he was going instead of getting caught in thick briars. And not once had he asked about Baldwin's condition.

"Let's go," Christian said. As his brother lurched out of the room, Christian paused and added, "Thank you, Avisa."

"Thank me after Baldwin is healed."

He came back to where she stood. With one crooked finger, he tipped her lips up to his. This kiss was as gentle as the other had been desperate, but the same pulse of craving reverberated through her. Her right hand slid up his chest, and his eyes lit again with those silvery flames.

"I owe you a debt, Avisa, not only for tending to Baldwin. I owe you a debt for your daring to do what my brother could not. You saved our lives."

"I was lucky."

He shook his head. "It was not luck, but preparation. If Pyt had discovered you also did not have what he was seeking—"

"But I did." She reached beneath her skirt and pulled out her dagger. Fishing the ring out of the sheath, she held it up. "He wanted this."

"I heard him talk about a ring, but I did not think of this one."

"It has a bead just like the ones he and his men wear."

He took the ring. "He believes *this* will give him the power to force the king from his throne? He is crazier than I guessed."

"Maybe he is not." She touched the stone. "There are old ways that still cling to the shadows."

"Don't tell me that you really are superstitious," he said in disbelief.

"I am not superstitious. Others are, and what they believe in, they may be willing to risk their lives to make come true."

He put the ring in the pouch on his belt. "I must greet de Sommeville and ask for his hospitality. We will speak more about this later, Avisa." He caught her chin in his hand. "And how you came to be so prepared to fight Pyt and his men."

She nodded, hoping she would have more lies ready then.

Christian left his sword outside the hall as requested. He smiled. Would Avisa be willing to part with her weapon? It was as much a part of her as her sparkling eyes and soft hair, which he wanted falling along his naked skin. All of him reacted to the image of her eyes closing as she breathed in tempo with him while he moved deep inside her.

"Sir, this way."

He shoved the fantasy aside as he went with a servant who was taking him to meet de Sommeville after nearly an hour of waiting. But that delay had not been as unbearable

as the wait to hold Avisa again. Really hold her—not just
for a quick kiss, but while he explored every curve accented
so enticingly by her gown. How much longer could he go
without making that fantasy come alive? She was a baron's
daughter, a woman he had offered to assist and safeguard. It
was ironic that she was quite capable of protecting herself
from outlaws and his greatest challenge was protecting her
from himself.

Christian followed the servant along the hallway, edging
to the side when a boy servant hurried past him in the other
direction. He ignored the child's curious expression as he
pondered how de Sommeville would receive him.

Tell him you travel with me, and you will be welcome.
Avisa had spoken the words with the ease of someone who
knew she would be greeted warmly anywhere she went. Did
she know how lucky she was?

Not lucky, but prepared. Those had been his own words,
and he was more certain of them now than ever. From the
night she had led them to the clearing after hiding in the briars, he had known she was concealing something. Was it her
amazing skills? Or was it how she had learned them?

As he was ushered into de Sommeville's presence, Christian knew answers would have to wait. The baron stood
from where he had been reading. The scroll in front of him
rolled closed with a snap. He paid no attention to it, but a
scribe hovered over it like a bird watching its nest.

De Sommeville was a hulking man, standing a head taller
than Christian. His tunic reached to his toes and was of a
pale green wool. A small cap covered the top of his curly
brown hair. His cloak was closed with a gold and blue-
gemmed pin with the seal of his family's lands on both sides
of the Channel. The front of his tunic opened to reveal cross-
garters above his low boots.

The baron bent down when the servant rushed forward to
whisper in his ear. De Sommeville's brows rose, then he
nodded. Motioning the servant aside, he crossed the room.

"You are Christian Lovell?" the baron asked. "Son of Robert Lovell?"

"Yes," Christian replied. "I am seeking shelter for my traveling party and medical attention for my page."

"We never turn anyone in need from our door." The answer was grudging.

"I am glad to hear that," said the voice that was so breathless in Christian's fantasies.

He turned to see Avisa in the doorway. Her gown was spotted with blood. She walked into the room and said, "Milord, I am Lady Avisa de Vere."

"You?" The baron stared, wide-eyed. "Have you been injured, milady?"

"The blood is not mine. We were set upon while we traveled the forest road."

"Bring a bench for the lady to sit on," de Sommeville ordered.

"I am fine, but Sir Christian's page was wounded and needs a chance to recover."

"Most certainly. You are all welcome." He glanced at Christian, but added nothing more. There was no need. His expression said everything. The sooner the Lovells were gone from within his walls, the happier de Sommeville would be.

Chapter 17

A visa rubbed her forehead with fingers that would not stop shaking. The ache had started there when she up-ended the man with the knife, and with each passing hour the pain had strengthened. It flowed down the left side of her neck and across her shoulder. Even the sound of her voice as she whispered to Baldwin to rest hurt as it resonated through her.

She blew out the lamp in the room where Baldwin slept and went into the room that opened from it. A third chamber was beyond the center room. It contained a bed more luxurious than the one where the boy was asleep. Guy had claimed it.

The middle room held a table and a pair of chests. Christian had not returned, and she sat on the bench, leaning her elbows on the table and her forehead on her palms. She needed to think. Having Christian nearby led her thoughts to him, and she had to focus on the problem she had not expected at Lord de Sommeville's castle.

No one from her supposedly overrun home had come asking for a haven. Had she misunderstood? She thought that the abbess had told her to make sure their journey took them to Lord de Sommeville's fief no earlier than a fortnight after she had met Christian. It was days past that because the week of Christmas had begun. She was here, but there was no sign of anybody from St. Jude's Abbey. She had to create some story to prevent Christian from leaving.

As if she had called his name, Christian walked in. He was carrying a tray with a dusty bottle and several goblets. Setting them on the table, he kneaded his swollen wrist.

"Does it still hurt?" she asked, folding her hands in her lap to hide their quivering.

"I am fine. How is Baldwin?"

"He is resting. The wound is deep, and he lost a lot of blood."

"And my brother?"

Her smile became a taut frown. "I gave him a portion of the same sleeping herbs. He was whining about his newest wound, which appears to have been inflicted by a thorn."

"That is a harsh accusation."

"You are welcome to check his so-called wound yourself if you think I am wrong."

"You are probably right, Avisa. You seem to be right about everything." He sighed. "Forgive me. It has been the worst week of my life."

"I have not enjoyed it either."

"None of it?"

She bit her lower lip to keep from giving him the answer she knew he wanted. She *had* enjoyed being in his arms and his kisses that were as changing as his moods. He was such a contradiction, angry and yet gentle. Demanding that Baldwin stand up to every task the boy was given, even as he worried about his page. So focused on the damage done to his family's honor, while at the same time able to endure insults made by those who should be his allies.

When she did not answer, he went to the door opening onto Baldwin's chamber. "Will he live?"

"If no bad humors get into his wound. I am going to change his bandage again soon, and I will see how he fares then. A lad of his age heals swiftly." She rose and went to him. She reached out, then drew back when she saw how her fingers shook. "Baldwin will not make the same mistake again of lowering his arm when facing a foe."

"He does not yet have the skills to fight against a more experienced opponent. You should not have asked him to do so."

"I did not. His orders were to watch over me. Orders that you gave him."

"You should have insisted he stay behind."

"What do you think would have happened if I had? He would have snuck after us."

He turned to face her. "He is little more than a child. He could have been killed."

"But he was not. He fought well and valiantly. And at the risk of you becoming furious with me again, let me remind you that Lovell blood beats through him."

"I cannot forget that. Nor can I forget that Lovell blood was spilled today."

"You should never forget that."

Her words startled him, she could tell, because he gave her a long look before walking to the table where the bottle waited. She went into the other room to draw the blanket up to Baldwin's chin. He mumbled something in his sleep, and she smiled. Every sound he made was proof he was alive.

As she came back into the middle chamber, Christian was filling two tankards with amber wine. He offered her one. Taking it, she raised it to her lips. Even though the wine warmed her mouth, its heat could not thaw the icy ball of fear around her heart. She put the goblet on the table.

"Drink it, Avisa," Christian said, handing it to her again. "Mulled *bastarde* is soothing."

She recognized the name of the Spanish wine enjoyed by the peerage. Sipping, she said, "I need something soothing."

"What is bothering you?" He gave her a lopsided grin. "Other than Baldwin's injuries and the incidents of the past days, what is bothering you?"

"That is enough."

He shook his head. "Not for you, Avisa. Guy told me that

at the inn you held every eye as you raised your sword over your head."

"Your brother always exaggerates."

"Not this time. You persuaded those peasants to follow you to what could have been their deaths."

"To their deaths was not where I wished to lead them." She put the wine on the table once more as the dull ache in her head deepened. "But if I inspired them not to cower at Pyt's attempts to terrorize them, I am glad."

"You have been as strong as an oak until we reached de Sommeville's castle. Since then, you have acted like a criminal facing his ordeal at court. You peer into every corner and flinch at any sound."

"I am fine." Picking up the bottle, she filled her glass again. She drank deeply, but stopped when she realized the wine seemed to add to her hands' tremor. If they had shaken as they did now when she faced Pyt and his outlaw band, she would not have been able to fight off a single man.

"Don't lie to me, Avisa." He took her goblet and set it beside his on the table. Folding her hand between his, he whispered, "You are shaking as if you have become only a leaf on that strong oak. What is unsettling you now when you should be rejoicing that you have reached de Sommeville's castle safely?"

"I must face how much I yet could lose," she answered as softly.

"You know I have vowed to help you rescue your sister. I will do as I promised." He lifted her hand to his lips, which were damp from the wine.

A fiery shiver coursed through her when his tongue swirled along her skin, and her fingers clenched his tightly. Afraid of being swept away by the potent passion swelling inside her like a molten river, she leaned toward him, wanting to bask in his touch.

His tender smile brought forth the yearning that was becoming an ungovernable need. Knowing it was madness, she ached for his lips on hers, demanding, blazing, offering

a joy that she wanted to be more than a dream. Her breath
burned in her throat as her heartbeat pounded so loudly she
was sure he could hear it.

"Avisa . . ." His breath was as tattered as hers. "If you did
not have to watch over Baldwin, I would have you heal me."

"Your injuries—"

"Can be cured by the touch of your skin against mine. We
will tend to Baldwin tonight, Avisa, but once he is past danger, I need you to tend to me." He placed a blistering kiss on
her lips before releasing her.

She groped for her goblet as he went into the room where
his page slept. Her fingers were quivering so hard that she
splashed wine across the table. In the past day she had defeated a feared outlaw by using the skills she had been
taught. But the battle within her, the longing for Christian, at
odds with her vows to the Abbey, was one she had not been
taught how to fight. It was a battle she did not want to fight
any longer. She wanted to surrender to pleasure in his arms.

*You belong to St. Jude's Abbey. You are a sister within the
Abbey. It is not right for you to be with him.*

"Be silent," she snarled at the voice she wished she knew
how to silence—at least for one night.

Baldwin drank the potion and handed the bowl back to
Avisa. He grimaced as he said, "I am tired of sleeping."

"Sleep heals best." She drew the pelt back up over the
blanket as he settled back into the bed. "Soon you will be
enjoying the Christmas festivities."

He mumbled something.

Carrying the bowl out of the room, she was glad her
shoulder no longer ached. She bent to wash the bowl in the
bucket by the shuttered window. Two days had passed since
their arrival at Lord de Sommeville's castle. Two days with
Baldwin growing stronger and her hopes for help from St.
Jude's Abbey growing weaker. When the castle's great hall
was decorated with greens for the holiday, she could not join
in with the anticipation of the revels to come.

Footsteps paused outside the door. She looked up to see a tall shadow there. Her heart thudded against her chest, then deflated when she realized the silhouette belonged to Guy. He was alone. That startled her. Now that he could not linger in bed, pretending to be greatly wounded, she had assumed he would be pursuing the castle's maidservants, intent on seducing each one.

Rising, she said, "If you seek Christian, he is not here."

"I know that. I saw him talking with de Sommeville in the hall." He smiled. "It seems our host has changed his mind about my brother's worthiness to lodge beneath his roof."

"If you wish to rest," she said, gesturing toward the far room, "I will leave."

"There is no need for you to leave." He held out his hand. "You could come with me."

She gave him a withering scowl.

It had no effect, because his smile did not waver. "Fair Avisa, there is no need for you to deny the truth."

"And what truth is that?"

"That you do not belong to my brother."

"I can agree with that." She continued to be amazed at how her life in the Abbey had shielded her from the hopeless state of so many women. She was disgusted by the idea that if she had not been sent to the Abbey she would have belonged to her father until he arranged for a marriage, and after that she would have belonged to her husband, as did his dog and horse. But she wanted to be *with* Christian, a part of his life.

He rested his hand on the edge of the deep windowsill. "Hearing you say that is very pleasing, fair Avisa."

Leaning away from him and his ale-thickened breath, she discovered he had placed his other hand on the opposite side of the sill. She had no escape unless she wanted to scamper up the narrowing area to the window.

"I need to check on Baldwin," she said.

"You just checked him." He leaned closer to her, pinning her against the wall.

The sill cut into her back, and she tried to push him aside. "Release me!"

"Why?" He smiled. "You have yet to see my very best skills."

"I do not need to see them. I have heard about them."

He preened like a woodcock before a hen. "From other women who told you that you have been silly to deny yourself the thrills we could share?"

She wondered how she could ever have considered Christian arrogant. His brother exceeded him.

"Denial is good for the soul," she fired back.

"Is that why you are not in Christian's bed?"

"I did not say I wished Christian's attentions either."

"But you do." He trailed a fingertip along her neck. When she turned her head away, he grasped her chin and twisted her face back toward him. "But don't you realize that you are denying *him* the very thing he wants more than he wants you?"

She stopped trying to pull away. "What do you mean?"

"Christian longs to be touted as a great champion. How can that ever happen when you save his life time and again?"

She raised her chin. "I would not have to do so, if you, as his brother, were not too inept to fight by his side."

"He has Baldwin to follow him blindly into every battle. He does not need me." His finger curved up behind her ear. "Nor does he need you, fair Avisa, in his quest to rid his honor of the tarnish left by our father's decision to abandon Henry Curtmantle at his darkest hour. Don't you see? Each time you come to Christian's rescue, you are reminding him of how he has failed just as Father did."

She stared at him, wanting to deny his words. She could not. Even knowing of Christian's greatest hope, she had found herself proving her courage rather than his. She had foiled the outlaws the day they met, and she had freed him

from Pyt's captivity. But if she had not, he could be dead.
She had vowed to protect him, doing whatever was necessary. She never had guessed that complying with that pledge
would mean destroying his hopes for honor.

When Guy began to grin, she spat, "You serpent! You tell
lies with a bit of truth in an effort to make others agree with
you."

"I will tell you whatever you wish to hear if you come
with me." Grabbing her right arm, he stepped toward the far
bedchamber.

"Release me!"

"You will find the sweetest relief with me, fair Avisa."

"Get out!"

He pulled her to him.

Her reaction was automatic. Grabbing his left sleeve, she
drove her other fist into his gut. He bent, groaning, but did
not release her. She put her arm beneath his left arm and
squatted, pulling him up over her back and slamming him to
the stone floor. He moaned once and was silent.

She turned on her heel and walked out of the room. She
was trembling as she had in the wake of the confrontation
with Pyt. Going to the stillroom to get more herbs for Baldwin would give her a chance to regain her composure. Not
from Guy's heavy-handed attempt at seduction, but from his
assertion that *she* was the reason Christian continued to believe he needed to prove his courage.

Avisa paused as her name was called. Looking across the
hall that was decorated with swags of mistletoe and yew,
she saw Lord de Sommeville motioning frantically to her.
She gathered up her skirt and rushed to see what the baron
wished. The longer she could avoid returning to their
rooms, the greater the chance that Guy would have crawled
away to find someone to comfort him.

Suddenly she was grabbed. She started to raise her hands
to fight off her attackers, then gasped as she realized she was

being hugged by two women. Two women she knew by the name of sister.

The taller one, who was half a head shorter than Avisa, whispered, "I am sorry we were delayed. A storm kept us from traveling for several days."

Drawing back, Avisa did not have to force a smile when she looked at two of her sisters from St. Jude's Abbey. Sister Mavise, who had whispered to her, had hair only a shade darker than Avisa's. She was built like a hedgehog. Her face was round and her arms were round. Her whole body was round. Sister Mavise's appearance often fooled someone who had not practiced fighting with her, for she moved like a fleet fox.

Avisa was amazed to see Sister Ermangardine beside her. As dark as Avisa was light, Sister Ermangardine was no older than Baldwin. She had an innocent face, which suited her, because she was less worldly than the other girls her age in the Abbey. Why had the abbess sent her?

Telling her sisters to meet her at a table in one corner where they would have a good view of the whole hall, Avisa went to thank Lord de Sommeville for letting her know they had arrived. She pretended not to see the baron's curiosity about why two young women had come to his castle, asking for Avisa. From his comments, she surmised the queen had told him nothing more than to expect Avisa.

Sister Mavise was warning their younger sister to hold her tongue when Avisa joined them at the table. "You must curb your outbursts," Sister Mavise said, then smiled as Avisa sat beside her. "You have been much missed, dear sister, at the Abbey. We were worried about your absence until we learned why St. Jude's Abbey was founded."

"Everyone knows?"

"The abbess told us shortly after your departure." She laughed, the lyrical sound floating up among the greenery. "There were so many rumors racing rampant through the Abbey that she decided she must be honest with us."

Sister Ermangardine interjected, "We are so proud."

"Pride is a sin," Sister Mavise reminded her. "You must remember what you were told, Sis— Ermangardine." She flushed. "We cannot forget to address each other as those beyond the Abbey's walls do."

Avisa nodded. A lesson she must learn, too, for a single careless word could betray the truth she had struggled to hide. "I am glad you are here."

"I was surprised when the abbess asked me to come to pretend to be your birth sister, even though our coloring is much the same. The abbess would have preferred to send Sister Mallory, I do believe. However, her hair is as ebon as my young companion's." Mavise laughed as she reached for a piece of bread that had been left on the table. Breaking it in half, she offered the other piece to Ermangardine.

The girl leaned forward to ask, "Where is the garderobe? I will burst if I take another bite."

Avisa gave her directions, then waited for the girl to rush out of earshot before asking, "I can understand why the abbess sent you, but why Ermangardine?"

"I have been curious about that, too. Ermangardine is either avoiding giving me an answer, or she is being truthful when she says the abbess told her nothing but to accompany me in the role of my servant."

"It would be seemly for you to have a servant."

"And her presence allows my tale of escaping from our family's enemies to appear possible."

"Tell me what your tale is, so I will not speak wrongly when asked."

Mavise hurriedly outlined a tale of sneaking out of Wain of Moorburgh's holding in the guise of a peasant during the festival to celebrate the baron's upcoming nuptials to the daughter of his enemy. The story made sense, because by marrying his enemy's daughter, the baron would have a greater claim on the lands he had taken by force.

"How did you escape the guards the baron had at your door?" Avisa asked just as Ermangardine returned to slide back onto the bench and picked up the piece of bread.

"I-I don't remember."

The girl piped up, saying with a mouthful of bread, "You drugged their wine with a sleeping potion you got from a sympathetic ally in the baron's stillroom."

With a laugh, Mavise hugged the girl. "Maybe remembering those details is why the abbess sent you with me. Tell us, Avisa, what has happened to you since you left the Abbey."

Avisa did so, but she left out many of the details other than that she had kept Christian from going to Canterbury. Details such as Pyt's attempt to trade Christian for the ring. Details such as how she had had to reveal the skills she had been taught. And most important, details such as how she longed to make love with Christian. Did she hesitate because she thought her sisters would chide her for being weak or because she feared they would denounce her?

"You admire Sir Christian greatly," Mavise said as she folded her arms on the table. "It is obvious in how you smile each time you speak his name."

"He is an admirable man."

"It is well that you have succeeded in your subterfuge with him." Mavise lowered her voice. "The situation in Canterbury grows more troubled."

"What has happened?"

"The archbishop has returned to the cathedral, but there are rumors he intends to excommunicate any church member who sides with the king. There are even rumors that he will excommunicate the king."

Avisa whispered a quick prayer. If such rumors were true—or even if they were not—when they reached the king on the other side of the Channel, Henry might not be able to restrain his well-known temper. He could be goaded into doing something that could tear England apart. Then, no story that Avisa could invent would keep Christian from throwing in his lot with the king's men.

"Is *that* him?" asked Mavise.

Avisa turned on the bench. Although fifteen feet or more

separated her from the arch where Christian stood, she could see his face as clearly as if he held her in his arms. He had become such a part of her life that he was a part of her thoughts, waking and sleeping.

Did he sense her staring at him? She could not be sure, but he began to walk toward them.

"Is *that* him?" asked Mavise again, grabbing Avisa's arm.

"Yes."

"You did not say he was so . . . so . . ." She giggled as if she were as young as Ermangardine.

Avisa nodded. Christian *was* so . . . everything. So strong, so handsome, so set on proving his courage, so arrogant, so vexing, so . . . everything. Watching his easy steps as he crossed the uneven stone floor, she knew he was also so deeply within her heart. When had he slipped past her resolve to keep her mind focused on her task? The moment she first saw him? The moment he first kissed her? The moment when she had first stood nose to nose with him to argue about her sword? It could have been any of those moments or some other one entirely. She did not know.

"He is coming here." Ermangardine sounded panicked.

"Take a deep breath." Avisa wanted to warn both sisters to guard their reactions when they spoke with Christian, but he was close enough to hear whatever else she said. So she had to content herself with a cautionary frown in their direction.

"I hear you have the very best of news, Avisa," he said with a smile broader than any other she had ever seen him wear.

"The very best." She stood and motioned to Mavise to do the same. "My sister and her servant."

"Milady . . ." He bowed over Mavise's hand, and color raced up her face. Another giggle came from Ermangardine.

"My dear sister," Avisa said with a smile, "allow me to introduce Sir Christian Lovell, knight in service to King Henry."

"It is an honor to meet you," Mavise choked out. She

cleared her throat, then said in a more normal voice, "Avisa has been telling us how you pledged to help her rescue me. Our family will always be grateful to yours, Sir Christian."

"The debt is mine." He bowed his head again. "If I may ask you to excuse Avisa and me, there is something I must discuss with her."

Mavise glanced at Avisa before saying, "Most certainly. I need to thank Lord de Sommeville for welcoming me, a courtesy that was overlooked in the midst of my pleasure at seeing my sister. Do return as soon as you can so we may share more tales of our adventures."

When Christian held out his hand, Avisa put hers on it. She gave her sisters a bolstering smile before crossing the hall with him. He did not reply when she asked him what he wanted. Instead, he led her up the stairs to the rooms they were using. He entered the center one and closed the door after them. Going to the door that opened into the room where Baldwin still slept, he shut that one, too. The door to the third room was already closed.

"You must be greatly relieved, Avisa," he said, his face as shuttered as the window. "I spoke with de Sommeville, and he has assured me that you and your sister are welcome to remain here."

"And you?"

"I am going nowhere until Baldwin heals."

She breathed a silent sigh of relief.

"So you can stay with de Sommeville," he went on, "until you ascertain what you wish to do next."

"Next?"

His brow furrowed. "You cannot return to your familial home while Lord Wain of Moorburgh controls those lands. He will only achieve what he has hoped for since the beginning."

"You sound quite certain of that."

"No matter how well you fight, Avisa, you cannot defeat a garrison of armed soldiers alone."

She snorted a laugh, not caring how unladylike it

sounded. "Do you think so little of me that you believe I would do something so absurd?"

"No, I think very highly of you and your skills. So tell me what happened, Avisa," he said.

"Lord de Sommeville called to me that my sister—"

"Not below, Avisa. In here." He pointed to the floor beside the window. "I found my brother senseless there. He mumbled your name when I was finally able to rouse him."

"Maybe you should have sent for a woman. It seems any woman finds rousing him an easy task."

He sat on the edge of the table. "Especially you."

"If you think I enticed him, you are mistaken."

"I don't think that." He smiled and slipped his fingers through hers. "You have done nothing to encourage him. I would ask that you treat him more gently if he is foolish enough to try to woo you again."

"Nothing was broken, was it?"

He laughed. "No, but only because I suspect you were careful not to do more than try to teach him his manners." He drew her closer. "Avisa, promise me you will be gentle with my brother."

"If he leaves me alone."

"He will. He has learned his lesson." His hand slipped up her back. "But I have not."

She grabbed the front of his tunic and whispered, "I am glad." As she pressed her mouth to his, all thoughts of his brother vanished. All thoughts of her deception vanished. Only one thought remained to weave through the pleasure. She would do anything that was necessary to keep this man alive.

Anything.

Chapter 18

"A cross." Avisa swung the broadsword parallel to the ground, striking Ermangardine's blade. "You cannot use a broadsword as if it is a dagger. You must make the length of the blade an extension of your arm, but it is an arm that cannot bend."

The girl nodded and hefted her sword. She matched Avisa's motions in a strange dance whose music was the clang of steel. Around and around, they went, their eyes locked and the swords sparking off each other.

For the first time in the five days since Mavise and the girl had arrived at Lord de Sommeville's castle, Avisa was not worried about their practice being seen. Most of the castle was still asleep. It was two days until Christmas, but the celebrations had already begun. Last night, kegs of ale had been emptied. When she and Ermangardine had passed through the hall, more than a score of people had still been sleeping where they fell in their drunken stupor.

In addition, they were practicing in a yard behind the armory, where the clank of steel would not be an unusual sound. The yard was deserted at sunrise.

"Good . . . Good . . ." Avisa did not attack when Ermangardine left an opening. Later, she would show the girl where she had put herself at risk.

Ermangardine had been eager to resume her lessons with Avisa, and Avisa was pleased to have a practice partner, even though the girl's skills offered no challenge. When she lowered her sword, motioning for Ermangardine to do the same, Avisa watched the girl wipe beads of sweat from her forehead. The morning air was cold enough to freeze water in the barrels by the stable, but the lesson had been strenuous.

"Did I do better?" Ermangardine asked, as eager as a puppy for a pat on the head.

Avisa smiled at the girl, who pulled at her knee-length cotte. The tunic, worn by yeomen beyond the walls of St. Jude's Abbey, at first disconcerted novices more accustomed to a gown that brushed their shoes. In early training, novices were given simple clothes. Later, when they had learned to wield a broadsword, they would practice in women's clothing as Avisa did. They must be as agile in a gown as they were in a short cotte and cross-gartered hose, although Avisa wondered if anyone could handle a sword well while wearing the floor-length cuffs that were so popular.

"You are improving, Ermangardine." She handed the girl the dress she had discarded for practice. "I suspect that before much longer you will defeat me at practice."

"Never!" She pulled her gown over her head and smoothed it along her perfectly straight body. "I could never be as good as you, Avisa."

"You will be. It is every teacher's wish that her students will surpass her, and I believe you shall be the first of my students to do so."

Turning so Avisa could tie the laces up the back, Ermangardine replied, "I am blessed to have you as my teacher. I pray I can one day be adept as you."

"It takes no more than practice."

"So much practice." She rubbed her hip. "I vow there is not an inch of me that is not sore."

Avisa laughed. "That never changes."

The girl started to laugh, then cried, "Look out!"

Having seen the motion from the corner of her eye, Avisa had already raised her sword to meet the one swinging toward her. As she blocked the blow, she stared in disbelief at the man holding it.

"Christian! Have you lost your mind?" she cried.

"It is possible." He kept his sword up, jabbing it at her randomly. As she knocked aside each parry, he laughed. "I have watched you do battle with others, Avisa. Now I think it is time I find out which of us is the more skilled."

"*You* want to fight me?"

"Why not?" He kept the sword between them as he circled her, forcing her to turn at the same time. "I can beat you."

"You should not be so sure of that, Christian." Gripping her sword, she held it up at ready.

"We shall see who is the better swordsman."

"Or swordswoman."

"I meant what I said." He continued to edge around in a circle.

"What are you waiting for?"

He gave her a cool smile. "I am a knight sworn to King Henry, Avisa. As such, I am vowed to offer a woman every courtesy." He wagged his sword. "You first."

"You may come to regret that."

"I doubt it."

She gauged how his steps were taken on the balls of his feet and how he held his sword with ease. She had seen him fight, and she knew he was skilled. But was he more skilled than she was?

She slashed out with her sword. He stymied her attack with a simple motion. Spinning away, she knocked aside his sword. The clang echoed through the courtyard, and Ermangardine cheered.

"Well done, Avisa," he said as he prepared for her next blow.

She did not make him wait. She swung at him, taking care to keep the tip of the sword far enough away from his tunic so it would not cut him. He matched every motion she made.

"Can you read my thoughts to know what I plan to do next?" she asked as she circled away from him again.

He laughed. "If I could do that, there would be many fewer questions in my head. Such as how you learned to do what you do with ease."

Ermangardine choked back a gasp.

"And," he said, glancing at the girl, "why you teach others."

She carefully poked his side with her sword, and he yelped as he looked back at her. "The first lesson I teach is never to allow your attention to wander while you are facing an adversary."

"Is that what we are, Avisa? Adversaries?" He blocked her sword, knocking her back a few steps.

"We are not friends." She steadied herself. "You made a point of telling me that you do not like me."

He laughed. "Why did you listen to that when you heed nothing else I tell you? You know you can be very unlikable."

"That is cruel." Tears blossomed into her eyes. She blinked them away, hating her own weakness. She needed to use her anger, not let it control her. She swept her sword toward Christian, but he halted it in midswing.

"A chink in your mail, Avisa?" He pressed his attack, forcing her back toward the stable wall.

She fought aside his blows, but her arms were growing heavy and slow. Ermangardine shouted something. She paid no attention. She could think only of the sword flashing in front of her in the ever-stronger light of the rising sun.

Her right foot slipped in something on the stones. Manure, from the smell. She crashed back into the stable wall. Her sword halted his as it swung toward her.

He pressed his sword against hers, holding her against the wall. With his face close to hers, he whispered, "Don't you understand? I cannot feel anything as tepid as like for you."

"Does that mean you love me?" Her heart was singing

within her with the power of every voice in the Abbey's choir.

"Only a fool would love a woman who is trying to slice through him with her sword."

"You *are* a fool."

"That is cruel," he said, but he grinned and kissed her playfully. "Shall we strike a bargain? I will be honest with you if you will tell me the truth you have hidden from me."

"Why don't you be honest with me first?"

"You are the most exasperating woman in England."

With a laugh, she whirled away and crashed her sword down on his. He stopped it, but not quickly enough.

A scarlet line edged along his left sleeve. She stared at it in dismay.

"Christian, I am sorry."

"Never apologize to an adversary. Weren't you taught that as well?"

He came at her. She matched his motions, then took the offensive. As he raised his sword to ward her off, she twisted her sword beneath his. It flew out of his hand.

She lowered hers and stepped back. With a slight bow, keeping her eyes locked with his, she motioned with her sword toward his.

"Showing mercy is seldom wise, Avisa," he said.

"I think I can spare some for you." She balanced back on her feet and held her sword loosely to be ready for whatever he planned next.

He smiled and turned to pick up his sword. With a laugh, she slapped him on the rear end with the flat of her sword. Her laugh became a startled cry as he whirled and grabbed her wrist. He brought her hand down sharply against his thigh. Her sword fell out of her numb fingers to slide across the stones beyond his.

He grasped her arm. In disbelief, she found herself flying over his hip and striking the ground. Her breath burst out of her in a gasp of pain.

"Is that how it is done?" Christian knelt beside her.

"Yes," she answered with what little breath she had remaining inside her. "How did you learn to do that?"

"I watched you. The motion seemed logical enough, so I practiced with Guy." He chuckled. "He agreed only when he decided being able to take a man down like that would help him impress women."

She pushed herself up to sit. "So that is why he has been complaining of a sore knee during the past few days."

"He has also been very eager to practice with me, because he wants to repay you for what you did to him."

"That is not very chivalrous of him." She tried to laugh, but winced as Ermangardine rushed up and embraced her. "I am all right," she reassured the girl. "Go inside and get ready for breakfast."

"And leave you with *him*?" the girl asked.

"I will be fine."

"I know that, Avisa, but when you rejoin the battle and wound him again—"

"I will make sure you are there, so you may practice bandaging wounds." She chuckled as the girl nodded very seriously before she ran out of the yard.

Christian handed Avisa to her feet. "She has a great deal of faith in you."

"She is young."

"But she has two good eyes that tell her that you could have easily defeated me if you had not offered me a second chance."

"You were right. It was not wise of me." She winced again as she touched her aching hip. "I will not be so merciful again."

"I will keep that in mind." He picked up her sword and held it out to her, hilt first. "This is finely made."

"By a master armorer." She smiled as she put it in its sheath.

"You wield it well. Will you teach me that twist you did with your sword?"

"Of course."

"It is a clever trick."

"I have been taught well."

"By some swordmaster you fail to name."

She shrugged. "What does it matter? The name would not be one you know."

"But I remain curious why a woman has been taught such skills."

"I am curious why more women are not."

With a laugh, he shook his head. "Such talk would undermine a chivalrous society where women are supposed to let men protect them. However, I am beginning to see the advantages of your way."

"You are?" She doubted she could be more astounded.

"Yes, because I can foresee more lessons with you so I can learn more amazing moves with a sword or without."

"I would be glad to teach you what I know."

"Where did you learn such unusual ways to fight?"

As she pulled on her cloak to keep out the cold she had not noticed until now, she did not hesitate, for since she had needed to resort to such tactics against Pyt's man, she had had time to figure what she could tell him to explain her skills. "During the last Crusade, someone very dear to our family brought back to England a father and his daughter," she said as they went into the keep. "That father and daughter were from a land in the most distant east. Their family had traveled in search of knowledge across the sea and through deserts and over mountains that reach nearly to heaven."

"Knowledge of such martial skills?" He took her hand as they climbed the stairs to the upper floors.

"Yes, and they learned from everyone they met. However, the family was captured by slave traders not far from Persia. They were brought to the Holy Land, and that is where it was discovered how they could defeat someone with only their hands. Offered their freedom, they came to England and became teachers. The father died when I was quite young." Her voice caught. Nariko's father had been respected by everyone at St. Jude's Abbey, and his passing had left the Abbey doused in grief for many months.

"Did the daughter teach you?" Christian asked as he led her through a doorway.

"Yes, and I would be glad to teach you more of what I know."

He closed the door behind her, leaving them in the dusk of a room where the early-morning sunlight had not reached. "Later." He brushed his lips against her cheek. "Now I would like to teach you more of what *I* know."

Her breath caught as he loosened her sword belt and leaned the sheath against the door. He placed his own beside it before he took her hands.

"Christian, I am sweaty from fighting," she said.

He ran his tongue along her neck. As she quivered, he whispered, "You smell and taste wonderful." He gave her a roguish grin. "And I intend to make you far more sweaty as we explore every pleasure together."

"Together?" she breathed.

"Together. Two bodies soaked with perspiration stroking each other." He brushed her breast with a teasing touch. "Tell me that is what you want, too, Avisa."

You belong to St. Jude's Abbey. You are a sister within the Abbey. It is not right for you to be with him. The nagging filled her head. Then a softer voice, a voice she had never heard before, a voice lightened by easy laughter and joy, whispered, *But nothing else has ever felt so right. Do you want to lose what you could find in his arms?*

"No!" she choked out.

"What?"

She saw his astonishment and hurt, evident even in the dim light. "Christian . . ." She was uncertain what to say. On her tongue burned the desperate plea for him to take her to his bed and reveal to her what men and women shared.

"All right, if that is what you want." He stepped back.

"No!"

"No? It cannot be both." He tipped her chin toward him. "What do you want, Avisa?"

She raised her eyes. His face was taut with the craving gnawing at her, too. He wanted her—and not just to taunt her as he had before. He truly wanted her. Could she be less than honest now? She was tired of lies and half-truths and deception. She wanted to be honest, too.

"You," she whispered, ignoring the cranky voice in her head. She had heeded it too long. All her life she had been the one who did just as she was supposed to. The good daughter who accepted a cloistered life. The student who excelled at her studies. The queen's devoted servant who did as she was bid. For once, she wanted to shrug off duty and obligation. For once, she wanted to forget about unfulfilled vows. For once, she wanted to surrender to passion.

"Do not jest with me, Avisa."

Putting her hands on either side of his face, she said, "I am sincere."

"You must be more than sincere. You must be certain. I already owe you a debt for saving—"

"Forget about debts and responsibilities now!" She was speaking to herself as much as to him.

"Gladly, but there can be no stopping again." His fingers combed through her hair, pulling it back from where it had fallen into her eyes.

"Then don't stop."

He took the edges of her hood and lowered it to her shoulders. Untying it, he let the cloak fall behind her on the floor. She was caught by his blue-gray eyes as his hands cupped her shoulders. Did he feel the shiver racing along her? She was not shivering from the morning's cold, but in awe of the fire that seemed to spiral outward from his palms.

His eyes searched her face, lingering on her lips with a heated glow that she could sense in her very center. She had never felt anything like this, save when he touched her. When her hand slipped along his shoulder as his arm encircled her waist, she could think only of the yearning in his eyes, endlessly deep and vibrantly ablaze with potent emotions that both enticed and frightened her.

Frightened? How he would laugh if she told him she was overwhelmed by his longings! He would remind her of the many times she had vowed she was afraid of no man. That had not changed, but she was scared of how easily she could lose herself within passion.

As his fingers glided down her back, she longed to melt against him like sweetened oil in a lamp. Her lips parted with a nearly soundless sigh when he brought her against his chest. The firm line of his body welcomed her, even as it awed her with the very maleness of him.

Sifting her hand through his hair, she closed her eyes as she watched his mouth descend toward hers. She could imagine nothing she wanted more than his kiss. His mouth claimed hers, gently but with an urgency even stronger than any she had sensed before.

He whispered against her mouth, each movement of his lips an enticing caress, "Maybe I was wrong."

"Wrong?" She could not imagine him being mistaken about anything when his kisses were so perfect.

"Maybe I was wrong when I persuaded you to let me give the orders during our journey." A slow, sensual smile slid across his lips as his fingers played a silent melody along her spine.

As she swayed to that song, memory burst through her, succulent memories of when he had touched her before, strengthening the thrill of each caress now. She feared the flame within her was about to burn right through her skin. "Really?"

"When you look at a man with that combination of innocence and desire, you make him eager to do your bidding. Ask what you would of me."

"I want you to . . ." Her voice trailed away into unexpected shyness. "How can a maiden ask for what she has not yet experienced?"

He smiled. "Shall I do as I believe you wish, milady?"

"Yes."

"It will be my pleasure." His hand slid up over her breast. As her breath caught again, he whispered, "And I hope yours."

"You talk too much," she gasped as waves of delight washed over her.

"I shall keep that in mind." He bent to put an arm under her knees and lift her up against his chest.

"Be careful! You will hurt your arm more."

"Why don't you let me concern myself with my well-being for once?" His eyes glittered like living jewels. "And yours."

Her breath burned with his as she sought his mouth and the rapture waiting there. She pressed close to his chest's hard wall. With her arm looped around his shoulders and his at her waist and knees, she was surrounded by his strength.

He ran his fingers up her skirt. She closed her eyes, overpowered by his eyes and the magic swirling through her. Another mistake, for the sensation of his rough skin against her leg was pleasurable and breathtaking at the same time.

When he set her on her feet again, she stood by the grand bed that Guy had claimed for his own. She stiffened at the thought of lying where Guy had brought his women.

This time she was certain Christian could perceive her thoughts, because he said, "My brother has not returned to this bed since he was well enough to leave it. Nor will he return to it as long as we are using it."

"He will not be happy about that."

"True, but we shall be."

She lost herself in his amazing eyes as his fingers settled on her waist. Placing her on the bed, he leaned her back. Her arms around his shoulders brought him over her.

She expected him to kiss her eagerly, but he seemed intent on memorizing her face. She did not need to do the same. She knew every angle on his face, every expression from laughter to fury, for she had re-created it inch by inch in her dreams for the past fortnight.

"Is something amiss?" she whispered. She did not like to admit that she was unsure how to offer him the pleasure he gave her.

"No, save that I await the order to go ahead." He tipped her chin toward him.

"I thought *you* were in charge of orders." She laughed.

"When you are in my arms, I am yours to command."

"I command you to teach me all I should know to bring you joy."

"Gladly I will obey, milady. Here is your first lesson."

Framing her face with his hands, he brought his mouth down to hers. His tongue teased her lips open. The pulse of his breath captured hers, sharing it. It was an order she could not resist, and she sampled the flavors within his mouth.

She closed her eyes to savor the incredible sensations as his fingers skimmed along her. He pressed his mouth against the hollow between her breasts. His heated touch seemed to sear away the fabric separating her skin from his lips. When he drew back, she arched toward him in an invitation for more of the pleasure. A soft groan escaped from her.

He put his finger to her lips. "Hush. You told me you did not want to talk."

Rolling onto his back, he raised her over him. She bent to run her tongue along his ear as he had hers, each time stoking the need within her. His ragged breath scorched her skin, and he moaned her name. Nothing had ever sounded so tempting. Nothing had ever tasted so delicious.

He swiftly loosened the laces up the back of her gown. Hooking a single finger in the front, he drew it down to puddle around her hips. He smoothed her shift along her, and she quivered with the need that would not lie quiescent.

She had to touch him. Running her fingers down his chest, she knew that not even in her most sensual dreams had she imagined those muscles would react to her inexperienced touch. His heartbeat leaped when she reached his belt. Even so, she pulled back as she had never done before. Not knowing what to do was a peculiar sensation.

"Is something wrong?" he whispered.

"I am unsure what to do."

"Words I never thought I would hear you utter."

"Do not jest with me." Her voice caught. "Not now."

"You must grant me a chance to accustom myself to an Avisa I have never imagined. When you are so resolved to do as you wish and so skilled in every other aspect of your life, it is startling to discover you so uncertain now."

"And unskilled?" The word hurt even to speak.

"Is that what concerns you? You have trusted me to teach you even as we discover rapture together." He combed his fingers through her hair and sat, still holding her close. "Avisa, sweet Avisa, don't you realize? Anything you want to do while you are here with me is what you should do."

"I am unsure what I want to do."

"Are you? Let me give you some ideas." His mouth caressed her cheeks, her nose, her eyelids, along her chin. He drew back enough so he could gaze into her eyes.

In his, she saw everything she wanted.

He slipped her gown over her feet and ran his fingers up beneath her long shift. His hands, hardened by his training with sword and bow, were gentle as he loosened the garters holding her stockings to her knees. He drew off one, then the other. Raising her foot, he pressed his lips to her instep.

She leaned forward and grasped the front of his tunic. As his lips coursed along her ankle, she clung to him, buffeted by sensations she could not even name. He released her foot and slid his hands once more beneath her shift. He smiled as he unlashed the sheath where she kept her knife. Tossing it aside, he drew her shift up and over her head.

As he let it fall off his fingertips, he stared at her. She flushed and started to cover herself, but he caught her hands.

"Let me just look at your beauty," he said. "You are my favorite fantasy brought to life. What fantasies do you have?"

She started to answer, then realized she did not have words for what she had imagined in her dreams. Her dreams, she was discovering, that were tepid imitations of the thrill of his skin on hers.

"Teach me," she replied. "Teach me to touch you as you wish to be touched."

"In a moment."

"I thought you were going to obey my commands," she whispered.

Smiling, he said, "That is true, and so I shall." He drew off his tunic and the linen shirt beneath it. The glow from the fire burnished his skin to a ruddy gold when he pushed his breeches along his legs' strong sinews.

She stared, afraid to breathe. She had never seen a man's naked body before. It was the perfect complement to hers— broad where she was narrow, strong where she was soft.

"This way," he murmured as he pressed her hand to his chest and slowly guided her fingers down across his muscular abdomen. He laughed when she faltered, but she heard a husky roughness in his laugh that had not been there before. "Do not be afraid of what will soon be part of you."

In his eyes she saw the hunger that ached inside her. A hunger mixed with an exquisite need that throbbed through her and dared her to reach out a single, trembling fingertip to explore the hardness between his legs. Its silken texture pulsated against her touch.

With a desperate groan, he shoved her back into the pelts. His mouth was not gentle, but demanding. She responded with her own craving. He ran his tongue up the curve of her breast, drawing its tip into his mouth. She writhed beneath him, lost to everything but the rapture and the craving. The two blended and became an ache deep within her as his hand swept up her leg, setting her aquiver.

When his finger delved into her, she swayed with the rhythm he was teaching her, just as he had vowed. Ripples of flame consumed her. She gripped his shoulders, afraid she would be pulled away from him. Then everything exploded within her, and she could only tremble against him.

She opened her eyes at his command, and she saw his

smile. He was elated to give her this pleasure. He kissed her gently, and her body pressed to his, eager for more.

"I did not know," she whispered.

"But I taught you as you ordered. What next, milady? I am yours to command."

"And I am yours."

He raised himself over her. Lightning erupted through her when he brought them together. Pain sparked for a moment, and he halted. She reached up and stroked his face. As she murmured his name, he began to move slowly, then faster as they ignited into a single quest for satiation. She matched his motions, wanting to give him what he was offering her. When he claimed her mouth for a hard kiss, she barely had a chance to react before her ecstasy peaked again. As every thought shattered, she heard his gasps of gratification. It was the most wondrous sound she had ever imagined.

Avisa blinked her eyes open. Several pelts were soft beneath her, and another covered her. She stretched her toes, savoring the fur against her bare skin. Where was she? She smiled. She was in Christian's arms, her cheek on his shoulder.

Tilting her head, she saw he was watching her. He smoothed her hair back from her eyes as he whispered, "You are beautiful when you are sleeping, Avisa."

"Not when I am awake?"

He laughed. "It is not like you to try to bait a man to give you compliments."

"None of this is like me." She smiled. "I believe I shall change that."

"A fine idea." He kissed her lightly on the forehead.

She drew in a sharp breath.

"What is wrong?" he asked, his smile disappearing.

"I thought—that is, I guessed—" She spread her fingers across his chest. "I did not guess that, when I was with you, even such a chaste touch would excite me so."

"Did you think that once we were lovers the anticipation would no longer stir within us?"

"I don't know. I never thought about it."

"Then I think I should show you how often I have thought about it. You have been a good student, but I have so many more lessons for you."

He tipped her mouth beneath his, and the renewed passion on his lips sent a thrill through her. A thrill she wanted to share with only him for as long as she lived. That would not be possible, so she must enjoy it—and him—as long as she could.

Chapter 19

When she stepped into the chapel, Avisa was beyond the protective walls of the keep. The tall windows, two with stained glass and the third still unglazed, marked an easy route for any invader who scaled the walls, but nothing could be between the altar and heaven.

Four rows of pews were set in front of an altar rail decorated with winter greens. By the uncompleted window sat a stone baptismal font, carved with scenes of flowers and beasts. Beneath her feet, red and black tiles alternated. The room smelled of damp and gutted candles.

Sitting in a middle pew, she bowed her head and whispered the prayers that had always offered her comfort and strength. The Latin words flowed, but she did not say them by rote as she had so often while impatiently attending matins or evening services. She did not want to rush away from the quiet now. She needed serenity to sort out her thoughts.

Everything had been simple at St. Jude's Abbey. Lessons began with the first light and ended with dark. The sisters who wished to learn to use weapons worked together, while the rest served the Abbey in other ways. Nobody had ever questioned their lives until the queen arrived.

Would another be sent if it was learned that Avisa had broken her vows to be faithful first to the Abbey? She looked at her fingers clenching on the pew in front of her.

The queen had told her to do whatever she must to keep Christian from Canterbury, and the abbess had seconded that order. But Avisa doubted that either had intended for her to share his bed.

The Abbey might be closed to her now. It was her home, the only one she could remember. The ones living within were her family. A family she had believed she would always have, a family she had taken for granted until now.

Christian had made her no promises beyond last night's pleasures. She had not asked him to, not only because she had been swept up in the rapture, but also because she knew Christian would not make a vow he did not intend to keep. Was she afraid he would tell her that he had drawn her into his arms only because she was willing? Had Christian, unlike her, given thought to anything beyond the moment of sweet ecstasy?

She had given herself eagerly and without obligation. She closed her eyes and savored the memory of his fingers on her naked skin. Now she must live with the consequences. One thing had not changed. She would do as she promised the queen and keep Christian far from Canterbury until the king and the archbishop ended their quarrel.

"I want so much to serve you as I have promised," she whispered over her folded hands. She was unsure if she was speaking to the Abbey or the queen or both. "I almost failed when I let Christian go to free Guy. That will never happen again. I will do as I vowed."

She waited for the solace she had hoped those words would bring. Nothing came. She heard only her heartbeat. When Christian had held her, it had pounded as if it wanted to escape from her chest to become his.

Another low sound intruded. Raising her head, she looked over her shoulder.

Behind the last pew, his hands resting on its back, Christian stood. He was dressed in a clean tunic that must have come from one of the chests in the castle. Its rich blue wool emphasized his deep tan. His recently washed hair was in dark spikes. Wishing he had invited her to help him bathe, she was not surprised her fingers tingled as she recalled his hard muscles beneath them.

He stepped around the pew and walked toward her. At his side, his sword matched every motion. He said nothing as he stopped, edging into the pew behind her.

"How long have you been here?" she asked quietly.

"A few minutes. I did not want to intrude on your prayers." He ran his hand along the carved pew. "But it was more than that. I never have seen you like this, Avisa." He brushed her hair as lightly as he had the wood. "There is a joy and a quiet acceptance within you here that I would not have guessed you possessed."

"You did not expect me to slash about with my sword in the chapel, did you?"

He smiled. "I never am sure with you."

"I think that may be an insult."

"Don't look for insult where none was intended." His face became serious. "I am speaking from envy."

"Envy?" She was astonished. "Of what?"

"What else?" His hand curved down along her cheek as his thumb followed her jaw. "Your unvanquished courage. You are as brave as de Tracy or any of the king's best knights. I watch you, and I wonder what could frighten you."

"You frighten me."

"Me?"

"You and the feelings you create within me." She turned her face away.

"Frightening feelings?"

Edging past him, because being in the chapel made the words more difficult to say, she whispered, "The feelings are not frightening. That I have them is."

He slipped out of the pew and came to stand behind her. His hands on her shoulders kept her from walking out the door. When he spoke, his breath glided along her neck and teased her ear.

"Do you speak, Avisa, of how you quiver each time I draw you close? If so, then there is nothing frightening about such feelings. They are what men and women discover in each other's arms, creating a hunger that will be sated by no one else."

"But I should not feel that way!"

"Why?"

"I should think only of . . ." She glanced toward the front of the chapel.

He laughed, loud and hard.

"At least one of us finds this amusing," she fired back.

"Be honest, Avisa. The idea of a woman like you, a woman so filled with life and daring and, yes, courage, cloistered away from the world is absurd. I cannot imagine *you* living a nun's life. You like wearing a sword and being skilled with it. You like the power surging through you when you face an opponent. The exultation of victory thrills you. As you thrill me."

His fingers swept through her hair as he found her mouth with the ease they had learned last night. She pulled him closer, wanting him more than she had ever before. As he deepened the kiss, she ran her hands up his back. Too much wool was between her fingers and his skin.

"Fine way to use a chapel," came a sarcastic voice from the doorway.

Heat soared up Avisa's face as she saw a trio of men standing just inside the chapel door. One man stepped forward. His gold hair was woven with silver, and it was thinning on top. He wore a bright scarlet tunic, announcing that he was a rich lord of great importance. A quick glance in her direction before his eyes focused on Christian suggested she was of far less importance.

The man drew his sword, and Christian's hand went toward his scabbard. The man's sword blocked his way, and Christian pulled back his hand before it was pierced. He gave the man the same furious expression he had given Pyt.

Unlike the outlaw, this man faltered and glanced at his companions.

That gave her the opportunity she had been hoping for. When she inched her hand toward her own sword, nobody seemed to take note of her action. They would rue that error of underestimating her. Her fingers closed around the hilt just as the man spoke.

"What are you doing with my daughter, Lovell?"

"Daughter?" choked Avisa, jerking her hand away from her sword.

"Don't you recognize your own father?"

Avisa was unsure who spoke those words because she could only stare at the man in front of her. The man with the sword was her father? She searched her memory for any remnant of her father.

She remembered his voice as being deeper than that of the man standing before her, holding a sword to Christian's chest. His face might be more wrinkled or exactly as it was when he had arranged for her to be taken to St. Jude's Abbey. She could not recall. His hair was much like hers, but his eyes were darker.

"Do your father honor," Christian whispered from the side of his mouth.

She searched her mind again. Honor her father? How? She must once have known, but her family had become the sisters within the Abbey's walls, and she had forgotten the ways of families beyond it.

She stepped between Christian and her father, ignoring the sword. Kneeling in front of her father, she drew his hand to her forehead in the obeisance she would have offered the abbess. He jerked his hand away. She gasped when he pushed her out of the way. His sword did not waver.

"What are *you* doing with my daughter, Lovell?" he demanded.

"She asked for my assistance."

Avisa bit her lip as she stood. If Christian spoke of her "rescued sister," her father was sure to denounce Christian as a liar. The lie was hers, but the shame would be heaped on Christian.

"Your assistance?" Lord de Vere laughed derisively. "Why would my daughter need the assistance of a coward?"

Christian's expression did not change, but she knew he was outraged. She opened her mouth to defend him, then closed it. Her father was acting as if she did not exist. She must seek another way to end this confrontation before someone was hurt.

"Father . . ." She moaned, and putting the back of her hand against her forehead, she wobbled. Shouts came from every direction as she folded her knees in what she hoped looked like a swoon.

She was caught in strong arms before she could hit the floor. When she was lifted against a broad chest, she let her head loll. She opened her eyes a slit to confirm what she had guessed. Christian was holding her, and as he shifted her in his arms, she was able to sneak a look at her father.

Lord de Vere was nodding when Christian suggested that she should be taken to where she could regain her senses.

"Take my daughter, Griswold," ordered her father, motioning to one of his men. The huge man, both in height and in breadth, held out his arms to hold her. She wanted to cling to Christian, but she could not reveal that she was duping them.

"She should not be disturbed further," Christian argued. "She is delicate, and I am not sure how many more shocks she can endure."

Her father agreed reluctantly, and Christian carried her out of the chapel. The others must be following because he whispered to her to keep her sword from swinging without letting anyone know she was faking her faint.

"Thank you," he murmured when she slipped her fingers over the sheath, holding it against her leg. "A few more whacks with that, and you would have found me a disappointment tonight."

She smothered a laugh as she nestled against him. She

was sorry when after carrying her up the stairs he put her on the large bed. Staying in his arms was wonderful, but never more so than when she was unsure what to do now that her father had arrived. Why was he at Lord de Sommeville's castle?

"I will be in the other room," Christian whispered before raising his voice to call, "Baldwin, come with me."

Baldwin? What was the page doing out of bed? He needed to rest.

She had to exert every ounce of her will to keep from jumping down off the bed and seeing for herself how the boy fared. Hearing Christian's voice diminish into the distance as he spoke with Baldwin, she relaxed. Christian would watch over the boy. Just as he had over her.

"Shut and bar the door," Lord de Vere ordered. "Get some cold water to douse my daughter's face. That will wake her."

By St. Jude! She was not going to lie here and get drenched with ice water. Blinking her eyes open, she gave what she hoped sounded like a genuine moan.

Her father was at her side, taking her hand and breathing a prayer of gratitude. "How do you fare, Avisa?" he asked.

"I-I-I am fine." She looked past him to see that only one of the two men with him was still in the room. That man dropped the bar on the door connecting the chamber to the other rooms.

"Thank you, Griswold," her father said.

The man bowed his head and went out of the room, closing the hallway door behind him.

Avisa pushed herself up to sit. When her father cautioned her to go slowly, she held her head in her hands as if it was aching. She had to get some information without seeming too obvious. She did not know her father.

"It is a shock to find you here, Avisa," he said.

"I am sure it is."

"Why are you here?"

"I was sent by St. Jude's Abbey to meet two women

here." She hoped she could answer all his questions with the truth.

"You were sent alone?"

She shook her head. "I have been traveling with Sir Christian Lovell, his brother, and page. Sir Christian—"

Her father's mouth tightened. "You speak of him very formally, even though you were in his arms in the chapel."

"Christian," she corrected, knowing she must take care with everything she said, for her father would not be easily deceived, "is Queen Eleanor's godson, and, as you know, the Abbey was founded by the queen."

"Are you saying that the queen arranged for you to travel with that coward Lovell?"

She bristled as she swung her feet over the side of the bed. "Christian is not a coward!"

Lord de Vere's brows rose. "If he is no coward, then why does my cloistered daughter wear a sword?"

"The abbess sent a weapon with me. I did not question her orders." She stood and realized her eyes were at the same level as his. Her memories had made him gigantic, as he would have seemed when she was little more than a baby. "May I ask why you are here, milord?"

"I always spend the Christmas holidays with de Sommeville, as you should know." His frown deepened the lines on his face. "No, you would not know."

"I am glad we have had this chance to meet again."

He nodded, obviously uncomfortable at such emotion from a daughter he had believed cloistered and forgotten.

The hallway door opened, and the man he called Griswold came in. He glanced in her direction before bowing his head.

"Milord," Griswold said, "it is requested that you dine with Lord de Sommeville at his high table tonight."

"Thank you. Tell de Sommeville that I accept his kind invitation."

The man shifted uneasily from one foot to the other.

"Is there something further, Griswold?"

"Lord de Sommeville added that he would enjoy your company along with your daughter's and her companions."

Her father cursed. Waving aside his man with an order to hurry to de Sommeville with his response, he waited until the door closed. He faced her and snarled, "Because of you, I have to break bread with the whelps of a coward."

Avisa stepped forward, but his scowl warned her to stop. "I do not like having our first meeting in so many years filled with rancor, but, as I told you, Christian Lovell is no coward. He has proven his courage over and over."

"Do not defend Lovell to me. He is the son of a coward who nearly lost our king his rightful throne."

"King Henry has accepted Christian's pledge of loyalty."

"Henry Curtmantle is a wise man, but every man makes mistakes. Such as accepting any liege pledge from a Lovell."

"You are wrong."

"Wrong?" He faced her. "It is not a daughter's place to decide if her father is right or wrong."

"It is when you are wrong." She met his eyes steadily as he put his hand on his sword. If she let his rage daunt her now, he could very well prevent her from doing as she promised Queen Eleanor. "I know the stories told throughout the realm, milord, and I suspect they are not true."

"If Lovell has been whispering lies in your ear, then he is even less of a man than I guessed him to be. You will have nothing more to do with him."

"Milord—"

"I will find a man who will be glad to fill your ears with loving words suitable for a wife. A man who will bring more than dishonor to our family."

She forced down the eruption of panic as her father spoke so easily of using her to align their family more closely with those who had the king's greatest favor. She would not allow another man to touch her, kiss her, be a part of her as Christian had, but what say would she have if her father insisted?

"Milord, my place is—"

"*I* will determine where your place is, daughter! I can tell you it is not with Lovell."

"You are right."

Her acquiescence halted him. A smile inched along his lips. "I am pleased to hear you say that, Avisa. Perhaps you are not so spellbound by Lovell's lies as I had feared."

Christian is not the liar. I am. She silenced those thoughts.

"I am pleased, as well, to see you know your place as my daughter," her father continued. "With the coming of spring, I shall find—"

"That I have returned to St. Jude's Abbey, where I belong."

"No! I will not allow you to return to a place where they put you in such danger."

"I am in no danger."

"Not now, but to send you with Lovell . . ." He could not finish as his rage choked him.

"My place is at St. Jude's Abbey."

"Your place is where I tell you it is. You are pleasant to look at, so finding you a husband should not be difficult."

"But—"

"Do not argue with me. My mind is made up."

Her fingers tightened on her sword. To draw it against her own father was unthinkable, but so was the future he was choosing for her. Anything she said would infuriate him more. She turned and walked out the door. Closing it behind her, she wondered what she should do now.

The answer was easy. Fulfill her vow to the queen. That had not changed. She must not think of what would happen afterward when she was given to another man and never saw Christian again.

Christian sat on the floor in the room where Baldwin had been recuperating. The boy was lying on the bed, but only because Christian had ordered him to. Guy was pacing impatiently.

"She can wait," Christian said. "So can you."

His brother swore a vicious oath. "But why should I deny myself?"

"Because I asked it."

"And I am supposed to obey you as you obeyed de Vere?" His lips drew back in a sneer. "You ran away from him like the coward he labeled you."

From the bed Baldwin cried, "You cannot allow him to speak so of you."

Christian stretched his feet toward the fire. "What would you have me do? Challenge Lord de Vere?" He scowled at the flames. Had he been so enthralled by Avisa's beauty that he had failed to consider that she was Lord de Vere's daughter? Their blue eyes and light hair were almost the same.

"He belittled our whole family." The boy looked in desperation to Guy. "Our whole family."

"You are wasting your breath," Guy said as he brushed the front of his tunic. "Christian is under fair Avisa's spell. He will not risk her affection by risking de Vere's life."

The door opened, and Christian stood as Avisa came in. Had she heard what Guy said? Not that it mattered, because every word was true.

She faltered, fingering the pommel on her sword beneath her cloak. "I thought I might find you alone, Christian."

Guy chuckled coldly. "Or is the spell mutual, brother?" He motioned to Baldwin. "Let the lovemates coo at each other."

"Stay where you are, Baldwin," Christian ordered. Taking Avisa by the hand, he said, "We will talk somewhere else."

"Have fun with your *talking*." Guy laughed.

Avisa's shoulders stiffened, but she said nothing until Christian drew her out of the room. "Where are we going?" she asked.

"Somewhere I may speak to you without other ears overhearing."

"Good."

No one was on the stairs leading up to the wall separating the inner ward from the outer. As he led her onto the narrow walkway, wind swirled around Christian like a living thing. Bare branches rocked to its silent music.

"I wonder if a tree can feel the wind's scouring against its bark as we feel it against our faces," Avisa said. She lowered her hood and held out her arms.

"You are unpredictable," Christian said as he leaned on the rocky crenellation in front of him. "I brought you up here because I doubt anyone else will come out into the cold. Now, here you are, with your cloak flapping around you, offering you no protection from the wind."

"I do not need to be protected from the wind."

"You do when it is so cold."

She stepped closer to him and rested her hand on the same crenellation. "The wind is not as cold as my father's voice when he speaks of your family."

"Baldwin has been battering my ears with demands that I let your father's blood recompense me for his insults."

Her face lost what little color it had. "Christian, you cannot challenge my father. I doubt he is your match, but he would never surrender to you while he possessed a single breath of life."

"So I believe."

"There must be something else I can do."

"Are you suggesting I should fight you in his stead? I would never surrender to you while I possessed even a single breath of life."

"Are you asking if I would kill you to uphold my family's honor?"

"Would you?"

Her face became bleak as she turned away. "Don't ask me that, Christian!"

His finger brushed her cheek, drawing her face toward him. When he held his finger up, his skin glistened. She put her hand up to her face.

"I am sorry, Avisa," he murmured.

She wiped her knuckles against her eyes. "You do not need to apologize. Tears are a sign of weakness."

"You are not weak." Anger boiled in him. "What else did your father say?"

"He says I cannot go back to the . . . I cannot go back home."

"Why?"

"Because he intends to wed me to someone who will bring honor to the de Vere family." She looked away again.

Christian fisted his hands on the parapet. *Someone who will bring honor to the de Vere family.* No son of Robert Lovell would be able to do that. His name would bring only shame to his bride's family.

"I am not that man," he said as he stroked her quivering shoulders. She wiped away tears he knew she was as ashamed of as he was of his father's cowardice. As he touched her silky hair, he thought of her soft breaths caressing another man's skin or another man finding ecstasy deep within her. His stomach cramped.

She raised her eyes, and he wondered, as he had the first time he had seen her, if the sun had glowed in them. He saw many emotions. Anger, frustration, despair . . . and love.

When she leaned her head against his shoulder again as she wrapped her arms around him, she whispered, "Do you believe your father is a coward?"

"That is a silly question."

"It is not a silly question. You have spoken often of others turning their backs on him. You have never said if you believe it or not."

"It does not matter what I believe." He enfolded her to him and buried his face in her hair. "Everyone believes—"

"Why do you care," she asked, pulling back, "what everyone else believes? Just because an opinion is commonly held does not make it the truth!"

"You are talking nonsense."

"Am I?" She tapped the hilt of her sword. "I can fight with this. Yet *everyone else* believes that is impossible.

There is no difference between the mistakes you made about me and the mistakes made by the rest of the world about your father."

His brow lowered. "You have no idea what you are speaking about, Avisa! Your skills are a curiosity, an exception. My father betrayed his king."

"Are you sure of that?"

"If he did not, then why hasn't he denounced those who call him a coward?"

"I don't know."

Her simple answer deflated his rage, but only a bit. "I do not want to argue. You know nothing of what happened."

"Neither do you!" She grasped his arms. "Christian, your father never faltered before. Why did he do so that day?"

"It is said the battle was lost."

"He could have accepted honorable defeat as others did. No other lord who joined the king that day has been ostracized, even though each failed him. Why would your father leave the field *then*? It makes no sense."

"If he was thinking only of saving his skin, he would not be slowed by sense."

"But he is your father, Christian. You would sacrifice your life for honor. Even Guy was willing to risk his life to save you, and he cares nothing for honor. Why would your father run when he could have accepted an honorable defeat?"

"What are you suggesting?"

"I am suggesting there are facts about your father leaving King Henry that you do not know. Facts your father must know."

"I have asked. He will not speak of it."

"Your mother?"

He shook his head. "She is many years dead."

"His confessor?"

"The priest at Lovell Mote has been in our household for only a few years. I do not know whether Father James, the previous priest, traveled with my father to England in 1147."

"Where is Father James now?"

"I am not sure. He left Lovell Mote when I was a child to serve the archbishop."

"Which one?"

He hated to dampen the hope in her eyes. "Becket. Father James may have gone into exile with him."

"Oh." She looked away for a long moment, then turned back to him to ask, "Could he have returned to England with the archbishop?"

"He would be elderly now, if he is alive."

"So there may be no one other than your father who knows?" She sighed. "There must be someone else."

"Yes, but who?"

She rested against him again, and he held her close. She was the only person who cared as much as he did about removing the tarnish of cowardice from the Lovell name. He wished there was some answer he could give her, but he had none.

Chapter 20

Christian did not look up as his brother called his name. Maybe Guy would not see him in the armory's corner. Pausing with his hand above his sword, he wanted to be sure not even the soft sound of a polishing cloth against the metal would alert his brother. He had come here to gather his thoughts.

I am suggesting there are facts about your father leaving King Henry that you do not know. Facts your father must know.

Avisa's assertion echoed in his head. Could she be right?

"I know you are here!" Guy shouted across the armory. "I must speak with you now."

Tossing the cloth onto the table, Christian stood. Guy's petulant tone meant he would not leave until he aired whatever had raised his bile. Christian hoped his brother had not seduced someone's wife and needed help soothing the cuckolded husband . . . again.

"Back here!" he called.

Guy's curses were muffled by iron crashing to the floor. He had kicked aside a stack of arrow tips, scattering them like ebony leaves. He strode through the mess and did not slow until he reached Christian.

"When are we leaving?" Guy asked sharply. "I cannot tolerate any more of de Vere's snide comments."

"Pay them no mind. He is filled with more bluster than

wisdom." Christian chuckled. "It is amazing such a man could have sired an intelligent woman like Avisa."

His brother's face grew more grim. "Before you praise her, you should know she has been playing you for a fool."

"Simply because she chose me instead of—"

"You are welcome to the lying whelp of a cur."

Christian set his sword on the table between them. If he held it, he was not sure he could keep from using it to warn his brother not to insult Avisa. "Do not speak so of her."

"Are you afraid of the truth, brother?"

"I have no interest in hearing your whining because she would not let you into her bed."

"Why should she? She was not sent by the queen to distract *me*."

He stared at his brother in astonishment. "What?"

"You heard me, but I will repeat myself if that is what will let the truth reach through your thick skull. Queen Eleanor sent Avisa to distract you and keep you away from Canterbury until the situation with the archbishop is resolved." He wore a superior grin. "The queen did not wish her beloved godson to face any danger that might show he is, indeed, as untrustworthy as his father."

"Our father. You bear the shame as much as I do."

"But I care nothing of that burden. You do, and the queen knows that." He picked up the sword and fingered its hilt. "Just as she knows how you would agree to set every other duty aside to help a beautiful woman rescue her sister from an evil baron."

"You have lost your mind."

"Me? Avisa lied to you! Every word she has spoken to you, everything she has done to . . ." He chuckled harshly. "Everything she has done *with* you is a lie. For all we know, she may not even be de Vere's daughter. He may be part of the queen's scheme to keep you busy where there is no chance that her precious godson will be hurt."

"She is de Vere's daughter." He sounded witless, but his head was whirling with memories of Avisa's sparkling eyes meeting his without any sign that she had been false with him. A groan erupted through his gut. Could everything she had said and everything she had done be a lie? Everything? Had her whispers in his bed been lies?

"Why do you find this difficult to believe?" Guy asked. "She is not the first woman to speak lies in a man's ear while she was lying in his arms."

Christian turned away.

"You love her!" His brother made the words an accusation. "The wench has made a fool of you, and you love her!" He laughed hard.

Grabbing his sword off the table, Christian raised it. His brother paled and held up his hands as if to ward off a blow. Christian drove the sword into its sheath as he walked past his brother. Pausing, he put his hand on his brother's shoulder, then without a word left the armory.

"Keep the sword higher," Avisa called to Ermangardine.

Her student tried to obey, but Avisa was still able to knock it aside too easily.

"Again," she ordered.

Instead of balancing the sword in front of her, the girl let its tip fall. Her eyes widened as she looked past Avisa.

Turning, Avisa smiled when she saw Christian walking across the armory's small yard. "Just the man I needed!"

He did not smile. When he glanced at Ermangardine, the girl rushed away.

Avisa stared after her. "What is wrong with her?"

Christian closed the distance between them with measured steps. Every instinct urged her to reach for her sword. Her instincts had never been wrong, so why were they warning her against him?

"I know the truth," he said without emotion.

"The truth? About your father? That is wonderful!" She reached for him, but he batted her hand away.

"No. I know the truth that you were sent to keep me from going to Canterbury."

Avisa's knees threatened to fail her. She drove her sword's tip into the ground and leaned on the hilt, hoping it would hold her. "How? How did you find out?"

"You are not going to deny it?"

"No. I don't lie."

"Really?" He arched a single brow.

"Other than to honor my vow to the queen to say nothing about the truth, I have been honest."

He laughed, the sound so cold it froze her heart within her. "It must make your life simple when you can choose when and where and with whom you will be honest."

"Do you have any idea how difficult it has been not to tell you the truth? I have wanted to be honest. I could not."

"Because of the queen?"

"She asked me never to tell you why she had sent me from St. Jude's Abbey."

"Abbey?" he choked. "You are a nun?"

"I am Queen Eleanor's servant." She berated herself for revealing more than he knew. In her head she heard the queen's orders: *You are to keep him far from Canterbury at the same time you allow nothing to connect you to St. Jude's Abbey. The value of the Abbey to me would be lessened if anyone else was to learn of my true intention in founding it and having young women trained to serve me in times of trouble.* "That is how you should think of me, Christian."

"You are making no sense. Are you lying to me again?"

"No. Why should I? You already know why I am here." Guilt pierced her, but telling him more now could destroy the Abbey.

"To watch over me as if I were a babe not trusted to toddle across the hall."

"The queen wants no one she cares for involved in what may come to pass between her husband and the archbishop."

"She could have sent word to me to stay away from Canterbury until Henry and Becket meet again."

Avisa reached for his hand, but he clasped it behind his back. "Would you have heeded her request?"

"When I pledged my loyalty to the king, it was to his family as well."

"Don't you see? *That* is why the queen sent me to keep you from Canterbury. If a call goes out for the king's men to halt the archbishop from turning the people against the king, she knows you would answer it."

He did not reply.

"Will you do as she wishes?" Avisa asked.

He stared at her without answering.

"Christian, please tell me what you plan to do!"

For a moment, she thought he would answer, then he bowed his head and walked away. She started to call after him, but halted herself. He would not answer.

Gripping her sword's hilt, she slid down to her knees and pressed her face against its flat side. She wept, knowing she had lost the battle she had hoped most to win.

Joyous voices and laughter filled the hall. Ale splashed on the floor as chalices were tapped together to make salutes to the holiday. Minstrels played and twirled and tumbled, to the delight of the children, who were running about with pieces of greenery twisted through their hair.

Avisa walked through the gaiety, encased in her sorrow. A few of the merrymakers glanced at her, then rejoined the fun. Nobody wanted to be dispirited on the eve before Christmas. Even though the twelve days of feasting and folly did not officially begin until the completion of Mass at midnight, the household was ready to celebrate and did not intend to be distracted from the revelry.

Edging through the crowded hall, Avisa almost kept going when she heard her name called. She paused when she saw Mavise waving to her. Beside Mavise, Ermangardine stood, staring at the floor. Their faces were as abject as her heart.

As soon as Avisa reached where they waited beside one of the arches leading out into the inner ward, Mavise said, "We have to speak with you immediately."

"As I must to you." She stood at an angle that gave her a view of most of the hall. She did not want to chance anyone overhearing their conversation. The thought brought a bubble of pain-filled laughter up into her throat. Soon everyone in the castle could know how she had duped Christian, and once more he would be dishonored. "Christian knows that the queen sent me to keep him from going to Canterbury. Only three people here knew the truth."

Mavise looked at the girl by her side. "Tell her, Ermangardine."

The girl shrunk as tears rolled down her face.

"Why did you tell Christian the truth?" Avisa asked, trying to keep her voice serene.

"I did not tell him!" She grasped Avisa's hand. "I took a vow to keep Sir Christian from knowing the truth. I never would have told him."

"Did you tell someone else?"

She nodded.

"Who?"

"Sir Guy Lovell."

"But why would you tell *him* the truth?"

She dug her toe into the space between the stones and rocked back and forth as if a fierce wind was pulling her first one way and then another. Her loose hair could not hide her face completely. It was taut with fear. Remembered fear, Avisa realized. The sick feeling in her middle thickened like rotting milk.

"Ermangardine?" she asked more gently.

The girl looked up, revealing threads of tears.

"Ermangardine, tell me what happened with Guy Lovell."

"He tried to . . . That is, he cornered me away from everyone else and . . ." She bit her lower lip as more tears flooded along her face.

"I understand." Avisa put her arms around the trembling girl and drew her close. She did not want Ermangardine to see her face, for it must be twisted with rage.

Avisa had put an end to Guy's heavy-handed groping by knocking him senseless. Ermangardine had been forced to try another way, and Avisa could not fault the girl for telling him whatever she could to get him to leave her alone.

"We must leave with the rising sun tomorrow," Mavise said.

"Yes." Avisa smoothed Ermangardine's hair back from her wet face. "I will miss you, but it is too dangerous for you to remain here."

"Aren't you coming with us?" asked Ermangardine between her sobs.

"My task is not yet done."

The girl flung her arms around Avisa. "I am so sorry."

"I know." Kissing the girl on the forehead, she said, "Come and bid me farewell on the morrow before you leave."

Mavise nodded and, putting her arm around the younger woman, hurried her across the hall. Avisa did not move until they had vanished into the crowd. Then she slipped out of the hall. Alone.

Christian climbed the stairs. Nobody was in the upper corridor, because de Sommeville's household was enjoying a drunken celebration of Christmas. Not just of the holiday, he had become aware, but of what many feared would be the final festivities before the king and the archbishop's conflict consumed England.

That is why the queen sent me to keep you from Canterbury. If a call goes out for the king's men to halt the archbishop from turning the people against the king, she knows you would answer it. The words were Avisa's. He could ignore the warning, but not the pain that had weighted her voice. Because she had been unable to succeed in what the queen had sent her to do?

It had been more than her failing the queen, but he did not want to think of that. He had wanted to drink ale until he could no longer see or think or feel. All his efforts had been

for naught. He could still see her face when he confronted
her and could still think of her dismay as he walked away
and could still feel the sleek warmth of her skin beneath his
fingers.

Opening a door, he took a single step into the room before he realized his body's cravings had betrayed him. He
had entered the room where he had slept with Avisa at his
side, where he had discovered that all her passions were
powerful.

As he opened the door to leave, he heard, "Don't go."

"Avisa?"

She stepped out of the darkness by the bed, and the light
from the hearth sent gold fire weaving through her hair,
which was loose over her shoulders. Her thin linen shift revealed more of her curves than it hid, for he could see the
shadows of her breasts beneath it.

"Please don't send me away," she said.

"You should not be here." And he should not be aching
for her.

"I cannot sleep. Please don't send me away."

"You should not be here," he repeated.

"I will go, but first let me tell you the truth. The whole
truth."

"I know the truth."

"Only part of it." Avisa kept her chin high so the tears
burning at the back of her eyes would not fall. "I need to tell
you all of it, even though I may destroy St. Jude's Abbey.
Maybe then you will understand why I have done what I
have and why you must stay far from Canterbury."

"I am listening." Christian closed the door.

Avisa began to explain about her life at the Abbey, answering his questions that she had avoided since meeting
him. She watched his face, hoping to see some sign that he
was willing to listen. Really listen. She had debated for
hours whether to tell him the truth. Even though Queen
Eleanor wanted to keep the reality of St. Jude's Abbey a se-

cret, she had also told Avisa to do whatever was necessary to keep Christian from being killed.

Suddenly he grabbed her by the waist and captured her mouth. She tried to turn her head away, to tell him there was so much more he needed to know. He refused to let her lips escape his as he backed her, step by slow step, toward the bed.

As he lifted her onto the thick mattress, she wrapped her arms around his shoulders and brought him to her. His eager fingers pushed aside her shift's long sleeves and drew the linen down her breast. She gave a soft cry of wordless delight as he ran his tongue along her. As he pulled off her shift, the material tore at his impatience. He threw the pieces aside and reclaimed her mouth. His legs entwined with hers, his gartered hose rough against her skin.

She became lost in ecstasy as his tongue explored her breasts, her abdomen, the inside of her thigh before slipping inside her to sample her most feminine flavors. As sensation overpowered her, leaving her quivering beneath his masterful touch, he drew away only long enough to rid himself of his clothes.

She gazed up at him. "I have hated lying to you," she whispered.

With a growl, he clamped his mouth over hers. It was demanding and bedeviling. Not giving her a chance to catch her breath, he drove himself into her.

As he shook with the potent force racing through them, she ceded herself totally. It thundered through her, erupting deep within her for one perfect moment.

Christian looked back at the bed where Avisa was asleep, exhausted from their lovemaking. The starlight stripped the color from her hair, as if the stars were envious of its golden sheen. The light was cold, but her skin was deliciously warm. His pillow was clutched to her breast. He ached to replace that pillow in her arms. Maybe he should stay. One more night.

But one more night would lead to another after that, and he could not remain here by her side.

Hooking his cloak closed, he picked up the sack containing his mail. He would don it where the clinking would not wake Avisa. He left the room and shut the door behind him. She had bared her soul to him, but he had heard little of what she said as he tried to fight the craving to hold her. He had lost . . . and he had won a final night of rapture.

His hand lingered on the latch. He should not go without telling her why he had to leave. Her father had denounced him as a coward, and maybe he was—he could not bear to stay and see Avisa's shattered face when he told her everything she had done was for naught.

He took a step and tripped over someone lying in the passage. Hearing a grunt, he wondered which of the revelers had drunk himself senseless. He put down his sack and bent over to wake the man.

"Baldwin!" he gasped. "What are you doing out here? You should be in bed."

The boy sat. "As you should be, sir." Pushing himself to his feet, he winced and put his hand to his side where he had been wounded. "You cannot leave her here. Her father will give her to another."

"She belongs to St. Jude's Abbey." He almost gagged on the words, because he was unsure if she would be welcome back there after she had broken her vow of chastity. Or had she? He did not recall her saying if she had taken a nun's vows, but he had missed much of what she said while he savored the sight of her looking so delicious in her linen shift.

"She belongs with you." His page stamped his foot. "If you leave her here, you will next see her as some other man's wife. You know Lord de Vere will never let her return to the Abbey. Since he has seen how beautiful she is, he intends to marry her to whoever can help him gain more power."

"That is enough, Baldwin," he ordered in a tone he seldom used with the lad. He was not surprised at the boy's reaction. Only last year, Baldwin's sister had been betrothed to a man twice her age, a man she had never met.

The boy subsided.

"Go to bed," he said gruffly as he picked up the sack.

"But you are leaving. I should go with you."

"Guy will travel with me." He grimaced as he thought of dragging his brother out of whichever bed he had charmed his way into. "I want you to stay here with Lady Avisa. The trouble fermenting in Canterbury may soon spread through England. I trust you to keep her safe, Baldwin."

"And returned to St. Jude's Abbey?"

How could such a simple question cut like a dagger? He had no idea which would be worse—having such a vibrant woman cloistered once more or having her scrve her father's ambition in an ally's bed. Would she think of Christian while her husband enjoyed her lovely body? Whether she went behind the Abbey's walls or into another man's arms, she would be denied to him forever—unless he could prove he was worthy of being given de Vere's daughter. He *would* prove his courage, so nobody could denounce him or his family ever again. Then Avisa could be his.

Chapter 21

Avisa woke and knew instantly that she was alone. She did not want to believe it, but Christian was gone. A single glance at the empty corner where his sword should be confirmed it.

The only sign of him remaining in the cool gray light before dawn was a tunic folded at the foot of the bed. She pulled it over her head and lashed it closed. His scent rose from the wool, and she wanted to bury her face in it. No, she wanted him, not just a piece of clothing.

She settled one of the pelts on her shoulders as she stepped over her tattered shift. Opening the door to the other room, she saw no one. She hurried to the third room and threw open the door. On the bed was Baldwin, lying on his back and staring up at the plank that held the bed-curtains. Her heart soared. If the page was still within the castle, surely Christian was, too. Maybe her account of life at St. Jude's Abbey and why the queen had founded the Abbey had shown him how desperate the situation was.

The boy turned to look at her. Her hope vanished with the speed of summer lightning when she saw his despair.

"Christian is gone?" she asked.

"Yes, milady." He sat and swung his legs over the side of the bed.

She turned away, wanting nobody, not even Baldwin, to see her pain. She had not guessed that Christian would forsake her after a night filled with such rapture. She would expect that of Guy, but not Christian.

Taking a deep breath, she released it as she faced Baldwin. "Where is he going?"

"He told me not to tell you his destination." He looked past her as if he could not bear to meet her eyes. "My orders are to remain with you and offer you what protection I can."

"From what?"

His shoulders were as stiff as a fence post. "I know I am not a great warrior like Sir Christian"—his eyes flicked toward her and away—"or like you, milady, but I pledge my life to safeguard yours."

She walked to the hearth. Bending to stir up the fire, she said, "Do not belittle yourself, Baldwin. You have already accomplished much. If you studied the warrior's arts with me, I would have you instructing the younger students."

"Students? You are a teacher? I thought you had been cloistered at St. Jude's Abbey."

"St. Jude's Abbey is unique." She did not give him a chance to ask another question. "Did Guy go with him?"

Baldwin nodded, his face rigid with frustration. "Yes, he took Guy and left me here."

"Christian knows he can trust *you* to watch over me and keep me safe. He knows *you* have a sense of honor."

"Oh."

She almost laughed at the boy's comprehension and his shock with what he had not considered. But she had never felt less like laughing.

"Where did Guy go?" she asked.

"But, milady, I told you that a vow was exacted from me not to—"

"Tell me where Christian went. That is why I am not asking you." She held the pelt close as cold wind whistled around the shutters. "I am asking you to tell me where Guy went. Or did Guy ask you to keep that a secret, too?"

The boy's eyes twinkled. "*He* did not order me not to reveal that, milady. He is riding to Canterbury."

"Why? To attend Philip de Boisvert's wedding?" Her stomach cramped because she was certain of the answer.

His expression became somber again. "Last night in the hall, Lord de Sommeville announced there has been a call throughout the south to prepare for battle if Becket decides to fight, as he did before he was elevated to archbishop."

"How could Christian be so foolish?" She had hoped the queen's greatest fear for her godson would not be realized, but it had.

Baldwin scowled, resembling his cousin more than ever. "Milady, don't you understand? He is being foolish because he knows your father would never give you to a man of questionable courage."

"When did he leave?"

"Two hours past midnight."

"And it is almost dawn. If we—"

The door opened, and Lord de Vere walked in. He scanned the room before his gaze settled on her. With a smile, he said, "I am glad to find you awake, Avisa."

She bowed her head. "Milord, happy Christmas."

He kissed her on each cheek. "Happy Christmas to you, daughter. I bring you joyous tidings on this special day. Put on your finest gown, and join me in the hall, where I will be announcing your betrothal to Lord Fitz-Allan's eldest son."

"Betrothal?" she choked. "But how could you have arranged a betrothal so quickly?"

"Fitz-Allan lost his brother in the debacle when Lovell's cowardice humiliated the king. He knows how eager I am to have my gullible daughter escape the influence of a craven's son." He ignored Baldwin's grumble at the insult. "His son is well respected and resides at the king's court. Your marriage will bring even more honor to our family."

"Must the betrothal be announced immediately?" she asked, searching her mind for an excuse to postpone it long enough for her to slip out of the castle.

"Why delay? Can you think of a better way to celebrate Christmas?"

"I have not yet attended Mass."

"That can wait. There will be a Mass with your wedding."

She shook her head. "The abbess reminds us every year that Christmas came from Christ's Mass, and we must never fail to celebrate that special Mass amidst the other festivities."

"You are not in the Abbey now."

"Please." She dropped to her knees and held up her hands. "It means so much to me."

Her father clasped her hands. "Very well. Griswold will wait in the corridor to escort you to Mass and then to the hall."

"Thank you." She stared at the floor, so he did not see her dismay. Her father did not trust her, and she had to admit he was wise not to. Leaving the castle would be much more complicated than she had hoped. "I need to dress and change Baldwin's bandaging before attending Mass."

Her father frowned at the page, but nodded. As he drew her to her feet, he kissed her again on each cheek. "Fitz-Allan's son is a good man. You will be happy with him."

"Thank you, milord." She stared at the floor and did not raise her eyes until she heard the door shut behind her father. "Farewell, Father," she whispered. If she was successful, she doubted he would ever claim her again as his daughter.

Baldwin bounced off the bed. "Lady Avisa, you cannot be seriously considering that betrothal!"

"Hush!" She put her finger to her lips. "Can you ride?"

"I can if I must, but we do not have horses."

She smiled. "My father and his men would have brought good ones for such a long journey. They should be rested."

"But what good do they do us?"

"Not us. You. If you ride after Christian, you can let him know I need his help here."

"I cannot. I promised to remain with you."

"But—" She sighed, knowing the boy would not be budged from doing as he had vowed. "All right. Then we will have to try something else."

"What? You are under guard."

She considered the question as she paced the room. When the door opened again, she stiffened. Her shoulders relaxed when she saw her sisters from St. Jude's Abbey. They wore cloaks and carried small sacks. Ermangardine stared at the floor as she had the day before, but Mavise stepped forward.

"Avisa, I urge you to join us."

"I cannot. I have work still to do." Avisa put her arm around Baldwin's shoulders. "*We* have work to do."

"Sir Christian knows you were sent by the queen, so nothing you say or do will keep him from going to Canterbury."

"He has already left."

Mavise shuddered. "If the situation there is as incendiary as it is rumored to be, he may well arrive to find the archbishop's allies and the king's in battle."

"You have heard something?"

The blonde nodded. "It is being said throughout the hall that Becket believes himself to be more powerful than any one mortal man should be."

"That is true, for he challenges the king for England."

"I fear he has gone mad, Avisa, from suffering great pain left by a surgery during his exile. Not even prayer has released him from the scourge that compelled a doctor to remove pieces of rotten bone from his jaw."

"Only a madman would make the decisions he has made since his return. Everything he does seems aimed at infuriating people, so instead of gaining the people's love, he is estranging them with his single-minded resolve to force the king to acknowledge his omniscience."

"And that is infuriating the barons."

"I know. That is why I must stop Christian from going to Canterbury."

"But he will not heed you." She put her hand on Avisa's shoulder. "It is unfortunate that he learned the truth, but what has been said has been said, and it is too late to change it."

"It is not too late," Avisa argued.

"My sister, I have long admired how clearly you see. You must not let your heart cloud your eyes. It *is* too late."

"No!" She turned away. "The queen bid me to protect her godson, and I shall do that as long I possess a single breath of life." She bit her lip as she recalled speaking those same words to Christian on the wall.

"Because you love him."

Looking at Mavise in astonishment, Avisa whispered, "How did you know?"

"There is no question of the love between you."

"But that love cannot change my promise to the queen. I vowed to do whatever was necessary to keep Christian from Canterbury, and I shall."

"Be careful," Mavise said. "You could be hurt."

I can never be hurt worse than I have been. "I know."

"What can we do to help?"

Avisa smiled at her sisters and then at Baldwin, who was listening in openmouthed shock. He must not have heard the truth. She would explain to him later. For now . . . She paced the room, then paused when she saw the medical pouch on the bed. Opening it, she pulled out the ball of thick thread. She tossed it across the room, holding one end. There must be ten or more feet of thread.

"I am going to Mass," she said as she faced her three helpers. "The chapel will be full, so it should be easy to put some space between me and my father's man."

"Tell us what you wish us to do," Ermangardine said, her head rising at last.

"First, I have a task for Baldwin."

Excitement lit his face. "What do you wish me to do, mi-lady?"

"Use the thread with this fabric." She gave the bed-curtains a tug. "While I dress, take these down and slice them into strips. We will weave them and the thread into a rope."

With Mavise's help, it did not take Avisa long to change into her traveling clothes and collect her weapons. She explained her plan, and Mavise helped her refine it so there was a chance of such a wild idea working. Giving her sword and cloak to Baldwin, she lashed her dagger to her leg. He handed her the rope he had created, and she smiled. The embroidery on it was still visible. Wrapping it around her waist several times, she tied it so the ends just brushed the tops of her shoes.

"How do I look?" she asked.

The page grinned. "Like nothing is unusual."

"Good!" She put her hand on his shoulder. "After we leave for Mass, go to the stables. I will meet you there. Wait an hour, and if I have not come, return here."

Avisa opened the door and motioned to her sisters to follow. When her father's man stepped forward, neither she nor the other women acknowledged him. They walked down the stairs with Griswold following like a malevolent shadow. He opened the door to the chapel, and they went in.

As she had expected, the chapel was full. The priest and his assistant were standing by the altar, and by their words she knew the service had just begun.

Lowering her voice, she said, "Griswold, I am going over to the side where there is more room."

"Milady—"

She ignored him and edged between the other worshipers who were standing shoulder to shoulder at the back of the chapel. Mavise and Ermangardine followed. Many of the worshipers moaned as she brushed past them, and she guessed they were suffering from too much ale. Glancing back, she saw Griswold watching her, but making no attempt to follow through the press of worshipers.

When the others knelt, she did the same. It was hard to be patient until they were brought to their feet again. She went to her knees and rose twice more before she reached the baptismal font.

"*Kyrie eleison, Christi eleison, Kyrie eleison,*" intoned the priest.

His assistant repeated the words before beginning a prayer.

Avisa loosened the knot of the sash around her waist. Letting each section of the rope slide slowly down, she was glad when the congregation knelt again. She drew one end of the rope around the base of the baptismal font. Her hands clenched at her sides when the worshipers were brought to their feet before she could secure the rope.

Her father's man was watching her closely. She kept her head bowed over her hands. She had to get one end of the rope tied and the other out the window before Mass was over. She had only one more opportunity.

When it came, she was on her knees instantly. She struggled to tie the thick rope in place before anyone noticed what she was doing. Looking at Griswold, she was pleased to see he was kneeling, too.

She knotted the rope and gave it a tug. Her elbow bumped into the person beside her. Murmuring an apology, she inched beneath the font with the other end of the rope. She had to grope for the window, because she did not dare to look. That might call attention to her.

She found the sill and shoved the rope onto it. Feeding the rope across the wide sill, she waited for the tension that would tell her the end had fallen out of the window. It did not come. What was wrong?

As the priest called to them to rise, she saw the rope snaked across the wide sill. A lip at the window's edge had kept it on the sill. Standing, she flicked the rope once, then a second time. She smiled as the rope pulled against her. It had fallen over the edge. She released the rope and let it drop its full length, taking care that it did not loosen the knots.

When the priest blessed the congregation, she made sure

she and her sisters were standing between the rope and Griswold's view. She took a cautious step toward the window, then halted when the priest called for the worshipers to share a kiss of peace. As the congregation began to comply with many wishes of peace and Christmas joy, she knew this was her best chance for escape.

Giving a pretty woman a kiss on the cheek and wishing her peace, Avisa added, "See that big man by the door? He is a stranger within these walls, and he should be made welcome on Christmas morn, don't you think?"

The woman smiled and pushed through the crowd to go to offer a kiss to Griswold.

Avisa smiled when she heard Mavise saying the same to another attractive maiden. That woman followed the first.

As soon as they reached him and caught his attention, Avisa bent to whisper, "Once I am on the ground, release the rope and let it fall through the window."

Ermangardine nodded as she squatted beneath the stone font.

"Give us an hour or two before you leave, so nobody connects you with us."

Mavise smiled. "Go! You are wasting time telling us what we already know."

Avisa kissed Mavise's cheek. "Travel with God's blessing." She turned to Ermangardine and smiled before stepping on the base of the font and swinging onto the windowsill. She sat there for a moment, offering kisses of peace to all around her. As they were busy sharing the good wishes with others, she motioned quickly to Mavise. The blonde sat on the sill as Avisa turned to swing her legs out the window.

Avisa smiled as her sister squeezed her hand for good luck. She hoped the others in the chapel were suffering enough from their night with so many tankards of ale that they would not notice a different blond woman sat on the sill. Whispering her thanks, she slid out the window and down the rope.

It reached to within five feet of the ground. She released the rope and dropped to roll down the grassy side of the dry moat. The impact almost knocked the breath out of her, but she scrambled to her feet as the makeshift rope tumbled to the ground. Gathering it up, she ran before someone looked out the chapel's window.

Baldwin was waiting at the stable when she arrived. His young face brightened, but he said nothing as, with a few half-truths, she persuaded a stableboy to bring Lord de Vere's horse and those of his companions to the baron's daughter. While she waited, she wrapped the rope back around her waist, although she hoped she would not need it again.

She led the horses, two grays and a black, out of the inner ward and through the outer ward. Few people were outside, and those who were appeared much the worse for the night's entertainments. Saying nothing to Baldwin, she went through the gate and out onto the road beyond the castle's walls. He gave her a curious look when she kept walking. She stopped when they entered a small copse.

"You succeeded, milady!" Baldwin regarded her with admiration. "Was it difficult to elude your guardian?"

"Not a problem at all, but we must go before someone gets the idea to check the stable. Let me give you a hand up."

He did not argue, and she hoped he was hale enough for the journey. With luck, they would not have to go all the way to Canterbury, but they must be prepared for the long ride.

When he was settled in the saddle atop the stronger gray, she drew the black horse toward a boulder. She clambered onto the rock and then onto the horse's back. The horse shifted beneath her, but she controlled him with a few calming words. Her father's destrier would be stronger and able to go farther at a faster pace than any horses Christian could have obtained for himself and his brother.

She hoped it would be fast enough to keep him from throwing away his life to prove his courage.

*   *   *

"Are you a coward like your father, Lovell, or are you going to show that you are different?" demanded the armed knight across the table from Christian. The room, in a filthy house just outside the Canterbury city wall, was barely lit. "Are you with us?"

Christian looked around the large table. More than a dozen men sat at it. He recognized most from the king's court on the other side of the Channel. He could tell by their salt-encrusted clothes that they had recently taken the twelve-hour journey across that stormy sea. Chain mail and weapons were stacked in the corners. Their leaders seemed to be William de Tracy, Richard le Bret, and Hugh de Morville, all men close to Christian's father's age. They were considered to be among the king's most faithful knights.

When Guy had met de Tracy on the street just as the sun was beginning to go down, the knight had insisted that he and Christian have a drink with him before going to de Boisvert's house. Hadn't they come to Canterbury, Guy had asked, to answer the king's call to protect England from the archbishop's machinations? De Tracy was sure to know where the king's allies were gathering.

Christian had agreed to come to this house near St. Augustine's Abbey, but instead of the grand heroes he had expected, he had found this cache of knights who were drinking heavily, with every swallow growing more confident of the king's wish to see Becket dead. All of them were now staring at Christian as they awaited his answer.

Guy jumped to his feet, holding up his tankard. "I am with you. It sounds like a grand adventure. Join us, Christian."

"For what?" Christian stood, too. "The king would not order the archbishop killed."

"He asked us to deal with Becket, whom he called a low-born clerk," de Tracy said, reaching for the jug to refill his tankard.

"King Henry is renowned for his temper. Did he say that in the midst of fury?"

De Tracy slammed his tankard on the table. "He has every reason to be enraged. Becket has been using excommunication as a weapon to undermine the throne." Taking a drink, he scowled. "We must do the king's will, or we will be the cowards he labeled us."

Guy put his hand on Christian's shoulder. To show brotherhood or to keep himself on his feet? "Why are you hesitating? Here is your opportunity to do exactly what you have said you must do. Join us, and you can prove to the king and the kingdom that you are a man of great courage."

"By cutting down an unarmed cleric?"

"By doing the king's will," snarled one of the men.

"And you shall have fair Avisa." Guy laughed as ale ran over his chin. "Isn't that what you want?"

"Who is Avisa?" someone asked.

Guy leaned one hand on the table, clearly enjoying his chance to be the focus of the conversation. "Avisa de Vere, a cloistered woman at St. Jude's Abbey, has broken my brother's heart even as he was breaking her maidenhead. She has played him for every kind of fool."

Christian's fist was driving into his brother's stomach before he even realized, through his blinding rage, what he was doing. Guy threw the tankard at him, and Christian ducked beneath his brother's wildly flailing fists. Thrusting Guy up against the wall, he held his brother's shoulders against the wide planks until Guy stopped trying to escape.

"You will," Christian said past clenched teeth, "always speak of Avisa with respect."

"I meant her no insult," Guy replied with a drunken grin. "She is a very shrewd woman. *You* are her fool."

Giving his brother another shove, Christian cursed.

"Are you done?" drawled de Tracy, wiping his hand across his mouth to brush away foam. "We are waiting for your answer, Lovell."

"I told you," Guy began, "that—"

"We know your answer." De Tracy grabbed Guy's arm in a warrior's clasp and pulled him down to sit at the table again. The bench rocked beneath them, and they roared a laugh. A full tankard was pushed toward Guy as the knight looked at Christian. "We are waiting on yours, Lovell. Your father failed Henry Curtmantle at one of his lowest hours." His voice dropped to a threatening growl. "Will you fail King Henry, too?"

"Never!" Christian took the ale someone pushed into his hand. "I have pledged to serve the king. I will not fail him, not tonight or ever."

"To glory and honor!" shouted someone.

All the men surged to their feet. "To glory and honor!" They clanked their tankards together and drank.

Christian wondered if anyone else's ale was as bitter as his.

Chapter 22

Canterbury was even grander than Avisa had imagined. Within the city walls, the buildings gathered together on streets that reached out from the cathedral. As she walked with the tired horses and the exhausted page through the dark, cramped streets, she saw no one. The doorways were bedecked with greenery, but no voices were raised in song, no games were spilling out into the street to mark the coming of midnight and the next day of revelry, no trickery was bringing laughs from passersby. The usual Christmas celebrations had vanished, leaving a sense of imminent disaster hanging in the air along with the thick smoke.

At St. Jude's Abbey, the sisters would be celebrating the feast day of St. Albert, the founder of a Benedictine abbey. December 29 was always a feast day. It should have been a feast day in Canterbury, too, because the cloistered brothers within the cathedral's walls were Benedictines.

The silence was ominous, and Avisa found herself looking over her shoulder often. She saw nobody but Baldwin.

"This way," the page said, turning to the left into a small courtyard not far from the wall separating the cathedral from the rest of the city.

The house at the back of the empty yard was lit well against the winter darkness. A pair of wagons were parked in front of it, and there were signs in the frozen mud of many people and horses coming and going.

The page hammered his fist on the front door. When it opened, he spoke in a low voice to the man in the doorway before motioning to Avisa to join him. A boy rushed out to take the horses. She nodded her thanks to him.

When she entered the house, she closed her eyes and relished escaping the cold night's wind. Relaxing must wait. She needed to find out if Christian was here.

"I am Lady Avisa de Vere," she said when the servant asked why they had come to the door. She glanced around the entry. A staircase led up from the left side, and a single low door was half open on the other. The wall in front of them held a niche with a pair of candles burning in it. "My companion is Baldwin Lovell, who serves as a page to Sir Christian Lovell. Sir Christian is an invited guest to the wedding to be held in this house."

The man bowed deeply. "Milady, you are welcome on such a cold night. If you will wait here, I will have a chamber prepared for you."

"Has Sir Christian Lovell arrived?" she called as the man started up the narrow stairs.

"Not yet, milady."

Beside her, Baldwin snarled Christian's favorite oath. She was tempted to repeat it. They had not passed Christian and Guy on the road to Canterbury. Could they have gone somewhere else? Where? To Lovell Mote? That made no sense. The boy had been unshakably certain that Christian and his brother were bound for this city.

"Would they be staying with someone else in Canterbury?" Avisa asked.

Baldwin rubbed his hands. "He always stays here."

"Is there another place they might have stopped?"

"Each time you asked along the way if Sir Christian had passed that way, we were always told yes."

"Then where are they, Baldwin? Does Lord Lovell keep a house in the city?"

"Baldwin? Lord Lovell?" asked a man who was stepping out of the room to the right. His brown robes and the cruci-

fix on his chest identified him as a holy man. The few wisps
of hair still on his head were pale white. With a face as wrinkled as tree bark, he moved with the caution of a man who
had brittle bones. He peered at them, then smiled. "Baldwin
Lovell, you were little more than a suckling when I last saw
you."

"Who are you?" asked the boy.

He laughed. "I am not surprised you do not remember
me, for, other than that quick trip back to Lovell Mote
around the time you were born, I have been serving in the
archbishop's household. I am Father James, your uncle's
priest."

Avisa stared in amazement. Father James was one of the
people Christian had suggested might know the truth about
what had happened the day Lord Lovell was condemned as
a coward.

"Who is your companion, Baldwin?" Father James
smiled.

Barely waiting for the boy to introduce them, Avisa
asked, "Have you seen Sir Christian?"

The priest shook his head. "Not for many years. I had
hoped for a chance to see him one final time before I die."

"To tell him the truth about what happened in 1147?" she
asked, knowing she had nothing left to lose.

He glanced at the door to the street, then motioned for
them to follow him into the room to the right. It was barely
more than a cupboard with a hearth. A bench was set beside
the fire. An unlighted lamp hung from the rafters, rocking in
the heat rising from the flames. He drew the door closed, but
it would not shut completely.

Baldwin opened it again and stepped outside, his determined expression showing he would allow no one past to in-
terrupt them.

"He is a Lovell," Father James said with a proud smile.
"Not one in that family lacks for courage, as well as a sense
of doing what is right, no matter the cost."

Avisa was tempted to ask the priest if he had met Guy

lately, but she was not going to waste this chance to find out the truth. "You speak with confidence of their courage, Father. What do you know that others don't?"

"As you know, milady, I cannot speak of what was shared in the confessional." He motioned for her to sit.

She continued to stand. If she sat, fatigue might overcome her. "I understand that, but can't you tell me something? It is imperative. Christian may be risking his life needlessly in an effort to show he has courage."

"It is fortunate that I was a witness to the events myself, so I may be able to tell you what you want to know." He folded his hands behind him.

"You will?" She should not be questioning her good fortune.

"Yes." He glanced at the bench with obvious longing.

Avisa sat, knowing Father James would not while she stood.

As soon as he was sitting, the priest said, "You are curious why I would tell you what I know."

"Yes." She added nothing else, because any word could be the one that persuaded him to change his mind about divulging the truth.

"I have seen too many battles, but none have upset me more than the one between the king and Archbishop Thomas. This afternoon, I heard that the king has sent knights to slay the archbishop."

"No!" She could not imagine King Henry ordering something so terrible.

"It is a rumor being whispered behind closed doors throughout the city. I do not want any Lovell pulled into the maelstrom if the cathedral is attacked."

"To prove his courage?" she choked.

"Needlessly." He slanted toward her, lowering his voice. "I recall that day in 1147 more clearly than any other day before or since. Henry was losing badly. If someone did not change the course of the foray against Stephen, he would have had to acknowledge the claim of Stephen and

Stephen's heirs to the throne. That was when Lord Lovell made an astonishing decision to go to King Stephen."

"And that is why he left the king?"

"Yes. I traveled with him when he went to speak with King Stephen. Unbeknownst to anyone, Lord Lovell arranged for Henry and his men to leave England in exchange for Henry's not returning for at least five years. Lord Lovell even persuaded Stephen to fund the costs of King Henry's return to the Continent. He saved the king at the cost of his own name."

Avisa whispered, "Why have you kept this a secret?"

"Lord Lovell did not want to humiliate King Henry. He felt it was better to be a dishonored baron than to have a dishonored king."

"And that must never change," said a voice from behind her.

Avisa came to her feet as Baldwin bowed his head and closed the door behind a man who had to be Lord Lovell. He had the same dark hair as his sons, and she could easily imagine Christian looking like him in twenty years.

"Father James," he said in the tightly controlled voice she had heard Christian use when he was furious, "I had not guessed you would repeat that story."

The priest stood and pyramided his fingers in front of him. "Milord, your son is the king's man. I am Becket's man. I had hoped, if your son knew the truth, he would not raise a weapon against the archbishop."

Lord Lovell said nothing, and the two men stared at each other. The priest lowered his eyes first. He pulled open the door and walked out.

"You must be Lady Avisa de Vere," the baron said as he bowed over her hand. "You have chosen a poor time to come to Canterbury."

"I came in search of your sons and the truth."

"My sons?"

"Christian heard of the king's call to his lieges to halt Becket's attempts to divide the country, and he has traveled to Canterbury to serve the king and show he is not a coward as you were falsely labeled." She bowed. "Milord, you must excuse me."

"Where do you go?"

"To find Christian."

"If you intend to tell him what Father James has told you, you cannot. No one else must know the truth."

She stared, sure she had misunderstood. "But why would you want me to keep the truth a secret any longer?"

"For the same reason it has not been spoken of for twenty-three years."

"But the king securely holds his throne now."

"Does he?" He bent forward to stir the fire. "If Henry believed that, do you think he would have had the young king coronated in June? He is anxious that his heir have the support of the barons and the church."

"Not even the archbishop would be so bold as to excommunicate the king."

He laughed humorlessly. "Becket has nothing to lose, except his life, so who knows what he might do when each breath may be his last?"

Avisa waved that aside. The archbishop had dozens of people watching over him. "Christian needs to know the truth."

"My son is strong enough to endure what he has endured all his life. If the truth becomes widely known, the barons might revolt against the king, sending the country into civil war again."

"I understand that, milord. What you do not understand is that Christian has another reason for needing to show his courage."

"To win you?"

"Not to win me, for he has my heart, but to persuade my father he is worthy of marrying his daughter."

A shout came from the hall. The door slammed against the wall, and two lads rolled into the room, wrestling.

Lord Lovell grasped each by the tunic and yanked them

apart. Baldwin's face was red where he had been struck. The other boy, his brown hair falling in his eyes, was bleeding from the nose. He wiped it on his brown wool sleeve.

"He would not stop!" Baldwin shouted.

"I must see Father James," the other boy said.

"Who are you?" asked the baron, releasing both boys.

"Eustace of the archbishop's household. I must speak with Father James. I must warn him to stay away from the cathedral."

Avisa asked, "Why?"

"There are four knights in the archbishop's bedchamber. They intend to do him harm."

"Are they armed?"

"No, but they are angry." He wiped his sleeve across his nose. "They must plan to do my master harm, because they have weapons stacked by a mulberry tree in the courtyard. They are saying they will prove to the king they are not cowards by ridding the world of Archbishop Thomas."

"Who are they?" asked Lord Lovell.

The boy shook his head. "I heard only one named. William de Tracy."

"De Tracy," she repeated in a whisper. She had heard Christian speak his name several times with respect. If that brave knight was in Canterbury, it was likely that Christian was at his side. But would Christian be part of a plan to hurt the archbishop? Was being labeled a brave knight worth the risk of eternal damnation?

Lord Lovell sent Baldwin to bring the priest. As the baron continued to question the boy, Avisa slipped out into the darkness. She stared at the cathedral walls. Somewhere within its grounds, Christian could be participating in the murder of a holy man.

People crowded the street, drawn out of their shuttered homes by tales of knights within the cathedral. They held brands high to light the street. Some were heading toward the cathedral, but she pushed past them, hurrying along the curving street. The people slowed as they approached the cathedral's gate. She did not.

Nobody stood within the gate. The brothers must have sought a place to hide. As Avisa entered the precincts, she looked at a large building which must be the Archbishop's Palace. She drew her sword when she heard footfalls behind her. Whirling, she saw nobody. The shadows could have concealed an army.

"*Réaux, réaux!*" The shout echoed through the cathedral's precincts.

She halted in midstep. That was the call for the king's men to gather. How many knights were descending on the cathedral?

Her arm was grabbed by a monk. "Run, if you value your life, maiden!"

"Where are the intruders?"

He pointed at the hall before fleeing.

Avisa ran toward the large building. Knights were answering the call. She drew aside and watched them pass. With the four who had entered the archbishop's hall, there must be a dozen of the king's men within the cathedral's walls. But she had not seen Christian.

She followed the men into a wide yard. A mulberry tree grew near the hall's door. The knights were assembling there. Their shouts rang through the courtyard like bizarre bells.

"Christian Lovell!" she called.

The men froze as they were dressing for battle, save for one who stepped forward when she reached the tree. Beneath his blue tunic, Christian was dressed in full mail that glistened in the light from the hall.

"Avisa! What are you doing here?"

"I gave the queen a vow that I would protect you," she said.

As some of the men chortled, he took her by the arm and led her away from the knights. "Avisa, you are not a knight. You should not be here."

"Neither should you."

"These are the king's men. They were given orders to stop Becket from destroying England."

"By killing a priest?"

He kept pulling her farther from the other men. "Avisa, it is a matter of honor."

"You don't believe that! You know it is wrong to slay an unarmed man. What sort of honor is there in that?"

"The king wills it," he said. Then, looking over his shoulder, he lowered his voice. "I don't think anyone can hear us here. Avisa, you must go now!"

"Not until you do. Sometimes a courageous man must stand up to his king and say he will not do another wrong."

"God's blood, Avisa! I do not need you acting as my conscience."

"Because you know it is wrong?"

"Of course it is wrong." He pulled her to him and kissed her with the longing honed by their days apart.

She wanted to stay in his arms, but she drew back. "You know it is wrong? So why are you here?"

"To keep Guy from damning himself."

"Where is he?"

"That is what I am trying to discover."

"But I vowed to stay with you, to protect you," she whispered.

He touched her face lightly with his fingers covered with chain mail. "There are times when vows have to be set aside. I vowed to the king to obey his orders without question, but I cannot kill the archbishop. You vowed to the queen to protect me, but my brother needs greater protection. Would following our vows tonight please those to whom we have pledged?"

"No," she choked out. "Go, and save him!"

"When I know you are safe."

Even though she wanted to stay to help him, she nodded. She shoved her sword in its scabbard and kissed him quickly. As he turned to join the other knights, she ran back toward the gate. Every step was harder than the previous one.

"Forgive me, my queen," she whispered.

The gate was filled with people curious about what was happening within the cathedral but too frightened to find out for themselves. Questions were shouted at her. She ignored them as she pushed through the gate.

"Lady Avisa!"

She looked around and gasped when she saw Father James standing on the street corner across from the gate. In the light of the brands, he appeared even older.

"Father," she said as she put her hand under his elbow, "you should not be out here. Let me take you back to—"

"Did you see the boy?"

"Eustace? Yes."

"No! Baldwin! Did you see him within the cathedral's grounds?"

Avisa reeled back as if the priest had struck her. "Baldwin?"

"He is not in the house, and a boy matching his description was seen by several of the brothers who have left the cathedral grounds."

"He is in there, too?"

"Too? You found Sir Christian?"

She did not wait to answer his question. Elbowing her way back through the crowd, she winced when someone stepped on her toes. She kept going. When she burst out of the press beneath the gate, she saw several monks hiding behind bushes.

Only one man stood beneath the mulberry tree. He tilted a bare sword to catch the light as she neared. "Go home, wench," he snarled.

"I am looking for a boy!" she called. "Baldwin Lovell, page to Sir Christian Lovell."

"Go home!"

She tried to edge around him, but his sword halted her. He laughed when she drew her own. His laugh vanished moments later when she knocked his sword from his hand and ran past him. He shouted after her. She did not slow. He would not follow because then he would have to admit that he had been beaten by a woman.

Avisa pressed back against a wall when she saw a group of men skulking between what she guessed were the cloisters and the cathedral. The monks peered from the windows, but did nothing to halt the knights.

She ran parallel to the knights, looking for Christian. The mail coifs and the darkness made it difficult to tell one man from another.

A hand clamped over her mouth as she was pulled back against the cathedral's walls. The mail pressed against her lips, and she tasted her own blood. The arm around her kept her from swinging her sword. She rammed her foot into her captor's leg and heard the clink of more mail.

"God's breath, Avisa!" came a hiss close to her ear. "You don't have the good sense God gave an ox."

Christian! She halted her efforts to escape and nodded as he told her to be silent when he released her.

He drew her into the shadows. "Why didn't you leave?"

"I did, but Baldwin is somewhere in here."

He swore savagely. "I will find him."

"I will help you."

"Avisa, these men are intent on murder. You cannot be a part of that."

She knew he was making sense, but she could not leave when Baldwin might be hurt or worse. "Where are they bound?"

"The archbishop was seen going into the Chapel of St. Benedict." He pointed toward a door on a section of the building jutting into the yard. "It is in the cross-aisle there. I will search for Baldwin near the chapel."

"I will look in the nave."

"Why would he go there?"

She smiled. "Because he is as pigheaded as the rest of the Lovells and just as cunning. He suspects you and Guy are with your fellow knights, and that you would stop him if he encounters you."

"So he would sneak in another way?"

"Yes."

"Lovell, where are you?" called a voice from the darkness.

"Go," she urged.

"Take care, Avisa." He kissed her before vanishing into the night.

She hurried in the opposite direction. Entering the nave, she pressed back in the shadows when she saw two knights talking a few feet away. They were passing a flask between them and bragging how they would stop anyone from coming to Becket's aid.

She glanced at the gallery above and saw no one. Clinging to the shadows, she found the closest staircase and climbed. She rushed along the gallery when she saw a motion at the far end near the Lady Chapel. Another knight? Or could it be Baldwin?

It was both, she realized, when she got closer. The boy was fighting off a knight who was laughing drunkenly. When Baldwin's sword was knocked from his hand, rattling across the stone floor, the knight crowed with triumph.

Avisa started to draw her sword, then realized she could not reach him in time. She untied the rope the boy had made from around her waist. Checking the distance and angle, she lashed it to a pillar supporting the upper gallery. She quickly tested the knots, then holding the other end, she climbed onto the stone railing just as the knight raised his sword to drive it into the boy.

"Leave him alone!" she shouted, her voice echoing off the roof far above her head.

The knight looked up, startled, then laughed again.

Holding the rope tightly, she jumped from the railing at the same moment he started to swing the sword. Every muscle in her shoulders protested, but she held her feet out in front of her. She struck the knight in the shoulders. He crashed forward into an iron lamp. As she released the rope before she could swing back up toward the other side of the nave, she drew her sword.

There was no need, for the man was motionless on the floor.

Looking at Baldwin, she started to smile.

"Behind you, milady!" he shouted.

Avisa spun to see the two knights by the door charging them. She hoped they were as intoxicated as the knight who had attacked Baldwin.

As the closer one swung at her, she knew he was almost sober. He hit her sword, knocking her back against the unconscious knight. He pressed his advantage as she tried to edge around the body. Behind her, she heard frantic shouts. Had the knights found the archbishop?

Agony flared through her when his sword sliced through her cloak and into her left side. She tumbled backward over the knight. Baldwin screamed for help, but the pain was even louder in her. Where was her sword? She had not even realized she had let go of it. Where was it?

The knight planted one foot on either side of her and lifted his sword to drive it into her heart. She groped for her knife. Was this her punishment for breaking her vow to the queen by letting Christian go with the other knights? She could not die. Not now. Not when there was so much left unsaid between them.

"Christian," she moaned, fearing it would be her last word.

"For King Henry!" shouted the knight. "Die, you—"

The knight abruptly staggered to one side and collapsed on the floor. He did not move, and she heard pounding feet fleeing along the nave. Had Baldwin escaped?

She struggled to get to her feet. Hands under her right arm brought her up slowly. She looked over her shoulder to see Christian behind her. Beside him, Baldwin was holding the makeshift rope.

"I heard your shouts," Christian said as he carefully lifted her into his arms and against the tunic over his mail. "I came into the nave just in time to see you swinging down to rescue Baldwin."

"So you thought you should try it yourself?" She smiled, then winced as pain shot through her.

"Baldwin, cut the rope down. Bring it with you and meet us at de Boisvert's house. There can be no signs of what happened here."

The boy sprinted toward the stairs as Christian stepped over the prone bodies.

More shouts came from behind them.

"Archbishop Thomas!" she gasped, then groaned as every breath hurt more.

"He is already dead," Christian said grimly. "There was nothing anyone could do to stop them in their drunken madness."

"Guy—"

"Was with them. I could not stop him either. That is why, when I heard you shouting, I came to help you." He bent his head into the cold wind that swirled around them as they emerged from the cathedral. "So it seems you may have done as you promised the queen after all, Avisa."

She strained to speak, not wanting to lose consciousness along with the blood seeping down her side. "What do you mean?"

"Your shouts saved me from taking part in murdering a defenseless man, a most dishonorable act. Guy has tarnished our family's name further tonight."

"Not further. Father James told me . . ." She moaned.

"Tell me later. Just be silent until we get you back to de Boisvert's where we can tend to your wound. You have tended to so many of ours, we owe you much care."

"Christian—"

"Hush, Avisa. Save your strength for healing."

"But I have to tell you that I love you."

"Avisa . . ."

She looked up at his face, lit by the torches they passed.

They must already be beyond the cathedral's gate. "You do not need to say anything, Christian, but I had to tell you. I love you."

"But I must say something," he said as softly as she had spoken. "These past days without you have left me with an empty feeling inside. I had intended to return to tell your father that he could not marry you to another nor could he send you back to St. Jude's Abbey. I love you, Avisa. You belong to me."

"*With* you," she corrected weakly. "I am not anyone's possession."

He laughed. "You are right. You belong *with* me, Avisa."

Epilogue

The grounds of St. Jude's Abbey were bright with spring blossoms, and every face was filled with joy. Music swirled on the breeze while minstrels performed tricks, to the delight of those gathered in front of the chapel.

Avisa checked the flowers in her hair, which was loose around her shoulders. Her gown was scarlet silk, a gift from her father, who had given his blessing for her wedding now that the truth about the Lovell family was being spread across England. Around her neck, she wore a gold chain, a gift from the queen.

"You look perfect," Christian said as he took her hand. In his finest clothes, his tunic the same color as her gown, he was so handsome she wondered if she could tear her eyes from him long enough to acknowledge the priest during the wedding ceremony. He bent to kiss her.

"A vow once taken into the heart cannot be broken."

At the unfamiliar voice, Christian released her. She reached for her sword as she saw a man who looked as ancient as the stones in the Abbey's walls. His hair and his robe were the same dirty gray. He leaned on a thick branch. He was no stranger. She had seen him in the great hall at Castle Orxted.

"Now you understand, don't you, young Lovell?" the old man asked.

"You were speaking of what my father did for the king," Christian said quietly.

"And of you, for you are much like he was before he accepted dishonor to save his king."

"How do you know of this?"

"Like Pyt, I was once King Stephen's man." He straightened. "I stood by the king's side when a brash young man named Robert Lovell came with an astounding offer to allow his king to live and King Stephen to hold the throne a while longer. He saved many lives that day. I see you took my advice, young Lovell, and your lady remains alive."

Christian laughed. "She taught Pyt a lesson all on her own."

"So I have heard in great detail." The old man smiled. "Her courage is already legendary among the outlawed. She is a worthy match for the son of Robert Lovell."

"Why are you here?"

"To ask you to even the debt you owe me."

"Ask what you will, and, if it is in my power, it shall be yours."

The old man's smile widened. "You are a man of honor, just like your father." He held out his hand. "You have something that belongs to me, something your brother stole upon our first meeting."

Avisa watched as Christian drew the ring with the glass bead from the pouch he always wore. He placed it in the old man's hand. The swirling lines seemed to float in the reflection of the sunlight on the glass.

"Use it with care," Christian said. "You said it has great power."

"It does, but not within the borders of England. It belongs to the misty moors and mountains of Wales. I will return it there to its rightful owner." He bowed his head and, leaning on the branch, hobbled away.

"I hope that was the right thing to do," Christian mused.

"It was the honorable thing to do." Avisa grinned. "And you are most honorable, my brave knight." She started to add more, but paused when a bouquet of flowers was held out to her. She smiled and took them from the girl who knelt, holding up her hands as if she held the small sword beginning students used.

"Thank you, Fayre," she said. She had not been surprised to find the young farm girl at St. Jude's Abbey when she returned a month ago after a lengthy recovery from the wound inflicted in the cathedral. Fayre had been eager to learn what St. Jude's Abbey had to teach.

"Thank *you*, milady." She bounced to her feet and ran toward the chapel's porch, where the wedding guests were gathering.

"*My* lady of St. Jude's Abbey," Queen Eleanor corrected as she readjusted the flowers in Avisa's hair.

Avisa knelt along with Christian, astonished that the king was standing beside Queen Eleanor. It had been said that the king would not set foot in England again until he was ready to do penance for Becket's murder. She doubted anyone else had known of his plans to return secretly to England, and she was speechless that he had come to St. Jude's Abbey on this special day.

The king ordered them to rise. He was no longer the resplendent, arrogant young man the queen had wed. Time had stolen the color from his hair and lined his face. She wondered how many wrinkles had appeared since he had heard of his knights slaying his onetime friend.

"We are honored, your majesty," Christian said, squeezing her hand.

"I thought you would like to know what has happened to your brother and the others who at Christmas mistook my angry words for an order."

She bit her lip. There had been many rumors flying about that the knights would be executed for killing the archbishop.

"Do not look so dismayed, Lady Avisa," the king said, smiling as his gaze swept along her. She recalled that the king's reputation for enjoying women other than his wife in his bed had not changed with the passing of time. "They have been sent to the Holy Land, where they may atone for their sins by serving in the Crusade."

Avisa was unsure how more killing would wipe away the horror of killing the archbishop. She glanced at Christian and saw the same uneasy expression—quickly masked—on his face.

"Thank you for telling us, your majesty," Christian said.

"Thank you, Christian, son of Robert Lovell. Your efforts that night were as courageous as your father's twenty-three years ago, for, like him, you did what you believed to be right instead of listening blindly to what others said." He arched a brow. "Even your king."

Avisa squeezed Christian's fingers as he had hers. It had not been easy for Christian to discover how his father had not told him the truth for so many years.

The king smiled. "Do you think I would have accepted your service if I believed your family had disappointed me already? There was a time when I cursed the mention of the Lovell name, but then I learned that I owe my life and my throne to your father. It is a debt I shall never forget."

"It is our honor to serve."

"I trust I can count on you to continue to do so. I have been trying to bring unified justice to England, and a loyal and fair-minded man like you would be the best to aid me."

"I am honored, your majesty."

Before the king could say more, the queen said, "We are delaying the wedding." She kissed Avisa's cheek, then Christian's. "Take good care of my lady of St. Jude's Abbey, Sir Christian."

"I will endeavor to take as good care of her as she has of me."

"A momentous vow." The queen smiled again and turned to walk with her husband to the chapel porch.

Avisa saw Christian was smiling as well.

"It is a huge vow," he whispered, putting his arm around her waist and tilting her toward him. "You saved my life and my honor and all you have asked for in return is my heart, which I gladly give you to safeguard."

"And I gladly take it if you will keep mine."

"A fair bargain, Lady Avisa." He tapped the top of her sword. "I know there will never be a lack of courage in my family from this point forward, because it has just gained a knight like no other."

She pressed her mouth to his. The guests waiting for the wedding ceremony would have to wait a little longer.

Read on for a preview of
Jocelyn Kelley's next exciting historical romance

One Knight Stands

Coming from Signet Eclipse in October 2005

The sea was blood-red beneath the rays from the setting sun that peeked from under a line of dark clouds just above the horizon.

"Isn't it wondrous?" asked a hushed voice. "I have never seen anything so beautiful."

"You certainly do not believe that, Vala." Tarran ap Llyr looked past the trees surrounding them to gaze out at the sea. He hated the color red. Once he had paid no more mind to it than any other shade. That had been before he saw how it spread across the floor of his home.

Pulling his eyes from the crimson sea, he heard a chirp from the goshawk riding on his left hand. He had raised Heliwr almost from the egg, and the bird seemed attuned to his strongest, darkest emotions. Maybe it was because the hawk thought of the hunt and prey, too.

Tarran slowed his horse to match the pace of the old woman's. Her brows were nearly as white as her hair, and her moon-shaped face was lined with years of living upon the shores of the western sea. Although the afternoon was warm, she wore a voluminous cloak of black wool.

Vala laughed. "But I do believe it. I have heard so much of *Cymru*'s beauty from those who have traveled before us. I want to savor every image of it, so I might enjoy the memories over and over."

His friend, Seith ap Mil, drew his horse up to ride beside

them. Tarran nodded to Seith, who looked as garish as the flowers in the field with his bright red tunic and deep blue cloak. Even his stockings, which were as dusty as Tarran's from their days of riding, were still a grotesque green and looked like bulbs on his round legs.

"Do you think we can beg shelter from the lord in the castle that is supposed to be just past these trees?" Seith rubbed his hand on his generous expanse of stomach. "I would enjoy a meal not of my own cooking."

"I have not seen you turning up your nose at anything we have snared so far."

"Hare makes a tasty meal. Thanks to Heliwr, we have enjoyed the occasional grouse, but a man wishes for something more civilized, like spitted chicken or a joint of mutton."

Vala laughed. "It would seem, Tarran, you are the only one among us who prefers the rough life."

Shaking his head, Tarran gave his horse a command at the same time he tightened his hold on the hawk's jesses. His steed leaped to a trot.

Behind him, he heard Seith ask, "What did I say wrong now?"

Tarran owed his friend an apology. Later he would see Seith received it. Seith had been loyal even when Tarran had been unworthy of a friend. Yet, Seith did not understand why Tarran preferred the quiet of his own company and a few friends to a large household where someone was certain to say something that brought forth the memories he was trying to submerge where they never could be retrieved. So far, he had been unsuccessful, for the red of the setting sun had sent pain through him, a pain as strong as if *he* had been the one stabbed.

Shadows beneath the trees held the dampness of the past winter. His hand went to the knife he carried in his belt. He fingered the dragon and leeks carved into the haft, ready to draw it. Such shadows welcomed thieves. Behind him, the men and Vala grew silent as they rode through the wood and crossed a wide, fast-flowing stream. In the west of *Cymru*, the laws of England were obeyed only by those who believed they could gain from abiding by the king's authority.

Tarran released the breath he had been holding when, minutes later, they emerged into the sunshine. Attack now could not come without warning, and he doubted anyone would be bold enough to ambush them within view of the castle. Robbers would fear retaliation from within the walls surrounding the foursquare tower that rose like a stone challenge. The lord who held the castle would be a fool to attack travelers within his fief's boundaries, for that could focus the king's displeasure on him.

The castle on the hill looked puny compared to the vast mountains rising above its parapets. A darker gray than the raw stone overlooking it, Castell Glyn Niwl sat in an area cleared of trees. The walls were edged with sharp rocks. No greenery softened at the bases, because it could be easily set ablaze or conceal invaders.

And a woman hung out of an arrow slit.

Tarran did not want to believe his eyes. It could not be— It was! A woman hung from the narrow opening. Her slender legs dangled against the wall, kicking wildly as she tried to find a toehold on the wall. Beneath her on serrated rocks, one long wooden pole lay across a pair the same length.

He exhorted his horse to a run up the hill at the same time he tightened his grip on the jesses holding the hawk on his left hand. Heliwr chirped, preparing for the moment Tarran would send him aloft. He did not release the bird as he stopped next to the poles. What were they? No time to check. The woman might fall at any moment.

He stretched up his right hand. Her feet were beyond his fingers. Standing in the stirrups, he clamped his legs against the horse's sides. The horse shifted, and he growled a warning for it to stand still. Hoofbeats and raised voices came from behind him, but he did not glance back. He looked up at the woman.

"Let go!" he shouted.

She looked down at him and frowned. She shook her

head, sending her russet hair swirling around her, and tried to dig her toes into a crevice between the stones.

Did she not understand Welsh? Maybe she was of a Marcher household.

"Let go!" he called in the Anglo-Norman language of the English lands east of Offa's Dyke. He had learned it as a child at the same time he had Welsh. "I will catch you!"

"Go away!" she ordered. "I have no need of your help, so leave now!"

"Is she mad?" Seith grasped the reins of Tarran's horse to keep it from moving. He took the hawk, balancing the bird on his left arm, which was as fleshy as his thick legs.

"Probably, but even a madwoman does not deserve to fall to her death." Tarran clenched his teeth. By St. David, he never wanted to see another woman broken and bloody and dead. The sight of Addfwyn, lying in her own blood, lines of pain dug into her face, leaped out of his memories. He wrestled it away. There was no time to think of his plans for vengeance now.

He pulled his broadsword. Stretching up, he tapped the woman on the buttocks with the flat side. "Let go!"

Instead of obeying, she kicked at him and clung like a burr to the arrow slit. "Will you go away? I don't need your help. I don't want your help. I want you to go away. Will you go now?"

She must be mad!

Maybe he should just leave her to stew in the juices of her insanity. No, he could not do that. More memories of death raced through his mind. Open eyes that no longer could look into his with yearning, blood pooled beneath a body he once had held against his, an impotent rage that had no focus, the acidic taste of the craving for vengeance.

He raised the sword again. This time, he struck her sharply on the right elbow.

She screamed as the fingers on her right hand lost their hold. For a second, she hung by her left hand as she grappled to get another hold with her right. Her fingers slipped, and she groaned. Then she was falling. He reached up, catching her before she could strike the rocks. Her legs hit his chest, and his breath exploded out in a gasp. He gathered her flailing limbs to him. Her hand smacked his chin. Pulling her tightly to him, he dropped back into the saddle. Pain raced along his thighs as they absorbed the force of her fall. The horse whinnied in fear. He murmured to it, but looked down at the woman in his arms.

Red hair framed her face and curled around the shoulders of the slate-gray gown she wore over a light blue undertunic. It was a simple gown without much embroidery, but the fabric was finer than anything a peasant could possess. Her body, pressing against him, was curvaceous, but as firm and trim as a well-trained warrior's. Her delicate face urged a man to look at it and then want to look again and again. Her lips, parted as she panted with her exertions, were soft and lush. No sign of madness dimmed her dazzling, green eyes. She closed them, and her body strained against his as she struggled to breathe.

"How does she fare?" asked Vala, dismay heightening the old woman's voice.

"She lives." Tarran took a deep breath and released it slowly.

About the Author

Jocelyn Kelley has always had a weakness for strong heroines and dashing heroes. For as long as she can remember, she's been telling stories of great adventures. She has had a few great adventures of her own, including serving as an officer in the U.S. Army and singing with a local group of Up with People. She lives in Massachusetts with her husband, three children, and three chubby cats. She's not sure who's the most spoiled.

Learn more about Jocelyn and her future books at: www.jocelynkelley.com.